UPON A STAR

JAMES MANGANAIS

bookhouse PUBLISHING

BELLINGHAM, WA

bookhouse
PUBLISHING

2950 Newmarket St., Suite 101-358 | Bellingham, WA 98226
Ph: 206.226.3588 | www.bookhouserules.com

Upon a Star
Copyright © 2025 by James Manganais

10 9 8 7 6 5 4 3 2 1

Printed in the United States of America

Library of Congress Control Number: 2025911680

ISBN: 978-1-952483-97-4 (Paperback)
ISBN: 978-1-952483-98-1 (eBook)

Editor: Julie Scandora
Book design: Scott Book & Melissa Vail Coffman

This book is dedicated to my son Sam,

I love you and always will.

Pain and suffering never end. They are merely pauses between the struggle where we can look around and see the world and its people are beautiful. These moments are what give value to everything we go through.

ACKNOWLEDGMENTS

THIS BOOK WOULD NOT BE POSSIBLE without the generous tips given by the patrons of The Lucky Moose Casino and Tavern. New Hampshire casinos must give away 35 percent of profit to charity, and those who are regulars at my place of work are very giving people.

Without the help of Andy Ivey and Rod Robertson, I most likely would have gotten the raw end of a book deal, ended up with a very different result, or not published at all. These two men directed me to a good publishing house. Thank you.

A big thank you to all the teachers whom I never bothered to listen to. Your background noise made the walls of school more interesting to look at. I managed to have a vivid imagination such as this only because I had to find some way to entertain myself.

Thank you to my editor, Julie Scandora, for wading through a sea of trash and letting the beauty shine through.

To my friends and family, who helped me by reading and offering feedback, thank you for your support.

Shout-out to my number one fan, Jake Tremblay.

1

THE FAIR FOLK

"WE WERE ALL MEANT FOR MORE than this. The shackles I wear grate upon my very soul, as I'm sure they do to all of you. Pain has ever been the teacher of past, and if suffering is meant to make humanity strong, then perhaps these dark days of the spirit will launch us to a plane of glory beyond our wildest dreams," says the dwarf, standing in the moonlight that shines down into the sandstone slave house from square holes in the roof to everyone inside. Thick ruddy ears adorn the sides of his bald and splotched head. Rags, tied through his long, thick beard, hang over the soiled cloth that covers his body.

The other dejected souls of the slave house watch the dwarf as he turns in place to look at everyone, his feet kicking hay and sand in his doing so.

"We've all seen it, the smoke rising from Kurin Forest to the north. We've all heard the way the guards have been speaking—hushed and full of worry. Something is coming, and when that something is here, I say we take whatever opportunity we get."

"Birkin's right," says a voice from the crowd. "We could finally have our freedoms back. We could escape."

Birkin snaps his head at the voice, looking to the man who spoke. "Freedom, yes, but escape, no."

Murmuring shoots through the slaves, and in a back corner also hit by moonlight, a human woman and a short half-elf child stir in uncertainty.

Birkin raises a hand to silence everyone, pointing upward. Heavy boot-steps sound on the roof, and a man in chainmail, covered by a red tunic with a depiction of barley, peers into the hole, his head protected with a kettle helm. "Keep it quiet down there!"

Hearing the guard retreat, Birkin returns to speaking, now in a lower voice. "Escape means nothing when we're escaping into a place with hundreds of folk looking for us. We rally the other houses and take Effilnem. There are too many of us for them if we surprise them."

Quiet voices go through the crowd once more. One speaks up, "We'll be killed for sure!"

Birkin slashes his hand towards the voice. "Are we not already dead? Or worse? I'd rather be killed and meet my fate in the heavens or hells than remain with these shackles upon wrists and soul. We fight, we take back our rights, and if not, then we die free." Birkin looks over everyone in the house, his eyes lingering on the woman and half-elf boy in the corner. "Think on it." With his final words, Birkin moves to lie down on an unoccupied space of the floor, speaking no more.

In the morning, loud banging comes from the slave house door, followed by the rattling of a lock and the swinging of the door with guards appearing by the exit. "Come on, you lot. Time for work."

In the corner, Kristo, the half-elf boy, and Mabel, the woman, stir, sitting up. The woman, with long brown hair braided down her back and a rag tied into the end, pats the boy's light-brown hair, looking at his sharp eyebrows that naturally turn downward. "You should be eating more. Lack of food is stunting your growth." The pair make their way out of the doorway with the other slaves and navigate through the coarse back-streets of sandstone houses to get to the main road where slaves from other houses are also being funneled into. Houses all have their shutters or curtains closed, and doors are locked tight while the crowd of slaves passes through.

Mabel's hand moves down to Kristo, and the boy puts his hand into hers to hold so they don't get separated.

"Being short is normal for me right now."

Mabel raises her eyebrows at this, giving an amused expression to him. "And who told you that?"

"The other half-elf in our house, Leffin. I asked him because one of the men in the mines yesterday said I might be short my whole life."

Mabel and Kristo continue to move forward, approaching the edge of the city where large, completely smooth sandstone walls run up into the sky. Guards line the walls and are pulling open a large gate to let the slaves out.

Mabel and Kristo pass through the gate, entering a wide sandy plane that has formations of red rock pillars occasionally sprouting up far ahead of them and to the right. In the distance to the left, a field of grass grows, and beyond that a thicket of trees goes into a denser forest. The black smoke of yesterday is not visible in the sky today.

"What exactly did Leffin tell you?"

"He said that half-elves grow slower than other races, just like elves do, and that my height is completely normal."

As the two walk on, the slaves diverge in their paths, with around a third escorted to the tree line, while the others proceed towards a large strip mine that burrows deep into the craggy ground. The encampment around the mine has a few buildings, mostly for food storage and for guards to take breaks. The main house has a large pulley that transports ore from the lower levels of the mine.

Mabel and Kristo, heading to the mine, start the winding walk downward as the sun begins to rise to beat the necks of the slaves. On the second spiral, there is a long flat stretch, home to a shack with an outdoor spot, shaded by a large cloth. Here female slaves are gathering. Under the shade, urns filled with water lie upon large, ruined rugs. The inside of the shack is similarly filled with the urns. Next to the shack, the wooden platform for the pulley has been lowered, which a second group of women have gathered about.

Mabel and Kristo enter the shack. Hanging on racks are knotted-rope backpacks that larger women remove and put on. Mabel grabs one as well, helping Kristo put it on, and then moves to grab an urn of water, shoving it into the open ropes for Kristo to carry. "Say hello to Temury for me and stay out of trouble with the men." Kristo nods his assent. Mabel bends down to give him a short hug and then pats him on the back, sending him out to deliver the urn of water.

The men of the mines have now all made their way to their places, hoisting pickaxes as they break rocks and then shoveling the muddy brown stone onto sleds. As loud, sharp ringing sounds go through the whole area, the guards on duty start packing cloth into the cowls near their ears to block the noise. Kristo walks by the guards and a few other slaves before getting to a group of men lucky enough to be in the shade.

One of them has greasy black hair and smiles at Kristo as he comes over. "Hello, little man. How are you today?"

Kristo moves to take off his packed urn, offering a ladle. "I'm good, Tem."

Temury takes the ladle and scoops some water to drink and then offers the ladle to the next man in line.

"Mabel says hello."

Temury gives a cock of his head and a smile. "Speaking of, do you think you can give her this?" He pulls out a piece of folded parchment from his cloth, using his body to hide it from the view of the guards.

Kristo raises his eyebrows, taking the parchment and shoving it under his shirt. "How did you get paper?"

Temury brings a finger up to his own lips. "Shush. Just say it's from me." Patting Kristo's back, Temury then moves off, going back to his work.

When the line of men is gone, Kristo puts his empty urn on his back and makes the return journey to the shack, passing by men who are pulling sleds of broken rock up to the pulley platform.

Inside the shack, Mabel, is helping a woman get a new urn into her pack.

"Hello, Mabel," Kristo says.

Mabel finishes with huffs from the effort, sending the woman on her way. "Welcome back," she says to Kristo. "We already need to start arranging the pots into empties and fulls. It's way too hot for spring, not that it matters out here."

Kristo puts his hand into his shirt and produces the piece of parchment. "From Tem."

Mabel looks up from her work. Seeing the parchment, she quickly comes over and snatches the paper with a big smile on her face. Finding a place to sit down, she opens it to read. As Mabel's eyes scan the paper, her hand comes to her mouth to cover a smile. Once she's done reading, she looks over to Kristo and coughs, hardening her expression. She wiggles the piece of paper in the air and then stuffs it into her shirt. "He shouldn't have given this to you. It would have been bad if you were caught with it." Mabel moves up from her spot on the ground. "Come and help me move the urns."

The two of them separate the empties from the fulls and help the other women with getting new urns. After a few hours of work, the pit workers stop for a breakfast of bread and mashed beans. Mabel and Kristo spend the next part of their day placing the empty urns on the platform to be hauled up and removing the full ones brought down below between the batches of slag being piled on.

Lunch, the same as breakfast, is sent down and distributed. When the sky starts to darken, a loud ringing bell travels throughout the mine, and the men cast down their pickaxes for the day to start the trek back to their houses. Kristo and Mabel help women remove their rope packs until the last one is done.

Outside the shack, an unusual group of guards forms about the winding way out of the strip mine. At its front, their black-haired captain, in full plate with a red tunic over it, eyes the slaves. As Kristo and Mabel leave the shack, his eyes fall upon them, and he raises a gauntleted hand at them. "You two! Come over here now!"

Mabel freezes in fear and then walks over, guiding Kristo over with her. "Yes, sir?"

"You, boy, what are you doing in there? There are to be no men in the water shack."

"He's only a boy, sir," says Mabel.

"He will work the mines with his fellow men, not with the water girls. Carry on back to your house."

"But sir he's—"

"Do not speak to me," he snaps. "Return to your house."

"Please, don—"

The captain strikes Mabel's face with the back of his gauntleted right hand, jerking her body back a step. A cut appears on her cheek with blood weeping from it. "Don't argue with me, criminal! Get back to your house before I draw steel on you!"

Mabel, still in frightened shock, pushes on the back of Kristo, moving him around the group of guards to return to their house. As they walk, Mabel grips her cheek, and the blood doesn't go unnoticed by the men who pass by her, each of them scowling from the sight but continuing forward.

Near the walls of Effilnem, where the great gate is opened, Kristo breaks the silence between the two. "Are you okay? I'm sorry you got hurt because of me."

Mabel shakes her head. "No, no, no. I wasn't hurt because of you." Mabel's face turns into a dark scowl with deep a furrowed-brow as they walk into the city with guards lining the streets. "I was hurt because of them." Mabel casts an arm out, swiping at the city, her eyes staring at the tall tower of Effilnem's keep, a red banner breezing from its majesty. "Cruel and heartless people! Blind your windows then, and keep us in the back of your minds, locked away so as to not have to confront what happens right in front of you!" Mabel casts her head down as she walks, the slaves about her and Kristo looking away and at the ground. Kristo stops moving now to turn, giving Mabel a hug around the waist, who returns it. Her face drips tears onto the harsh ground that erases them. After a moment, Mabel pats Kristo, who takes her by the hand.

At their house, the yoke over the door, signifying this is indeed for slaves, and the doorway itself are too low for people to enter without bowing, save for Kristo and Birkin. As the slaves enter it, a guard checks off a list. Once everyone is inside, he closes the door and locks it. When all are settled in, Birkin takes stock of them, stopping in front of Mabel. "What happened? Do you need to be tended to?"

Mabel shakes her head. "No, I got struck by the mine captain. He wants Kristo to go to work mining now instead of delivering water."

Birkin's eyes move to Kristo and then soften. "That is . . . awful." After giving a supportive look, the dwarf goes to look after the other slaves.

As night begins to take over, the door rattles open once more, and a guard points to a few people inside. "Come distribute the food." The slaves leave, take out urns from under the holes in the roof, and replace them with ones full of water. They leave once more, coming back with cabbage and bread for everyone. Once done, the door locks again, with the final click of the day.

As Kristo eats, he peers up out of a hole in the roof, looking at the main tower of Effilnem. "Do you think we could see the whole world from up there?"

Mabel turns her gaze up to the tower and huffs in light amusement. "No, the world is so much bigger than that. Didn't you say you were from the half-city? That's many leagues away from here, many days of travel."

Kristo nods. "I don't remember much of it, except the ocean."

Mabel nudges Kristo. "Being able to remember the ocean is nice, though I've never seen it. Halmin is smack between farmlands and massive forests."

Kristo leans himself against Mabel's side, biting into his cabbage while getting comfortable. "Do you miss Halmin?"

"Yes, I miss it very much. I miss eating the fruit dangling from every house. The little river that my friends and I used to jump into. The cherry blossoms in the church of Sutri. But I miss my house the most. It was the first farm outside the town to the east. Small but nice in a simple kind of way. Our main crop was strawberries."

Kristo scratches his head. "What's a strawberry?"

Mabel shuts her eyes. "It's a small red berry, shaped like a triangle that is sweet but also sour." She opens her eyes again, looking down at Kristo. "It's springtime so there must be many plants blooming in town. The trees in the burial forest are likely sending songs to one another, making the trees glow green."

Kristo munches through his food until there is nothing left, putting a hand over his stomach. "What about your friends?"

Mabel goes quiet for a time and then quietly answers. "I had a few. The kids that were growing up with me were nice enough." She notices Kristo holding his stomach and gives him the last of her cabbage to eat.

"Thank you. . . . Did you have a best friend?"

Silent for even longer, she finally says, "I did. She's the reason I'm here."

Kristo looks at her sadly. "I'm sorry. . . . What happened?"

Mabel gives a huff. "My family, despite being farmers and having food, was quite poor. We got sick, someone broke a leg, and other things that required money eventually put us in debt. My family turned to theft. Since I knew how to read, my father sent me to the town library to steal valuable books to sell to passing caravans. It wasn't long until my friend caught me taking books, and she told me to give them back. Instead of doing so, I ran home. She told the librarians, the inquisitors came, and soon my family was enslaved to serve our prison sentence. It was such a . . . foolish thing." Mabel looks up and out of the slave house to the stars. "Such a small incident, so little done. Yet so many days spent here, years. I don't think Sera knew what she was doing. We were little. She was probably thinking it was the right thing to do, but we were friends. She didn't have to make such a big deal of it."

Kristo nods into Mabels side, his eyelids getting heavy. "Do you hate her for telling on you?"

Mabel continues to stare up at the stars, causing Kristo to poke her legs for the answer. "I don't know, Kristo. I used to. I used to hate her with everything in my heart when I was younger. But being older, I know she didn't mean for this to happen. She just loved books. I think if she and I could talk about this, I would listen to what she had to say and make my mind up then."

The child yawns. "Well, if you don't have a best friend anymore, we could be best friends."

Mabel gives a short laugh, petting Kristo's head. "I thought we already were!"

2

A HAPPY BIRTHDAY

MABEL SITS UP IN THE MORNING, groaning and putting a hand over her stomach that gives out a loud growl as she leans against the wall of the slave house.

Soon enough the clacking of keys has all the slaves in the house getting up, making the same trip as yesterday and the day before and every day before that through the alley and along the main road. Shutters clack closed as the first slaves pass and remain so until all have passed.

Mabel has her hand down to hold Kristo's, and instead of leading him through the stone arch of the gateway, she pulls him off to the side under it. Kristo goes along but looks up at Mabel questioningly until Temury comes into view through the crowd and meets them both.

Instead of a greeting, Temury looks at the cut on Mabel's cheek, to which she shakes her head at his questioning eyes. He puts his arms around her, pulling her into a hug. Other slaves notice but quickly turn their heads forward. "I've wanted to do this for a very long time." Temury gives Mabel a tighter squeeze for a moment and then lets go. A smile is clear on his face, but the one on Mabel's starts to falter. He motions forward for them all to walk. "What's the matter?"

Mabel drops Kristo's hand to place her hand on his back. "I need a favor."

"Anything."

"I need you to take care of Kristo. He is supposed to join the miners now. I'll meet you at the gate every day before and after work."

Temury frowns, his eyebrows raised, looking down at Kristo. "Look at the size of him! Scrawny and barely higher than my waist! Who ordered this?"

Kristo points his hand at the mining pits ahead of them. "A new captain. I never saw him in the pits before."

Temury runs a hand through his greasy hair, shaking his head. "There is less mercy here than before. I will look after him. I'll have him help pull a sled. Not too much work, and old Thop will be glad to have the help."

Mabel nods, breathing a sigh of relief. "That's good. If he had to do regular labor, I'd have to try to find a way to give him even more food than I already do. I wish there were hanging fruits like back home or rich bread straight from the bakery to give him."

Temury looks up, squinting his eyes at a few vultures moving through the sky near the thicket of the north. "If it were my city of Rosen, there would be fresh petals to give him by the bagful, the vendor lane stoking fires for roasts, and the Green Apple market constantly buzzing." Temury looks down to Kristo. "I'd have you try the biggest pancakes there are. Bigger than your head and stacks up to your knees!"

Mabel gives a giggle at the thought.

But Kristo blinks a bit confused. "What are pancakes?"

Temury gives a sad expression but then nudges Kristo. "Tell you what. When all of this is over, I'll take you and Mabel to Rosen and show you what they are, okay?"

Kristo thinks for a moment and then gives a smile. "I'd love to go. How about you, Mabel?" he asks, turning his head to look up at her.

She smiles down at him. "I'd love to. I would go anywhere with my two favorite people."

Before long, the trio pass in front of the water house, which causes them to stop. Mabel looks down to Kristo, putting a hand on his shoulder. "Kristo, you be good today. Do everything Temury says, okay?"

Kristo gives a nod in response. "Okay."

Mabel moves her head to look up at Temury. "Keep him safe."

Temury puts a hand on Kristo's head and then pats his back. "Of course I will. You make sure you keep yourself from worrying."

Mabel rubs her brow at the thought and then motions that's she's going inside since a few guards are going by. "I'll try."

Temury looks down at Kristo, who is gazing at him expectantly. "Pulling a sled won't be too bad, just a bunch of walking and waiting." Temury moves forward, motioning for Kristo to follow as they make their way down the slope of the mine. When they arrive, a few men are already picking away at the stone. Temury moves to a pickaxe and hoists it up. "Go on and find someplace comfy until the sled is filled, Kristo."

Kristo moves to a broken boulder nearby, sitting on it and looking out on the mine. Hundreds of people are similarly chipping away at the walls of the strip mine. So many of them are dirty, each of them toiling, all of them showing anger or sadness on their greasy faces. "Pain has ever been the teacher of past, and if suffering is meant to make humanity strong, then perhaps these dark days of the spirit will launch us to a plane of glory beyond our wildest dreams." Kristo says these words slowly, struggling to process what the leader of his slave house meant when he spoke them. From behind him the sound of pickaxes and chisels, coupled with the grunts of the men using them, fades. His light-brown eyes move from guard to guard, watching them walk by or chastise men. The chainmail armor on top of the guards' thick padded clothing particularly stands out.

"Kristo!"

With a jerk of his head, the half-elf looks at the speaker.

Temury has been calling for a while. Once he notices Kristo is paying attention, a tired smile spreads across the man's face while he leans on his pickaxe. "Daydreaming, huh? I wish I had your spirit." The man's head then flicks towards a few planks of wood that are kept together with brackets of iron with a rope stuck through an outcropping metal ring. On top of the sled is a pile of rocks ready to be moved with an old man finishing the pile. "That's as much as you and old Thop should manage. Help him bring it up, and then tell Mabel we'd like some water."

Kristo nods without a word and goes over to the sled to help the old man. Two of the other miners look at him through their unkempt hair with eyes as distressed as a dog watching its favorite toy get thrown from a cliff. The frowns upon them seem permanently etched there as if they had chiseled it right with the stone they tirelessly work upon. Turning away from the gazes, Kristo takes the rope of the sled with both hands and puts it over his shoulder, starting the trudge up the small incline of the iron pits with Thop in front of him. As they go up the winding path, the men working at the red stone sometimes stare, arms hanging limp by their sides. On more than one occasion, the guards must whip the men back to work.

The boy's feet continue moving their way up to the halfway point of the mine. There, women gather around the sled to take the cracked stone and place it onto the wooden platform for it to be pulled upward. Kristo leaves to help Thop with the sled, starting the march back down the slope to his group. Upon arrival, another full sled of rocks lies waiting for him. And so the day goes, dragging a load up and an empty sled down until the sun hangs low, with a brief respite for bread and beans. As sunlight begins to give out, the bell is rung, and guards herd the workers up, shaking their spears for the slaves to move faster so they can end their own day.

Temury moves to Kristo, and the two make their way out of the pit. At the top, Effilnem's sandstone walls, as uninteresting as the rest of the land-scape, greet them. Outcropping rocks of the same tan-red roll along till, in the distance, trees and brush can just be seen with another stream of slaves coming from the direction of the tree line. Both groups meet and become one outside the gate that opens to devour the unhappy souls. Normal citi-zens are once again off the street at this hour, not wanting to know or be associated with the dealings of such a vile class of people. Temury and Kristo wait just under the arches of the gate.

When Mabel arrives, she gives Temury a hug, who relaxes into it. "Thank you for taking care of Kristo."

Temury hums, acknowledging her, but the two soon break, having to part as a group of guards is walking through. "I'll see you both tomorrow," he says with a wave as he moves off.

Once Kristo passes through the door, he rushes over to secure his favorite spot—the prime piece of land in a corner of the building, which has a bit more hay than the rest. Today it seems no one has tried to lay claim to it, but an occasional glance from other housemates gives Kristo the impression his spot isn't as secure as he'd like.

Mabel gives a curious expression at the extra hay. "Looks like you're back in your nest."

The boy moves over to allow Mabel to sit and have a less bumpy part of the wall to use as support, even pushing over some extra hay for her, which she acknowledges with a grateful smile.

Instead of immediately responding, Kristo looks up at the red sky to eye the main tower of Effilnem's keep that has a shine on the top from a guard's kettle helm. "Mabel, could you tell me more of what your town Halmin was like? You told me already it was okay in size and the buildings grew food and even the surrounding area was filled with farms. But I want to know what the people were like. Did you all have something you did for fun?"

A screech from the iron door signifies it's closing, followed by the gentle ticking of a lock.

"The people, huh? Well, they were happy. The only time they were especially upset was when we would have a visit from the inquisitors. Of course, there were times when we had lesser troubles. The bee population was always a problem for the strawberry patch my family kept. But it was a small town, so the people helped one another if they could. That was when I was very little, though. As I grew older and people were getting sent off, fewer people would offer help; suspicion got the better of pleasantries."

Her words cause the nearby section of the slave house to fall silent.

Although also listening, Kristo isn't looking at Mabel; he is instead staring off into the darkening sky, as if trying to picture life going on in her town.

Mabel notices those around her listening and adjusts herself so she no longer faces Kristo's corner. She continues to speak, talking a little louder, "As for fun, we would play by skipping rocks or pretending we were mages. One boy I used to play with insisted we sword fight with sticks whenever the kids of the town got together. He and his friend Demio were always getting into trouble, but it was the type of trouble that didn't cause harm." Seeing out of the corner of her eye Kristo look up at the sky, Mabel continues with more enthusiasm. "That wasn't the most fun, though. Every year a traveling troupe would come to town. A swath of resting land would be chosen, and the families would build stalls there to sell their signature food. Once the travelling band arrived, a massive tent would be erected. For the next two days, children would run from stall to stall, buying all their favorite foods from the different households. I think families made as much money selling as they lost to their children buying. The only people that could have made money were the traveling troupe and the Marmuin family since they were the best cooks in town."

As Mabel checks to see if Kristo is still listening, she notices the other slaves are staring off, looking at something in the distance they can't quite see, a few of them smiling from her story. "The entertainers would perform miraculous feats. Inside their tent, it was like they created their own little world where the rules were whatever they wanted. From that world, those miracles would bleed out into our town's sea of stalls. Performers would come out and levitate chunks of the ground or display other minor stunts to attract people to the main show in their tent." Mabel takes a breath to look about at everyone. Staring at the ground, taking a moment to chew her lip, she then continues, her voice cracking. "One year, an illusionist ordered from a couple of stalls. When the people gave her the food, it fell through what was her hand and hit the ground. People weren't too thrilled at that one, and she had to stop doing that very quickly." Mabel pauses to look up at the tower that Kristo is staring vacantly at.

Rubbing her hand at the aches of her shoulders, she continues. "The inside of the tent is where the wonders were, as I said. There, large poles with ropes strung across them had people running back and forth. Another time the performers created a human bridge for other acrobats to walk across. One year, a mage pulled an impossibly sheer rock wall with large holes in it from the dirt. People were allowed to try to climb over it, and if they made the journey, they would get all the troupe's profits for the three days they were there. Many men tried to scale the wall, but no one in our town was able to do it. At the end of the third day, the troupe sent out a pale, skinny helper to climb through a low hole in the rock wall and declared him the winner. Everyone in town was so disappointed, and those who had attempted the climb complained about it for weeks."

Mabel smiles as she remembers her past life, but that smile doesn't reach her eyes. "At the end of the traveling troupe's stay in town, their tent would be brought down. In its place, the earth mage of the troupe would create a grand fire pit. Stalls and stands would be broken down and cast into it. A service would be held in honor of Pelina, the goddess of trade; then the troupe's pyromancer would set the piled wood ablaze for everyone to enjoy. The pyromancer would show off by sending phoenixes and other animals made of pure fire soaring over the crowds or running through the air till they flickered out. One year, a storyteller performed. An illusionist amplified that storyteller's voice for the whole town to hear while the pyromancer made characters of fire, depicting what was being described for kids to enjoy. I'm pretty sure that made the adults a little annoyed. They would always sit with their lovers to watch the flames. Parents would set their children out to hassle packing performers for tricks so they could have some alone time. It was normal for loving couples to propose at the fire. As a little girl, I joined my friends in gossiping about who was proposed to. Now I wish I could be proposed to near that fire. I used to make fun of it, but it's taken on a different light now."

Mabel stops and looks down at her hands and then at Kristo again. "I hope that gives you something to think about while you stare up at that tower, Kristo." Giving the daydreaming half-elf a few pats upon the head, she goes silent, keeping Kristo company while he daydreams. With the memories of her prior life just out of her view, Mabel sits in confinement, staring up at the same tower that Kristo is smiling at, trying to picture everything she said.

Dinner is delivered as before, and then the workers start nestling into what little bit of ground they have. Heat is shared between strangers, friends, or enemies to keep each other warm through the night. The guards overhead can be heard creaking in their chairs, talking to one another about their daily struggles. Then a faint noise can be heard, steadily growing till it encompasses the whole city. Every slave, some shaken awake by their sleepless neighbors, hears the music seeping in from Effilnem's keep. Notes from a distant piano drift across the night air, followed by the soothing sounds of a violin as they intermingle in the moonlight. Silenced to better hear the music, all look up at the tower as the sound calls to them.

"Mabel?" Kristo's voice is a whisper as he tries to listen to the sound he's never heard before. "How old were you when you came here?"

The human woman looks down at the boy to place a hand upon his head. "I was around your age . . . I think. How old are you, Kristo?"

The pointed tips of the half-elf's ears seem sharper as they listen to the piano leading the violin. "I don't know. No one ever told me my age."

A crash of a small crescendo sets the next pattern of the two instruments. Mabel asks, "Do you know your birthday?"

Kristo shakes his head, not knowing that either.

"Then how about we make today your birthday? Happy birthday, Kristo." The woman pulls the child into her side for a short while to give him a hug before releasing him, the pair looking up once more at the imposing tower.

Out from one side of the rain hole, a bright red flame passes overhead towards the high tower, twinkling in the night sky. "Look, Kristo, a shooting star. On your birthday, no less. Make a wish, and it'll come true."

The child has a smile on his face as he calls out to the star. "I hope I'll get to see your home town, Mabel, to eat all the food hanging from the houses, and to experience the festival."

Mabel rubs the child's head, giving him a gentle scolding. "You're supposed to keep it to yourself, or it won't come true. . . . Oh, but here come a few more. It must be a shower. Go ahead and make your wish again, but this time do it in your head."

Kristo nods, concentrating hard and making the same wish for each ball of light that flies across his little window to the rest of the world.

3

ASK AND RECEIVE

A THUNDEROUS BOOM SOUNDS THROUGHOUT EFFILNEM. The entire slave house bursts to life at the noise, and all see the proud tower blown out of the starry sky in a violent combustion, sending debris onto the city and keep below. Guards on top of the slave house look on in terror as more explosions cascade over the keep, blowing chunks from its stone face into the city below.

"Fireball! Get the hell down!" one of the guards yells, grabbing his partner and throwing him into the alley near the prison house and then jumping into it himself.

The debris of the keep continues raining down into the city and into the slave house. Mabel scrambles to cover Kristo, her face next to his as he is huddled up in the corner, looking at her.

"Kristo, just look at me, all right? Just me, nothing else is worth worrying about, okay?"

The child nods. "Mabel . . . what's happening? Where did the tower go?"

As Mabel's mouth opens to answer, a loud thwack hits the center of her shoulders, and crimson liquid dribbles from her mouth onto the boy's clothing. More debris falls onto the slave house, a giant stone breaking open the wall near the pair, revealing the alleys. Mabel strains her arms to push up without falling on Kristo, rolling onto the hay where she lets her head loll in his direction. His expression is filled with shock and confusion. Seeing Kristo safe from harm, Mabel smiles faintly. "I love you . . .

little one . . ." Seeing the woman die, the already destitute house becomes a shell of something it never knew it was, the slaves feeling more alone, more abandoned, more forgotten than before. Mabel's soul departs from its broken walls with her final breath, leaving her staring with proud affection at Kristo.

The slaves all look at Mabel and then at the gaping hole near her body and get up. Through the hole, the slaves spot the two watch guards on the ground, scrambling to get up after ducking for cover. Birkin rises from the slave house floor, his eyes leering at the two men, grasping for their spears, terrified of the freedom-craving slaves.

Kristo calls to Birkin in a cracked voice. "Birkin . . . Mabel she's . . . she's hurt. Please do something . . ."

The dwarf turns his head to look upon the corpse of the human woman, his lips in a deep frown. "I'm sorry, boy. There is nothing that can be done." He then points at the guards on the ground, yelling with the anger built by the many years of labor. "If it's wearing red, kill it!" With bloodthirsty rage, the dwarf lets out a cry of anger, causing the other slaves to scream as they charge the guards through the rubble. Each slave's face looks like a wolf's, seeing prey for the first time in years.

The ravenous pack of slaves, smelling fear in the air, descends upon the pair of guards, dashing for the end of the alley. When one slips on a piece of rubble and falls, the slaves reach him. They rip his kettle helm from his head and smash it against his skull until his body stops twitching. The thief adorns his head with the bloody metal helm. The guard's body is stripped, the chainmail stolen, all but the colors taken from the once slave watcher. With him dead, the mob moves on, fueled by righteous rage as they are out for the blood of their once keepers, going like crazed hunters through the moonlight.

Kristo, unable to tear himself from Mabel's side, kneels over her with his head pounding. The blinding wall of sound from battle going on in the city overwhelms him as he stares at the body of his friend, tears streaming down his cheeks as his fists start pounding on her chest. "Mabel! Mabel! Wake up! Mabel!" With her not responding, Kristo sits back, completely oblivious to the world around him, weeping next to her. It's not until he is shaken to the core that he comes back to reality.

"Hey! Kid!" A man who Kristo didn't notice comes up and grabs him by the shoulders, forcing the child to look at him. He has a simple nose-guard helmet and chainmail, covered with a yellow tunic, held down by a belt. His face is lightly chiseled from routine exercise, and his face is clean shaven. "You have to go. Leave through the front gate and keep running. There is a supply train if you keep going straight. Go now."

Kristo's brows turn downward, and he yells in the man's face. "No! I can't leave, not without Mabel!"

The man pushes Kristo's shoulder, trying to get the boy to come to his senses. "I'm sorry, but she's gone! Now go before you end up the same way!"

At the shouting, Kristo is too stunned to continue talking, his senses numb.

The man examines Kristo's eyes. With a softer tone, the man takes off his helmet, showing off dark-brown hair, and puts it on Kristo, covering his eyes. "Give me a sec, kid." The man removes the helmet, cuts a piece of his cloth off with the short sword by his side, and uses it to pad the helmet so it fits the child. "There, you're a soldier now, and I'm your captain. I'm giving you your first order. You're going to come with me back to camp."

Kristo looks at the man with a frightened face and then back at Mabel.

The man looks at her too and then back to Kristo. "I promise we'll give Mabel a proper funeral, but not right now. You need to be somewhere safe."

Kristo gives Mabel's hand a squeeze and then gets up as the soldier does.

The soldier nods to Kristo and picks up his short sword and round shield. "Follow me." He moves forward into the alley and around the house towards the exit of the city. On his right, a crowd of slaves, yellow-clad soldiers, and red-tunic guards are engaged in a melee in the main streets. Taking a detour, the man leads Kristo through alleyways toward the main gates, sticking to the shadows of the buildings. At the last building, the man looks to the right around the corner. "We're almost there, soldier. Your freedom is right around the corner." The man then ups the pace to a light jog, going around the corner.

Kristo hasn't turned the corner yet when a shout comes from the left. He sees a spear moving forward, followed by a red-tunicked guard. Kristo's eyes open wide.

"Behind you!" says Kristo as he charges the yellow soldier.

Kristo's heart drops in his chest as he bursts forward, freedom and anger burning in the child's mind as he slams into the guard and attempts to tackle him.

The guard's spear jerks as Kristo collides into him, causing it to scrape along the side of the yellow soldier's mail.

The brown-haired soldier grunts in surprise. He then turns back around, astonished to see Kristo has pushed the guard's attack aside. Going to the child's rescue, the soldier uses his shield to bash the guard's head. His kettle helm flies off as he falls backwards, and Kristo is knocked away. The guard tries to get up, but the soldier pushes his advantage, delivering a hard kick into the guard's stomach to roll him over on the ground. The soldier tosses his sword away and drops onto the guard's chest, balling a mailed fist and beating the man's head in, the mailed glove slicing the guard's face with each blow. When the soldier realizes the man isn't moving anymore, he rises, his chest heaving. He stares down at the man, groaning for life, whose face is pooling crimson onto the dusty stone alley. The soldier flicks his eyes to Kristo, a sorrow in them as he rises, leaning against a nearby wall. After a time, the yellow soldier speaks to Kristo. "You are brave, and I owe you my life." With a hard sigh, the soldier motions towards the gateway with a jerk of his head. "Your freedom, little elf."

The soldier moves through the alley towards the streets to the gate. Its great doors, broken, lie upon the ground. More yellow soldiers are moving into the city through Effilnem's once grand gate. Kristo moves towards the promise of safety, looking down at the great doors he's moving across and then at the soldier in front of him. Kristo's pace picks up to run closer to him, free of the city, free of chains, free of the slave house.

A group of riders spot Kristo and the soldier and dash upon them, soon surrounding the two with their brown horses standing proudly as a wall to block passage.

A blond-haired man dressed in yellow-themed, regal garb raises his hand up at the soldier. The rest of his contingent point spears at Kristo's savior. The hand of the blond man radiates a red aura that flickers like an out-of-control bonfire, ready to absolve the surrounded soldier of life. "Explain your cowardly actions immediately."

The surrounded soldier raises his hands, dropping his sword and shield. He motions towards the child. "My Lord Lenfro, I've found a young child and wished him no harm in the chaos."

The blond man seems to soften for a moment, eyeing Kristo in his slave garbs before steeling himself once more. "What about your fellow soldiers? You would abandon them during battle?"

The soldier hangs his head to show his neck to his superior. "My Lord, I have already felled two enemies, one with my boot and one with my gauntlet. If you so wish, I shall return to the fray after the child's safety is assured." A crimson-black stain on his boot confirms the soldier's words, and his mailed glove is still shining with the blood of the guard he beat half to death in front of Kristo.

Lenfro's eyes flick over the man's weapons of choice before lowering his hand. The red shimmering stops, and his accompanying knights raise their spears out of the way. "Two men killed with the evidence upon you and having a child in tow that you wish to save from the flames of war. That is quite the tale to tell." The nobleman then tosses his head back towards the camp, prancing his horse out of the way. "You have proven yourself chivalrous or at the very least lied yourself quite well into that reputation. You will give me your name first."

The soldier sighs with relief as he moves to pick up his sword and shield, sheathing his blade and putting a fist upon his breast. "I am Garrick, Your Lordship."

Lord Lenfro nods at Garrick. "You will come to the keep in the morning after our victory, Garrick. May your rest be a peaceful one." As his soldiers move forward into the city, the nobleman's attention turns back towards his troops, and he joins them to inspect the battle closer.

Garrick turns around and looks down at the boy, who is standing out in the open rocky terrain, staring back at the city and its destroyed tower. "Come here, soldier. You need rest. You've gone through enough tonight."

Kristo turns back towards the soldier slowly, his eyes not wanting to be torn away from the broken tower. "Mabel's back there . . ."

Hearing the child's sadness, Garrick moves forward and bends a knee to be more at Kristo's height, putting a hand up on the half-elf's shoulder. "I know, but we can't go running back. We'll be in the way or might get hurt. If Mabel loved you as much as you love her, she wouldn't want something bad to happen to you."

Garrick jostles Kristo's shoulder lightly, looking into his eyes. "I promise we will have a service for her. We will go back tomorrow and collect her."

Kristo sniffles, nodding at Garrick.

The soldier gets up from his knee and walks, with Kristo only a short distance behind, to the camp. There, a few of the women and feeble left behind to guard the camp are ensuring those dragged back receive medical attention. When the two reach a wagon, a round-cheeked, middle-aged woman with a bonnet comes to address the pair.

"Is either of you hurt? Do you need any help?"

Garrick gives the woman a dismissive wave of a hand. "No, we need a tent to sleep in and food for the both of us. This little one has seen enough tonight."

The woman looks at Kristo and then opens her arm in the direction she wants them to go, ushering the pair towards the back of the camp to a simple triangular tent with hide laid out on the dusty ground. "Here you are. I will come back as soon as I can."

Garrick gives her a quick thanks and then gets into the tent, keeping the flap open for Kristo. The child looks at Garrick, who gives a beckoning hand to him. "The desert chill will set in soon. Best to be under cover."

Kristo enters and takes a corner.

Garrick sits across from him and takes off the bloody glove from his right hand. He looks at it for a moment as if disappointed, then tosses it aside, and scratches his head.

A long pause ensues as if the two are trying to sense what the other is thinking before speaking.

Garrick sighs and takes off his other glove, throwing it down on top of the bloody one. "What's your name, kid?"

With another long pause the child examines Garrick's face, finding no malice in it. "Kristo." The child then looks towards the slit of an opening in the tent. "Why did Mabel have to die? She did nothing wrong. She worked hard, was kind to everyone in the pits, gave her food out to the sick. She didn't . . . she doesn't . . ." Kristo's rage and frustration boil over in his voice as he shouts to the world. "She should have had a better life! There was no reason for her to die like that! She should have been able to see Halmin again." Angry tears come to Kristo's eyes

Garrick looks at the ground in thought. At the name Halmin, Garrick's body perks up. "Halmin?"

Kristo nods and then shakes his head in a dejected manner. "It doesn't matter. She won't get the chance to, not anymore."

Garrick seems to deflate, his words being soft. "I don't have the answers, Kristo, but I wish to the gods above that I did. Or maybe those answers are best left not knowing. If there is a great plan, then I'm sure she is basking among the fruit trees up in the higher planes. May Sutri guide her soul." The man doesn't know if his words help.

Kristo starts to cry, his head hanging forward far enough that the helmet on his head falls to the hides covering the ground. Garrick looks away, letting Kristo cry till the tears stop coming.

The tent flap opens after a time, and the plump-cheeked woman comes in with a plate of cheese and bread, as well as a pitcher of water with two cups. Taking measure of the situation, she doesn't ask anything, leaving the two alone with their meal.

Garrick's head turns towards the tent flap, a deep frown on his face as the sounds of men screaming in pain get closer to camp.

The night goes by at a terrible pace. Moments inside of the tent stretch out for hours, and even as sleep finds the two of them when Kristo's tears give out, their slumber leaves them with little respite as the sun lights the tent. Garrick is the first to move, rubbing soreness from around his body at having worn his armor to bed. He finally undoes the chainmail's belt around his waist, casting all off in a heap.

Hearing the loud movements, Kristo comes to and downs the leftover water as his impromptu caregiver watches.

Garrick grabs his short sword and puts it on. As he makes sure his shield is with his chainmail, he addresses Kristo, "You need new clothes." The soldier moves out from the tent, a waning half-moon necklace dangling from his neck, showing now that his chainmail isn't on. He stands up and offers a hand into the tent to help Kristo out. "I hope you like yellow."

Kristo stares up at the man before taking his hand to get up.

Garrick looks about the series of tents that have been made for triage with women going about frantically with bandages and water. He gives a sigh from the sight, walking in the direction of a supply wagon that has a woman standing in it and various yellow clothing behind her. "Hello, Mari." Garrick pushes the child forward as if to offer him to the woman. "I need the shortest set of clothes you have."

The woman looks down at them both. Spying the blood stain on Kristo's clothing, she gives him an apologetic smile. She then looks through the crates and comes back with a pair of trousers and a bright-yellow, sleeved tunic. "Here you go, little lord."

Kristo takes them with a grateful nod of his head.

Garrick then puts a hand on the half-elf's shoulder. "Thank you, Mari."

The pair return to their tent where Kristo changes into his new clothes as Garrick waits outside. Once done, the child comes out with rolled-up pants and the sleeves of his shirt also in a massive ball of cloth by his wrists. On top of his head, he has the simple nasal helm Garrick gave him last night.

Looking at Kristo, Garrick gives him an amused grunt. "You look like a lighthouse."

Kristo doesn't understand why the man finds this humorous but doesn't mind it. "What's a lighthouse?"

Garrick knocks on Kristo's helm, motioning for him to follow as he grabs a shovel leaning on a blockade crate near the exit of camp. "A lighthouse is a tall building designed to help ships find the shore. They're common by coastlines." Garrick continues his walk out of camp, moving towards the city and its broken gate.

The sunlight on the gates clearly shows black scorch marks where the gates were blasted into and where its great hinges were on the great archway. Yellow-clad soldiers fill the streets, cleaning up the mess of bodies that are strewn about. As they walk, Garrick and Kristo notice closed shutters and locked doors, while more unfortunate residents are cautiously looking out from broken homes at their ruined city streets. Once at the slave house's alley, Kristo dashes down its length to the building. Among the debris is Mabel's body, stiff and blue tinted.

Garrick stands over her body, looking down at Kristo next to him. "You said she's from Halmin and her name was Mabel? Did she tell you anything about her life there?"

Kristo is silent for a moment, kneeling to hold one of her stiff, lifeless hands. "Yes, she said she lived on a strawberry farm and liked to have fun at a festival every year."

Garrick's eyes move to Mabel's face. His head hangs down as he whispers something like an apology to Mabel's corpse before addressing Kristo. "We'll have to walk to the trees for a proper grave. It's the custom."

"What about the man on the horse?" Kristo asks, sniffling.

As Garrick picks up Mabel's body, Kristo lets go of her hand. Garrick leaves the broken alleyway, stepping over the corpse of a stripped guardsman. "Sometimes you have to do things important to you first, even if that means getting into trouble." Garrick walks on, Kristo coming to him with a few fast-paced steps. The two walk away from the city and towards the northern tree line.

Birds Kristo never knew existed sing as if yesterday's bloodbath happened ages ago. The cool humidity of the first trees hits him, the child touching and experiencing all that is happening in the bustle of forest life. "I don't know if I've ever touched a tree before."

Garrick looks down to Kristo, who is feeling the bark on his fingers, and stops a moment to let the child experience it. "The world is in an awful place if a child your age can say such things."

Kristo looks up to Garrick, touching the tree still. "I can't say it anymore."

Garrick nods, and a satisfied look passes over his face for a moment. "Good."

Garrick and Kristo move through the trees, both trying to find a proper place for Mabel.

Soon Kristo finds a patch of soil that has a large rock with a thin, shiny vein running down it. "How about here?"

"This is a fine spot. Very well chosen." Garrick lays Mabel's body nearby, takes up the shovel, and plunges it into the ground. "Kristo, I need acorns and pinecones for the service."

The child, leaning against a tree and staring at his departed friend, looks towards Garrick with confusion.

After a few flicks of soil, Garrick stabs the shovel into the dirt and turns to see Kristo staring at him with a confused gaze. "Right . . . never mind." The soldier looks up at the sky with the sun barely in midday behind the leaves of the surrounding trees. The sun continues to move until an orange haze takes hold of the land, Garrick working all the while. As the hole is finally deep enough, Garrick carefully moves Mabel into it and goes off in search of seeds. Once back, he finds Kristo sitting on the side of the hole with his feet dangling in. "Hey! Get out of there!" The child looks up at the man in a shock. With nuts and seeds tucked in one arm, Garick pulls Kristo up to his feet by a hand hooking under the kid's shoulder. "This is Mabel's resting place. Respect it as if it was Mabel herself. Understand?" He points a stern, thick finger at the boy's face.

Kristo bows his head and looks down at Mabel again, "Yes, I understand," he says as a tear falls from his cheek to hit her left hand and he looks on Mabel for the last time.

Garrick starts shoveling soil back into the hole where Mabel's body will fertilize the next season's growth. When the hole is almost filled, he spreads the seeds he collected onto the grave and continues covering the turned ground with what's left of the pile of dirt. Once the soil has covered the seeds, he motions for Kristo to come near. "Close your eyes and think about your friend."

Kristo does as he's told. Garrick puts a hand on the boy's shoulder, and once Garrick sees Kristo's eyes close, the soldier does the same. The two stand in silence for a time.

Garrick shuffles his feet and speaks with a voice that is trying to sound holy. "Sutri, goddess of the high planes, patron mother of farmlands and forests alike, we humbly beseech you for your aid. Our friend Mabel has left our plane and searches for a new world to call home. Please guide her to your glory, let her bask in the flower fields close to your heart, and help her find respite under the fruit trees of your love. May the seeds planted upon her final plot of land find nourishment and bounty from the body that once thrived off the very land she now comes back to be one with. Return her will to your wonder, and let her spirit be known to be in good care by having one of these small seedlings grow to be a mighty king with branches fit to give the love she held for all things on earth." Garrick bows his head.

The half-elf boy doesn't fully understand what was said, but regardless, tears fall from his slightly sharp cheeks, hitting and darkening the ground.

Garrick adds, "And may the tears from those close to Mabel be the first rains to cause the seeds to crack."

Putting a hand upon Kristo's head, Garrick takes the boy's helmet off and offers his moon necklace in its place. "Kristo . . .? Would you like to come with me to my hometown of Halmin?"

4

FATE OR CHANCE

"You have the same hometown as Mabel?" The half-elf looks up at Garrick, whose brown eyes meet Kristo's.

"Yes, Mabel was a friend of mine when I was younger. We grew up together. I . . . I wish I found her again under better circumstances."

Kristo is looking between Garrick's eyes, as if to try to make sense of him. "Yes, I'd like to go to Halmin."

Garrick offers the necklace again.

Kristo looks at it. "What is this for?"

Garrick takes up the shovel once more, putting it over his shoulder. "It's a gift. Have you not gotten one before?"

Kristo shrugs and puts it on. "Yeah, but they were always food."

"I can see why; pretty things must not matter if you're hungry."

Kristo nods quickly. "I'm hungry right now."

Garrick gives a light chuckle, looking up at the sky turning black. "We did have only breakfast today. . . . When we get to camp, we'll go to the meal line. Plus, when we get to my home, I'll cook you up a fat piece of cow Marmuin style."

Kristo's sharp eyebrows scrunch together. "What's Marmuin style?"

Garrick tilts his head as if a little proud. "It's me, my family's style of cooking. I am Garrick Marmuin."

Kristo's eyes light up. "Mabel said the Marmuin family were great cooks. Can you cook me something now?"

Garrick shakes his head, amused from the enthusiasm behind Kristo's voice. "Calm down. I'll cook you as many meals as you want back in Halmin. Though, from the look and sound of you, you might chew through all my savings." Looking back at the grave, Garrick gives Kristo a nudge on the shoulder in its direction. "Say goodbye to Mabel."

Kristo turns to Mabel's resting site, taking in the surroundings. He stares at the large rock nearby as if to burn it into his memory. His gaze moves down at the grave. "Thank you, Mabel. I hope Sundri—"

"The goddess's name is Sutri," Garrick interjects in a calm tone.

Kristo nods, starting again. "I hope Sutri takes good care of you as you did for me."

Garrick ruffles Kristo's hair and begins to walk back to camp. Kristo gives the rock near Mabel's grave a final look over before turning away, running a few steps to get to Garrick's side. On the walk back, sunlight drains from the sky. A dark blue sheet with specks of lights dotted across it cradles the world. The moon is out with three distinct craters in a triangle scarring its face. A veil of black is coming over its right, the darkness creeping on it. The pair keep a quick pace, eventually coming to the camp once more. Passing through the surrounding barricade, Garrick puts his shovel back against a crate.

As the two move through the camp, Kristo keeps near Garrick, who looks to be heading to a bright spot near the heart of the tents. As the pair pass through the encampment and the tents, they hear groans and laughter. Clacking tankards and weeping hearts mingle in the air of the encampment, thousands of souls, each with his or her own motivation and worth.

Those walking through here, Kristo thinks, all have a comfortable sense of pride about them. He can see it especially in Garrick, in his steps.

Drawing closer to the light, Kristo sees it comes from fires' large flames with spits over them. Chefs move quickly around the nearby barrels and crates with boards across the tops for culinary stations. Garrick leads Kristo to a line for them to wait their turn for a meal. Victorious, drunk men call to each other at the heart of the camp. Around them, men and women are sitting in the dust to play games or are raising toasts to celebrate deeds. Kristo looks up at the scruffy-looking men and resolute-faced women, taking in the environment. A few of the army members give brow-raised expressions at Kristo.

"Garrick? Why don't we just ask for the woman from before to give us our food?"

The soldier looks up for a second to think about a response appropriate for Kristo, moving forward in line with everyone else. "The person before was a caretaker for the sick or injured. We are neither of those things. We just happened to come along when she was free earlier. By now, she is probably very busy doing what she signed up for."

The meal line moves, letting Kristo see an angular-faced woman with sharp ears and deep-black hair that gives no reflection standing in the center of the cooks. She is wearing an all-blue outfit of a pair of trousers and tunic with black trimmings, which looks almost regal compared to the outfits of her counterparts. A playful, blue, transparent glow rolls in the air around her hands until it dissipates off out into the world. From the heavens above her, Kristo can now make out thin slivers of water streaming out of the sky that weep into barrels about her. The chefs are dunking pitchers into the barrels to hand out. "Garrick! Do you see that!? It's amazing!"

Garrick looks about at the other soldiers with an apologetic smile and then answers Kristo. "She's our army's water weaver. She uses her magical ability to pull water out of her surroundings to do what she wants with it. The whole army likes her because, quite literally, she is the well we all drink from. Her name is Venitria. She's an elf."

A balding chef with a lame arm hands Garrick a pitcher of water, a board of meats, hard bread, and cabbage. The man then speaks in a monotone voice, bored from repeating his words numerous times. "Fine food for a fine victory. We'll be going back to stew tomorrow." The man is now looking at the greasy-haired kid in front of him who's next in line. "Who're you? Never seen you here before. You best not be trying to get a free bit of rations."

Garrick raises his pitcher to catch the man's attention. "He's an ex-slave. I'm taking care of him."

The man sucks his teeth and hands over a board of food with a pitcher of water. "Ain't right, a child having been here as a slave. Where's the justice in that? Damn king is a king of savages if this is what the loyalists fight to uphold." The man slaps another piece of meat onto Kristo's board.

Kristo looks at the chef with a thankful awe. "Thank you!"

The man points at Kristo, while addressing Garrick. "You make sure he puts on the pounds he ought to. Damn kid looks like a skeleton. Might spook the whole place."

Garrick gives the man an affirming nod and then makes for the duo's tent.

After getting a few steps from the line, Kristo turns back to watch the water weaver pull droplets of life from what looks to be the moon itself, the silvery liquid splashing down into the barrels surrounding her. "Garrick? Can we stay and watch?"

Garrick lets out a confused grunt as he turns to see what the boy wants to enjoy. The soldier shrugs and chooses a piece of stony earth out of the way of the happenings of the camp to sit down. Kristo looks back to Garrick, who pats a spot next to him, and the boy joins the soldier. Together the two enjoy the sight before them, Venitria working as if she is on the stage of a play. Her hands are calling to the sky for the respite of rain. The water, summoned out of sheer nothingness, is guided and pools in the barrels that offer their life-giving gift. The two eat and watch, Garrick turning his eyes aside to look at Kristo, who is watching the act as if it were a miracle.

In her performance, the elf feels the eyes of the two upon her actions and turns her head to see them enjoying her work. She looks at the stored water in the barrels near her and turns to them with a sly smile. With a flick of her finger at a barrel and then with a point at the two spectators, she sends three thick, shining butterflies over to them. Kristo turns his neck around and around as they circle his head. Garrick gives a soft smile to the child in his care. Then the soldier watches the butterflies flutter to him, abruptly splattering against his face in a sudden lurch forward. Kristo howls in laughter at Garrick's drenched face, pointing at him and smacking the ground with a balled fist. Garrick on the other hand has his eyes closed tight with teeth gritting.

Unbeknownst to both, Venitria has come next to the two and is relaxing on the ground. She speaks to them with a teasing voice, her hand outstretched with fingers calling to the water on Garrick's body. Her voice is one as cool as the liquid she has mastery over. "Did you both enjoy watching my magic in action? I never gave approval for spectators." The water that drenched Garrick's face begins traveling about his hair and then under his clothes, running over his being and sucking the grime out of him in response to the movement of the woman's fingers.

Garrick flicks open his eyes to look at the woman. "Thank you. I haven't had the chance to bathe since the crossing of Illidus." He moves his arms and legs about as the liquid rushes about him, the water soon sucked out of his left sleeve to then be tossed onto the dusty ground. Garrick gives a grateful nod to the woman.

Venitria then flicks her eyes to the half-elf, conjures a ball of water above her fingertips, and tosses it on Kristo before sucking it all back up off his skin. Cleansed, Kristo feels about his body as if a miracle was performed.

Looking at Kristo's hair and seeing flecks of gold in it now, Garrick says, "I would have never guessed your hair would be that color."

Venitria gives the boy a little more water for his pitcher and then does the same for Garrick. "It's the light of the eternal woods. All elves are born with golden hair. I suppose this half-thing also has it. He would grow out of it by his hundredth year if he was a full elf. For him, maybe his thirties or forties."

Kristo touches and pulls at his hair, trying to see it.

"How old do you think he is?" Garrick asks.

Venitria comes closer to Kristo, putting a hand on his head to examine him. "Given the question, I take it he's not yours."

Garrick scoffs at the question. "No, no. I would have had to be . . . what? Maybe fourteen to have a child this old."

Venitria turns to squint at Garrick now, examining his face. "I can never tell how old any of you humans are. I would have put you around three hundred."

Garrick shakes his head, looking away from Venitria to Kristo. "What I wouldn't give to live that long."

Venitria turns her eyes back to Kristo, taking her hand off his head. "Hard to say with half-things. Ancestry and blood mingling are never even. He might be anywhere from fourteen to twenty. Judging by the gold left in his hair, he might be going through growth spurts soon."

Kristo chews into his meat, looking up at Venitria. "Does being an elf mean I can cast magic like you?"

Giving a smile, Venitria pats Kristo's head. "No, little one, that is dependent on your blood."

One of Kristo's eyebrows rises as he looks down at his hands.

Venitria shakes her head, as if sensing his thought. "No, not like that. Your ancestors would have had to have the ability to cast magic, and even then, it might not have been passed to you. Were your parents casters?"

Kristo gives a shrug. "Don't know. I can't remember them."

Venitria casts a raised brow to Garrick as Kristo is picking at his food. "He was a slave." The elf looks down at Kristo with pity, the same as the chef did earlier. "It is good to be here, liberating this place then. If the old council heard of their lineage being enslaved, there would be hell to pay. I'm not sure why the throne watcher isn't more involved."

Garrick holds up his hand to her. "Best not send any letters about it. He is free now, and there is no need for them to get involved."

Venitria puts a hand on her head, as if discussing things with herself. After what feels like minutes, she stops her thoughts to address Garrick. "You're right, I suppose. Elves would be duty bound to aid their kin, but in doing so, the dwarfs might get odd ideas that we're moving in on their trade partners. Sometimes I wonder how the world would be different if they weren't crafted from stone."

Garrick's shoulders relax, and a hand moves to ruffle Kristo's hair. "He'll be in good company from now on. You and your people don't have to worry."

Venitria's eyes turn sharp, her gaze digging into Garrick. "I'll be holding you to that."

Her look and tone cause Garrick to blink, confused about what she means.

Before he speaks, Venitria turns around from the two, walking away. "Feel free to watch whenever you both like. Just remember to bathe more often."

Garrick and Kristo watch Venitria's work for a short while longer until Garrick leads Kristo to return the dinnerware and then guides him back to the tent where the soldier's chainmail and shield lie. Getting in, the pair lie upon the hides, Garrick adjusting his to get the creases out.

Lying down, Kristo looks over at the man who has been taking care of him for the last day and then closes his eyes. "Mabel would have liked Venitria."

Garrick grunts, a nod coming from him. "Yes, she always loved watching mages work their arts."

Kristo moves about on his hide, trying to find a comfy spot to settle into, feeling sleep take hold.

In the morning, the two are woken by a stern male voice blaring in their ears. "Garrick! Garrick Marmuin!" A shaved-headed man with a long red beard wearing a dark-grey plate has shoved his top half into their tent. The leathers of the man's mail are dyed a harsh red, and a sleeveless, vibrant-yellow tunic has been tossed on the outside. "Garrick Marmuin, you are ordered to appear before Lord Lenfro immediately." The shaved-headed man pulls himself back from the tent and tosses a burlap bag and a water skin through the cloth opening. "Breakfast for you both."

Grabbing his chainmail and leather belt, Garrick puts on the armor, along with his helmet and snatches the rations as he leaves. Kristo follows. Escorted by the bearded man with a mace in a loop at his waist, Garrick hands out a baked potato from the sack, as well as a bit of bread for Kristo, eating some of it himself. The trio walk through the blown-out gates that have soldiers repairing it. Ropes are tied about the giant doors as they are suspended from the ramparts above. Workers are calling which direction the doors need to be swung to refit them properly.

The rubble in the streets the day before has disappeared with not a pile or trace of dust to be seen. In fact, the sandstone houses aren't even damaged along the main road. Kristo is looking about, taking in his sur-roundings. "What happened to the houses?"

Garrick pats Kristo's shoulder, turning to start walking up a tan path-way on the hill that leads to the keep. "An earth sculptor must have done this. They are mages like the water weavers, but instead of summoning water to use to their fancy, they pull stone straight from the ground to bend to their will."

At Garrick's explanation, the child gets a pep in his step. "Do you think we'll be able to watch them like we did Venitria?"

The group moves farther up to a portion of flat ground next to tall walls that give the soldiers on the keep's ramparts a full view of all that come and go.

"Maybe. We'd have to find them first, and then they'd need to agree to demonstrate for us."

The design of the keep causes those entering to walk back around in a *U* shape between a second wall that forces people to funnel through like sheep. Once around the bend, the repetitive red and tan walls give way to a gorgeously designed gate with a symbol of a falcon etched and painted on it. Through the gate, a lawn of pure green stretches between the yard and the keep itself. Berry bushes are lined in rows near the wall of the courtyard, spaced far enough away for workers to pick their treasure at the easiest angles. Portions of the ground are cut to reveal the brown soil underneath. Tomato vines, grapes, potato plants, and other food crops pop out of the exposed soil in an impossible arrangement, given their individual growing seasons. Fruit trees occasionally impose their will on the grand sight, casting their shade upon grass or plants that require the mighty shadow. And a circular pool of water with reeds popping from it rests as the centerpiece of the area.

To Kristo the gate might as well have been a portal, an open gap in the world in front of him, revealing a place he could never have dreamed of existing. The boy pulls away from the other two to run through the gate to the yard so he can observe the awe-inspiring feat of dedication up close. Despite his excitement, the half-elf still hears the man who had woken him. "Leave the little one in the garden. Lenfro has something important to discuss with just you."

Garrick goes to Kristo, kneeling near him to watch the child touch a ripe cherry tomato. "Kristo, I'm going to be gone for a bit. I'm just going into the keep. I want you to stay out here. Don't leave the boundary of the gate."

The child looks up at the man who's been taking care of him and then darts his eyes around trying to think. Before he can speak, Garrick puts a hand on Kristo's shoulder to soothe his anxious demeanor. "No need to worry. I'll be back soon. Be good."

Kristo nods, letting Garrick take his leave to follow the bearded man through another pair of heavy-set oak doors at the end of the lush courtyard. Left to his own, Kristo turns around to look about the surrounding area. At his feet, he comes down to examine the plant with hairy leaves and feels a syrupy goo on its broken edge. Curious, the boy sucks on his finger, pulling it out in surprise. The syrup on his finger is sweet! Going deeper into the wonderland, Kristo leans over a bush with dark green serrated leaves that blow out from craggy branches. Near the center of the leaves, he picks one of the dozen or so violet oval berries the size of his thumbnail.

Before he can put the berry to his mouth, a sharp feminine voice pierces the air from behind. "Don't eat that!"

With a frightened yelp, the boy turns to see who yelled at him. In the shadow of a gnarly bark tree, a blond girl in a green dress is sitting at a table.

Next to her, leaning against a tree is a knight in polished plate armor with a pauldron on his left shoulder twice the size of the other. A belt holds in place the red cloth over his mail. Orderly black hair tops his trim, tan face. The knight's green eyes simply watch everything unfold. Kristo notices the gauntlet for the knight's right hand is missing and his scabbard is missing its sword.

Near the couple is an ornate metal table, surrounded by similar chairs with plush seats and backings tied to them. Upon the table is an arrangement of delicate plates, some with food, others barren.

The half-elf approaches the table, looking at the girl, and asks, "Why can't I eat the berries?"

The little lady keeps herself upright, one hand over the other in her lap. "They're not yours, and the berries are poisonous. You're supposed to boil the leaves." She sips from a cup in front of her and then places it back on the saucer.

Close to the table now, Kristo peers at oddly shaped breads and fruits. "What are those?"

The girl, unsure of what to make of the boy in her garden, scrunches her eyebrows together and looks at the knight, who shrugs to her in turn. Her words then come out slowly with confusion. "They're . . . biscuits," she says, pointing at the small, tan disks of bread. Moving her finger to indicate the small bowls of fruit, she says, "And those are fruit bowls."

Kristo lets out a curious hum as he eyes the treats on the table. He had breakfast only a short bit ago, but with food in front of him, his eyes can't hide his desire to taste the various treats he's never seen, let alone tasted, before. "Yes, but what's in the fruit bowl?"

The girl opens her hand out to offer the chair next to her. "A couple of different melon slices, with black and red raspberries. Would you like to sit and try them? Father told me to be a good host to everyone that steps foot in the courtyard." Although her question is friendly, the tone of her statement holds some resentment.

Too focused on the treats on the table, Kristo doesn't note the tone. Not one to miss such an opportunity, he scrambles under the table to get up into the chair the girl offered. Leaning forward over the table, he sits ready to attack the food laid out. As he reaches for a biscuit, the girl strikes his hand.

"You have no manners! Do you know how to act like a proper noble?"

Kristo yanks his arm back and rubs the red portion. "No."

The girl closes her eyes to calm herself, huffs through her nostrils, and opens her eyes at the staring half-elf in the corner of her vision. "Then I'll have to teach you." Centering herself with a breathing exercise, she gets ready to teach Kristo as if he was a mutt. "First, the approaching stranger introduces himself before taking a seat at the table. He does not run under the table like a dog. My name is Lady Amelia Loraine Desimay Tengress. And . . ." With a graceful hand, she motions to Kristo to speak.

The boy understands neither the motion nor what she has suggested he say.

Growing impatient, the girl huffs, "Your name?"

"Oh," he says softly, more to himself, the gears in his head turning. Then to the girl, he says, "Kristo."

In a bit of disappointment, the girl urges him to speak more. "Your last name?"

The prior slave thinks about this for a moment. Then a smile comes across his face. "I'm just Kristo, never had a last name."

The girl's brows rise. "That can't be true. Part of being noble is not keeping information in pleasant company."

Kristo shakes his head and says with a little annoyance, "I'm not keeping anything. My name is just Kristo."

The young girl looks at the knight next to her with curiosity, seeing the same expression on the knight's face. She continues, "I see. Well then, Kristo, where are you from?"

Kristo looks up at the branches of the trees over him, enjoying the sight of them. "I'm from the half-city. I came here when I was very little. I have no memory of that place. People tell me it's nice."

Amelia nods in agreement. "It is very nice. My father took my mother and me there a few years ago. The fish is very good, and there is always something to do."

The thought of fish causes Kristo's eyebrows to narrow as if remembering something. "Yes, it is." With a little pause, Kristo takes the lead. "Lady Amelia, can I have a biscuit now?"

"Not yet," she says firmly but without maliciousness. "I have offer to offer tea first."

With one more regulation, Kristo deflates back into his chair to stare at the food in front of him.

"Would you like some tea, Kristo?"

"Yes, I'd like to try some."

Amelia pours the golden liquid into the cup near Kristo. After setting down the pot, she takes up a tiny vase, bringing it over to Kristo's cup. Gauging Kristo's expression, she realizes she'll have to continue to explain. "It's Almenian sweet grass. People typically like to let it drip for two seconds and then stir their teacup with a spoon. It's what I saw you suck from your fingers earlier." The little lady then dribbles the syrup into Kristo's cup for him to try. Amelia pours herself more tea, stirs the contents with a little spoon, pinches the handle, and brings the cup to her mouth to sip.

Kristo, having carefully watched her, mimics her actions.

With the ritual complete, they put their teacups onto their saucers. Amelia then motions towards the biscuits. "Would you like something to eat, Kristo?"

The boy looks back and forth between his host and the tray, taking a treat as the girl does the same. Not wanting to upset her further, Kristo waits to watch the girl bring the food to her mouth with an open hand underneath the crumbly bread to catch what falls off. Kristo's face lights up to a big smile as he finally gets to enjoy the food.

With all of Amelia's boxes checked, she is enjoying herself now, a smile on her face. "Kristo, I hope you don't mind me asking, but where did you get your clothes? They look too big for you."

Kristo looks at himself, flapping arms about with the loose fabric dangling. "Garrick and I went to a cart and got them. The lady who gave them out was nice. I like the color."

The little lady motions for her guard to come to her side. "Sir Reginauld, please go to my room to retrieve my sewing notions."

The knight gives her a look with both eyebrows raised, but it's met with a stern face that makes the man put a hand over his chest. "Right away, Lady Amelia," and he departs to the keep.

Amelia continues to offer Kristo more food. With further instruction, she teaches him how to eat fruit from a bowl with a fork.

"Lady Amelia, why is this place so full of plants while the outside isn't?"

She gives an easy smile at the opportunity to discuss her favorite topic. "My father, Lord Tengress, is a nature speaker, or a green mage. He can bring life to plants and make them move as he wants. All the plants here are under his care. Eventually they will be mine to take care of too. I've had tests done at my father's discretion, and I will become a green mage as well."

The half-elf gets up out of his chair, puts hands on the table, and looks seriously at Amelia. "No way! Can you make the trees drop fruit? Or the bushes to cover the whole area? Please? I want to watch."

Amelia lets out a squeak at the boy's outburst before calming herself and patting her dress. With calm tone, the lady makes a gentle wave in the air for Kristo to take his seat again, which he does, starting to understand the hand movements. "I'd love to, but I can't. Father says that magic starts culminating after the body stops growing. It must pool for a time before it is able to be tapped into. They say I should be able to cast my first spell in my mid- or late twenties, but Father also says, by being around objects in tune to one's casting preference, the magic pools faster. That's why I like to sit in the courtyard."

Kristo pays attention to every word, nodding along to her explanation. "So . . . ," Kristo says as he gets up and stands close to the tree casting the shade upon Amelia's table, "if I stay here a long time, will I become a nature speaker too?"

With an amused wave of her hand, Amelia shakes her head. "No, people are born with an affinity for a type of magic; then exposure to things related to the affinity increase the rate in which mana pools."

Disappointed, Kristo comes back to take his seat by Amelia again. "Aw, that's the same thing Venitria told me. I hope I have some magic in me. Venitria is a mage I saw yesterday and watched her form something like a bird out of the water she pulled from the sky. Maybe I'll be a water weaver too or an earth sculptor like the one that fixed the city."

Sir Reginauld comes back and places Amelia's sewing supplies in front of her. "Your sewing notions, My Lady."

The girl nods at the knight. "Thank you. That's all I require for now."

The knight puts fist to breast and then moves to his place under the nearby tree.

Amelia picks up a pair of scissors. "Come here, Kristo. Move your chair closer and put your legs up in my lap." Kristo does, and Amelia cuts the extra cloth at the bottom of each leg of the trousers, folding it over for her to sew a cuff. With her work soon done, Amelia motions for the boy's arms.

As Amelia works on his sleeves, Kristo asks, "Have you seen many elves? I talked to one yesterday, but she seemed, I don't know, different, as if she was talking from far away."

Amelia nods in affirmation, focusing on the stitching. "A few have come to my father's court. I've seen the same thing. It's like they keep themselves distant. My father says they don't like making friends outside themselves."

Kristo gives his head a shake. "It's a good thing I'm only half like that. I like people. How would I be able to have biscuits if someone didn't make them?"

An amused smile comes to Amelia's face. "That's a very strange way to put it, but I understand."

5

BREAD MAKING

GARRICK PASSES THROUGH THE SECONDARY DOOR from the courtyard. Taking a moment to hold it for with the knight who summoned him directly behind, Garrick looks at the ruins of what once must have been a regal entryway. Cabinets and the fine plates they once held are broken and scattered across a singed rug that runs down the long hallway in front of him. Workers of the keep are sorting through the mess, maids trying to clear the wood and light debris, and butlers are taking care of the rubble of the sandstone walls from the holes blown into them. Garrick takes a few steps inside. Seeing a maid struggling to place some wood in a wheelbarrow, he goes over and helps her lift it.

"Thank you," she says.

Before Garrick can respond, the knight behind him puts a hand on Garrick's shoulder and says, "Leave the rubble be. You have an audience with Lenfro."

Garrick nods and follows the knight through the debris of the hallway to the right, where a set of great oak doors set into the wall have been shattered. Inside, in the banquet hall, a chandelier lies broken on a gorgeous rug, and more of the keep's workers are salvaging what they can of it. Stained-glass windows line the walls, which surprisingly have remained unscathed, despite the destruction around the keep.

At the end of the room, the feasting table, with as many of the remaining good chairs as possible around it, holds a wide array of food that must have been taken from the keep's stores. Knights from both warring sides are eating at the table, but those wearing red tunics are not carrying any weaponry. At the head of the table sits Lenfro, who is wearing a fancy yellow tunic and embroidered pants. Next to him sit two similarly regal-dressed people, a tall blond man with long hair in a ponytail and a woman in a green dress and beehive-looking wig.

Next to the table in a line is a procession of people that are all attempting to talk to Lenfro. At its forefront, a ruddy-eared dwarf with rags tied in his beard converses with Lord Lenfro and is saying, ". . . you've set free would be willing to fight with you, allow the men of the mines to fight alongside your army."

Lenfro shifts his sitting position. "And what would you want in return? To be made a knight? A seat at the table? Your own command?"

The dwarf shakes his head. "I want what every man and woman that has spent almost a decade in that pit wants. Blood and justice against our captors. I don't need your permission to have command. The men already follow me."

Lenfro raises his eyebrows and then looks at the well-dressed man next to him. "How about it, cousin? Should I set those that you've interned here loose against the crown's men?"

The man eyes Lenfro coldly while taking a few grapes to his plate. "You may do whatever you like. You are the victor here. I would caution you, though."

Lenfro chuckles. "You would caution me? I sit as the head of your table, eating your food stores after I decimated your forces, and you would think to caution me?"

The two lock eyes for a minute

Then Lenfro sits back, offering a hand forward to the ponytailed man. "Let's hear it, Vincent. What would you caution a would-be minister of war about?"

Vincent places his grapes down on the plate with enough force that a few of them smoosh into the silver, an action observed by Lenfro. "This man is a bandit leader. Do what you will with your army, cousin, but do not let this man lead anyone more than himself. Are you familiar with the long cliff incident?"

Lenfro stretches in his chair, eyeing the dwarf. "Yes, I studied it actually. Brilliant maneuverings to cause men—your men—to have their backs against the valley of reeds." Lenfro is having fun watching Vincent's expression. "Just a bit south of here if I remember right. Are you implying this is that dwarf?"

Vincent gives a curt nod, eyeing the dwarf, his gaze filled with contempt.

"Aye," the dwarf says disdainfully, "the name's Birkin if you'd like to use it."

Lenfro claps his hands together. "Then consider your request approved. You'll be a sergeant in the restoration army effective immediately." Lenfro motions towards one of the knights further down the table. "Thema, write up this dwarf's letter of command when you've finished eating, please."

The knight gives a slight bow to his lord.

Lenfro then gestures a hand at Birkin. "Come sit, my new ally. There is plenty of room at this table. I'd love to pick your brain about how you came up with that devious plan."

Vincent appears ready to boil over in rage as the dwarf smirks at him. "I'd love to."

Lenfro motions at the knight sitting across from Vincent. "Jema, I mean no disrespect in this, but could you move down just a hair so our new friend may sit there?" The knight obliges, giving a small nod, and then scoots his chair down as a servant comes in with a chair for the dwarf.

As soon as Birkin sits down, Vincent gets up, pounding a fist into the table, which causes Jema to get up and draw his blade. "Enough, Lenfro! I won't be made a mockery of in my own home!"

Lenfro gives a dismissive wave to Jema to sit down. "Relax, he isn't a threat. That ring on his finger binds his ability to control mana." Lenfro leans forward in his chair, a serious expression on his face. "My apologies, cousin." Vincent deflates slightly, and Lenfro continues. "Where, exactly, *would you* like to be made a mockery of?"

The knights around the table wearing yellow stifle their laughter, while those in red are keeping their tempers in check.

Vincent has had enough. He pushes his chair into the table with a slamming noise and then helps the woman next to him up as they move to leave the room. Guards at the end of the room move to stop them, but Lenfro waves them off, and the pair storm by Garrick and the knight escorting him.

Jema speaks to Lenfro but is still audible for all to hear. "My Lord, perhaps we are being too harsh to Lord Vincent?"

Lenfro raises his eyebrows and then shakes his head. "No, Sir Jema, I would have to disagree. You are first and foremost a courteous man, but that man deserves no courtesy." Lenfro gestures to Birkin. "He and many others were forced to strike stone for years on end under his orders and watch. That man deserves to clean latrines for the rest of his natural life. After that, I might have a necromancer raise his corpse to continue the work."

Then to Birkin, Lenfro says, "Speaking of work, the ore in the iron mines still needs to be mined. Our side needs metal."

"The men who just came from the mines will not go back."

Lenfro puts his hand up as if to stay Birkin's emotions. "Not as slaves. I'm not suggesting as workers either. What we need are overseers for the loyalist soldiers we captured. What fairer overseers for the imprisoned than those that they might have mistreated or not?"

Birkin nods at this in satisfaction. "Yes, you'll need someone in charge who knows how to read. I'll scrounge someone up and get volunteers."

A female voice clears her throat at the table, causing attention to turn to a woman in white wearing a porcelain mask with a flower depicted on it. "My Lord, we have a system of justice in place for such ordeals. It is to prevent mistreatment by those presiding over sentencing and oversight."

Lenfro nods. "You are right; we do. Though that very system caused this entire mess we all are fighting through. Perhaps a new precedent needs to be set, and for now, I can think of nothing fairer." There are no rebuttals to Lenfro's words, and soon the line of worried nobles and high-class citizens is being tended to once more.

Garrick, who had been held off to the side, is now ushered forward by the knight with both cutting to the front of the line. Lenfro waves the two over and says to Garrick, "This way." With a guiding hand, he ushers just Garrick further back into the banquet hall, which perplexes Garrick. "You were supposed to report to me yesterday. Explain yourself."

The soldier briefly recounts what transpired with Kristo.

Lenfro nods. "Noble of you. I believe I also saw you at the previous battle at Kurin's Retreat. Then on top of that, you were one of the first inside the walls of Effilnem. It's sad to say, but you might be one of the only survivors of that lot. Tell me, what was your profession before becoming a soldier?"

Garrick scratches at his growing beard, as if embarrassed to answer. "A baker, My Lord."

Lenfro's eyes rise. "To think that someone so valorous would be baking lovely treats!"

Garrick shakes his head. "It is nothing, My Lord. I have had a bit of sword training and used to hunt when I was younger."

With a wave of his hand, Lenfro dismisses the statement. "That type of background is common for men in this kingdom, but you still managed to survive the odds."

Garrick nods, his words a bit unsure. "I suppose so, My Lord."

"As it stands, my ranks of knights have been thinning of late," Lenfro says, motioning towards the table of knights, "and I require people true to this rebellion. The men know of you, especially after you've been chaperoning around the little half-elf, Kristo. I would have you join my table as a knight."

Garrick blinks at the proposition, eyeing the other knights, but then bows his head. "Thank you, My Lord, but I cannot. I was about to request absence to take Kristo back to town to be with my wife in Halmin."

Lenfro clasps onto one of Garrick's shoulders. "And why wouldn't I grant that to a knight? Just be back before we move out. Should be a week, maybe two. Halmin is close by."

Garrick's head comes up, and then he nods. "It would be an honor to be counted as one of your knights, My Lord."

Lenfro smiles at Garrick. "Good, let's get you knighted then." He motions at the knight that escorted Garrick. "Get me one of my good swords. We've a new knight to join our ranks."

6

WITHOUT WANT

THE HEAVY DOORS OF THE KEEP open again. Garrick speaks to the red-bearded man in the doorway, gives him a handshake, steps through, and hears the door shut behind him. His brows furrow in confusion at the sight of Kristo being tended to by the little lady of the keep. Garrick goes towards them, a hand upon the pommel of a new sword. "Hello, lady of the house. I am Sir Garrick Marmuin. May I have this seat?" Garrick rests a hand on the chair to the left of Amelia.

She looks at him and nods. "Of course, Sir Marmuin, I am Lady Amelia Tengress, Lord Tengress's daughter. My apologies, but I am in the middle of fixing Kristo's clothes. You are free to have anything on the table."

Garrick takes a seat, impressed by Amelia's grace. "You have my thanks for tending to Kristo's clothing, Lady Amelia."

The girl finishes with one sleeve, asks for Kristo's other arm, and says to Garrick, "It's not a problem. He's been an interesting guest, almost poisoning himself and then going under the table to reach his seat." Amelia's threaded needle goes through Kristo's new cuff in an exaggerated fashion to express the girl's feelings.

Garrick's arm twitches as if to go to smack his face, but he smooths this over by adjusting his hair and talking in a calm tone. "I see I will have to teach him table manners."

The half-elf fidgets in his seat at the conversation's track. "Are you in trouble with Lenfro, Garrick?"

With a smile, Garrick looks down at his new longsword and then at Kristo again. "I was but not any longer. I've been knighted for my service by Lord Lenfro."

As Amelia finishes her work, her eyes turn toward Garrick, trying to gauge his worth. The knight in the background leaning against the tree does the same and rolls his shoulders back before looking at Garrick.

The new knight continues his explanation. "I was given the sword I was knighted with, and in my coin pouch, I have a voucher for a horse that was captured in the siege."

Kristo's puzzled look shows he doesn't fully understand.

Garrick tilts his head just slightly as he explains. "It means I am in the service of House Strixwi now; the yellow winged horse will be placed on my shield."

Amelia claps her hands at the announcement. "Congratulations, Sir Marmuin, on your promotion to knight bachelor."

Garrick gives Amelia a courteous nod and continues. "I also requested a leave of absence, which was granted under the condition that I deliver you, Kristo, to Halmin and my family. Also, I am to make sure everything is going to be fine before I come back to my duties."

With the idea he will be going to the place in Mabel's stories, the child can't help but grin from ear to ear.

Garrick gets up and bows his head to Lady Amelia. "Thank you once more for the aid with Kristo's clothes. I must now beg our leave. If Kristo is ever in Effilnem again, I hope you might grant him the ability to call on you."

Amelia looks over Kristo fully to take stock of him. Taking a piece of embroidered cloth off the table in front of her, she holds it out for Kristo to take. In a very matter-of-fact tone, she says, "This piece of cloth is our bond. Don't ever lose it. If it's damaged, you need to just show me the cloth and I'll replace it. Don't think of this handkerchief as a promise; it is more of a thought."

Garrick witnesses this exchange with open mouth but quickly shuts his jaw with a soft clack of teeth.

The two bid farewell to Amelia, leave the keep of Effilnem, and make their way out of the city back to the camp. There, they request supplies from various personnel and then report to Garrick's captain about his promotion. Eventually, Garrick and Kristo reach an enclosure with shoulder-high stone walls. In the pen, a dozen and a half horses graze the area where grass has been made to spring up.

At the pair's approach, a pot-bellied man with dusty brown clothes and a cap raises his arm in greeting as a yellow scarf drapes towards the ground. Behind the man's station on the pen wall hang various saddles with different colored straps and leathers. "Hello, friends. What can I do you for?"

Garrick returns the gesture in greeting. Then he produces from his coin pouch the parchment authorizing his entitlement to a steed. Handing the paper to the man, Garrick says, "We're here to select a horse. Here's a note from Lord Lenfro."

Kristo has moved next to the wall of the pen and is petting the muzzle of a black horse with a dark-brown mane and tail.

The man in charge of the pen takes Garrick's note and reads it. "Uh . . . yup. That's the way *horse* is written, and that's Lord Lenfro's mark." The horse master takes a piece of parchment from his pocket to confirm the signature. "All right, head through those stable doors and pick yourself a good one."

The horse the boy is petting puts its lips to Kristo's hair, messing it all around as reward for the attention.

Garrick removes a wooden block keeping the stone doors shut and calls out, "Kristo, come inside, and don't approach the horses from behind or you'll risk getting kicked."

Kristo joins the knight. All the horses turn their heads to gaze at the people in their pen, with a few walking over to inspect them.

Viewing the options, Garrick puts a hand under his chin and scratches the two-day-old stubble. "Kristo, I have no clue how to gauge a good horse. My family never needed to keep one."

Kristo gives a shrug. "I don't know either. Some slaves tended to the horses, but I never got to."

Garrick sighs and watches the animals' demeanor, taking their size into account. After inspecting all at a distance for a few minutes, he goes around to greet the horses individually. After meeting the horse that Kristo was petting, it follows Garrick to the next horse the knight inspects and then toys with the man's hair with its lips. "You like attention that much?" Garrick says to it. With arms crossed, the knight looks over the steed, nods, and returns to the horse master.

Kristo tails his protector's steps.

"I'd like the black horse with the brown hair, sir," Garrick announces to the man in charge.

"The one that likes hair?"

Kristo nods eagerly. "I liked that one too."

With a humored sigh, the horse master claps his hands. "All right, I'll get the tack for you both." Scratching his cheek, the stable master surveys the equipment along the walls, picks up gear and a saddle that matches the horse's mane, and hands them off. "Here you are, sir. I'm certain this one fits."

"Thank you. I'll be sure to take good care of her." With everything needed in his arms, Garrick returns to the pen to approach the mare, putting the equipment on her with the help of the stable master, who explains everything.

The whole time, Kristo is scratching the forehead of the horse, which huffs when the child stops.

Once Garrick finishes, he pats the mare on the shoulders. To Kristo, he says, "Would you like to be the first to ride her?"

Kristo gives an immediate nod, getting closer to the horse. He attempts to use the stirrups but fails multiple times. Finally, Garrick picks the child up by the waist and positions him in the saddle.

The knight takes the reins to lead the horse out of the pen and back to his and Kristo's tent. Opening the flaps of their tent, Garrick picks up the ration sack the pair stored there for their trip and puts it on the back of the saddle, securing it with the drawstrings hanging on the knobs. The knight then takes his hides off the ground, tossing them over the back of the horse's saddle. He collapses the tent, wrapping the stakes in it, and adds it on top of the hides.

Garrick hands his helmet to Kristo and then playfully slaps the boy's knee. "All right. Now we go to Halmin. Ready to see all the plants?"

Kristo gives a curt nod. "Will it be like the garden Amelia was in?"

Garrick pulls at his horse's reins again to have her walk just a step behind him. "No, it's even bigger, and the plants are even brighter colors. Some houses have small flower gardens too." Garrick, knowing the roads, leads the pair away from the tan-red landscape with the slow-clopping hooves sounding their departure. The trio head toward a land sparsely filled with trees and then deeper into the forest where the humidity and scent of tree sap takes over their senses. Occasionally, they take breaks to rest or eat as needs arise. During lunch, human and half-elf sit against the same tree at different angles with occasional rays of light hitting the ground near them. Both pairs of eyes are on the horse, which is currently inspecting a bush near where she is tied.

"Garrick?"

The knight gives a hum. "What is it, Kristo?" Garrick breaks off a bit more bread for the two, holding a piece for the boy.

Kristo takes it, has a bite, and speaks with a mumbled voice. "What is your family like?"

The knight looks up at the tree branches, examining the leaves. "Don't speak with your mouth full of food. It's considered rude." Garrick gives a gentle hum again, this one with a question mark hanging off the end. After a short time to gather his thoughts, Garrick says, "It's small. My wife, her mother, her dad, and I are the only ones of my close family living in Halmin still. My brother and sister moved away to Plick around two years ago."

"What about your parents?"

Garrick shakes his head. "They died when I was little." He bites into his bread as if to signify the end of his answer.

Kristo turns his head away. "Why are you taking care of me?"

Garrick's eyebrows rise, and he look at the child. "I couldn't just leave you where I found you."

Kristo shakes his head, picking at the grass under him, and stares at it in his palm. "No, I mean why take me back to your hometown? Why make sure I'm fed?"

Garrick smiles and says sarcastically, "Well, I can take your bread away if you like."

Kristo frowns, looks at his bread, and then slowly offers it to Garrick.

"No, Kristo," he huffs, shaking his head. "I was just being sarcastic, you know . . . making a joke where I don't really mean something. I'm not going to take your bread from you."

Kristo immediately pulls his hand back with the bread.

With a sigh, Garrick says, "Mabel was a good friend of mine when I was younger. She was looking after you, right?"

Kristo nods.

Garrick nods too. "I want to continue that. You deserve more than what you've been dealt. Halmin is a good town with honest people; you'll have friends and a normal childhood."

Kristo tries to fully understand what Garrick said and turns his head to stare off into the woods. "It's so green here."

Garrick eyes the surroundings Kristo is looking at. "You'll be able to stare at the greenery for as long as you want when we get to Halmin."

"That's good. It's my favorite color." In a pause of the conversation, birds are heard singing, causing the child to look around in the trees. "What else is your family like?"

Garrick gives a shrug. "It's different from what you're probably expecting. My wife, Sera, is a quarter giant. She's taller than me by a few inches." Garrick puts his hand above his head to show how tall. "I like to poke fun at her every now and again, calling her a gentle giant. Just like the jeer, she's kind, and that kindness shows on her face." With a rub to the back of his head Garrick wonders for a second if he's giving a good description or not. "She has hair the color of wheat with strands of brown mixed in that is normally done up in a bun. Her eyes are the hue of the sky that around the edges turn a deeper blue." A deep smile spreads across Garrick's face. "Oh, and she loves children. Her mother is the head of the church to the goddess Sutri in Halmin. The nature gods church mandates that only women officiate. But men can be choir members. That's how Sera and I met. Due to her mother's station, Sera learned at the church to read and write. It took a while, but she managed to teach me too."

Kristo squirms uncomfortably. "Her name is Sera?"

Garrick notices the boy's change and says, "Yes. Is something the matter?"

The child searches Garrick's eyes for . . . something.

Now more confused, Garrick asks, "What is it, Kristo?"

The child stays silent for a time. "I'm just trying to picture her."

"She's a lovely woman. Don't let her height get to you. As I said, she loves children. She actually turned the front of our bakery into a little school where children of the town can go to practice their literacy." With Kristo's questions giving out for the moment, Garrick pats the child's shoulder to signify it's time to move out, the man eager to get back home.

As they continue their journey, Garrick every now and again checks to see if Kristo needs a break, but Kristo just shakes his head, telling him he's fine. It's not until the sun starts to give out that Garrick finally stops, finding sticks to prop his tent up. Finished, he tells Kristo, "We'll be walking this pace again tomorrow. We're getting closer. I remember the creek we passed by from the army's march south."

Unconcerned, Kristo says, "It's nice seeing the forest."

The next morning, Garrick is the first to wake up and soon has Kristo up and moving as well. After a quick breakfast, the two of them start moving out once more. At recognizing a halfway landmark—a tree with white flowers starting to bloom on it—Garrick gets a quick swing to his legs. Past the beautiful landmark, the birds' songs get weaker, and the scent of wet ash fills the air.

In the road to the left, the forest parts, revealing what must have been a natural thinning of trees. But the landscape now can only barely be remembered as such. A cruel black and grey force laid claim to the land before the eyes of the travelers. Trees caught in the maelstrom lack branches and show blackened bark their full length. Others less strong have trunks with huge jagged breaks or lie toppled over on the ashen ground. Along portions on the travelers' right, sturdy rock walls rise in tall unnatural lines, a feat capable only by mages. Countless black craters on both sides cut into nature. Garrick is staring absentmindedly at a weed sprouting a short distance away out of the ruined area.

"Garrick?" Kristo asks, bringing the knight back to his senses. "Why is the forest different here?"

For the first time since they met each other, the man has a furrowed brow, trying to pick the proper words for Kristo. "This is a battlefield. The land here was once called Kurin's Retreat." Garrick points a finger out towards a huge pile of ash. "There used to be a giant log cabin there. See the mound of ash? Its inhabitants would look over the rare flowers and beneficial herbs that used to grow here." Garrick moves to tie his mare to a tree, lifts Kristo off, and the two sit on the edge of the flames' rage to look at everything in depth.

Kristo is anxious to hear more. But Garrick doesn't speak, so Kristo poses another question. "What happened to the cabin?"

"Mages."

Kristo's sharp eyebrows show even more confusion than before. "Mages?"

Garrick sighs, looking at Kristo for a moment and then letting his eyes return to the battlefield. "Mages like Lord Lenfro and Venitria are great gifts to our world, but they are also great curses. They have the power to aid it in many ways that we normal folk can't even dream of. That power can be used, as you saw in camp, to bring life to a place that usually wouldn't support it or to build families shelters from the elements. At the same time, that power can be used for the opposite—taking life and joy from the world at a dizzying rate. Those black circular dents in the ash are places where fireballs fell, flung by mages from both armies, my own and those loyal to the crown."

Kristo turns his head to see so many black craters across the landscape in front of him.

Garrick continues, touching some of the ash. "The fire from the battle must have spread wider after both sides left and caused what we see here." Garrick gazes down at the line of stone running along the right side, picking out a spot of wall to point out. "I was right there behind a row of soldiers during the first part of the battle. The loyalist army ordered their archers to fire. In response, our stone sculptor pulled up rock that you see there from the dirt. Everyone I was in ranks with pressed themselves against that wall for cover while raising their shields. Fireballs were blasting about the field, and arrows rained onto our shields loud enough to make even a deaf man block his ears. It was like the world was out to kill every soldier on the field, not just on our side either. We were at the whims of powers beyond ourselves, mages with great gifts using them to kill men as if we were nothing but a flock of sick chickens. Each man was saying a prayer to what god he held dearest as we all listened to metal rain hitting our shields. I myself have to plant a fruit tree in Sutri's name when this mess is over."

Kristo notices how Garrick has a hardness to the eyes while recounting that day.

"When the quivers finally ran dry and the mana of the area was exhausted, we were ordered to advance, stepping through flames to clash with men like myself, maybe just a tad different. I . . . ," Garrick pauses not in sorrow but in remembrance, as if he can see everything playing out before his eyes, "I think I killed five in the heat that surrounded us after the mana in the air gave out. Mages are very powerful, but they're near useless if they're in a dead zone. Practicing magic means less time to practice swordsmanship."

Garrick turns to Kristo. "We ended up winning that battle; the loyalist army had to retreat to recruit more soldiers. I imagine they are still doing that. With the victory, Lord Lenfro ordered us on a march south, using our two illusionists to make it seem to the guards of Effilnem that it was just a normal night while we came upon the city."

The boy quietly contemplates what Garrick said and turns his eyes back to the aftermath. "How many people have you killed?"

The knight turns his face up at the nearest tree as if asking it for forgiveness. "That's not a question a child should be asking." Garrick turns to look at Kristo, seeing the child still searching his face. Garrick gives a sigh, grabs a piece of burnt wood, and tosses it. "Six in total, five here, two at Effilnem, but then I saved you, so I get to subtract one."

After a short while longer, Garrick looks across the ash field to see a woman dressed in furs. Braided in her hair, she wears a piece of antler, tied with colored yarn. She is looking at Garrick. Next to her stands a girl, similarly dressed, about the age of nine or ten. Garrick and the woman hold each other's gaze. Garrick points off to his right, and the woman nods, pointing first at Garrick and then in the same direction he is motioning towards.

"Kristo, we must leave. The nature mother demands it."

Kristo looks at the woman. "Why?"

Garrick gets up, patting Kristo's side to do the same. "Because she wants us to. She tends these woods, and it's better not to upset someone who could will a tree branch to fall on your head."

Kristo gets up, following Garrick to his horse. "She looked upset."

Garrick nods, looking over his shoulder at the woman. "She isn't wrong to be. The rebel army burned most of this area on purpose to corral the loyalists into a defeat." He helps Kristo back into the saddle and quickly guides the horse and boy down the road, away from the scar in nature. Garrick's pace slows to normal once they are a good distance down the road. Now the path cutting through trees becomes more pleasant as it meanders around the great growths.

At the very end of the day's trek, the trees are more sparse, the trees and brush being young slender things. Tree trunks, notched to indicate Halmin's border, take the place of oaks that would usually have been there. In the distance, large swaths of land have been sectioned out for growing with various crops. A wood-planked house with a sturdy rock foundation can be seen in the distance. A short distance away from that, an interweaving of dozens of trees come together in a tent-like shape with the branches of the trees grown so tightly together to form a roof that there are no cracks for the elements to enter.

Garrick takes the tent and hides off the horse once more, aids Kristo in getting down from the mare, and does his best to shoo off the hair-obsessed mare playing with his scruff of a beard.

"Garrick? What's that long building that looks like it's made from trees?"

Squinting in the darkening distance to spot the farm building, Garrick falls on the hides, pulls off his chainmail, and says, "That's a barn. We're on the very outskirts of Halmin. This is Tennly farm. Mrs. Melony Tennly won a bet with a traveling troupe three years ago to guess how many beans were in a glass box. In return for winning, she got to ask a favor of the troupe. Over the course of two weeks, a nature speaker planted acorns and then fused the resulting saplings together with magic. She said it took so long because she wanted to make sure the barn would stand the test of time, even going so far as to hit it with an axe with little effect to prove that it would."

Kristo settles onto the unoccupied hide and gazes up at the stars in the sky. "How much longer until we get to Halmin?"

The knight closes his eyes while talking to the boy, resting with his face towards the sky. "We'll be there in the morning. It's best not to walk the roads near farms at night. It gives the wrong idea." At the prospect of seeing his wife again, the knight has an easy look on his face. "Don't worry, Kristo; you'll love Halmin."

On the third day of travel, Garrick smiles at waking up to the sound of roosters crowing in the distance. As he is getting everything ready to move on, the mare next to him is turning her head closer to his hair, but after Garrick stares sternly at her, she backs off, turning her head to look the other way. He then takes the sack of rations, pulls out a hearty breakfast, and shakes Kristo gently to wake him up. Once the two finish eating, Kristo is helped back on the horse, Garrick puts on his armor, and the happy travelers march on.

Going by the giant-leafed barn, the half-elf can't stop looking at it, even turning around in the saddle to gaze at the structure until it leaves his field of view. Farmland surrounds Garrick and Kristo. Tracts teeming with the bounty of the land have farmhands harvesting the crops into wheelbarrows. Passing another set of farmhouses, the two finally set their sights on a town with buildings lacking walls and sporting new constructions on its outskirts, eating up former farmland. In the town, well-cropped grass replaces paved roads. The homes here are constructed like the surrounding farmhouses with the exception that some of them are a story or two taller. The wall facings aren't planks of cut-up trees; instead, they are trees themselves, grown to take the shape of the houses, some having small branches jutting outward. These branches eventually burst with blooms that turn into ripened orbs of fruit that passing people pluck to eat.

The town includes all the usual businesses and buildings—butchery, flower shop, church, and more. Next to the flower shop is a building created from magic that causes the bark of growing trees to weave their branches overhead and offer sheltering leaves to those that would wish to enter its grandeur. The open ground between this structure and the next has a voluminous garden where strange plants bloom, looking similar to the courtyard plants in Effilnem. Between the open partings of trees, long roots have been stretched out into benches that a few townspeople currently occupy. Near the back of the structure, a tree grows and sheds pink flowers onto the grassy floor. Before the tree, a woman with blond hair and streaks of light gray holds her hands closed as she offers her thoughts to the queen of nature. She has an air of authority, judging by the way caretakers here are giving her space. Another woman in a simple green robe has a rake to collect the fallen flowers to keep the lush ground clean and is clearly trying to work quietly so as to not disturb the woman in front of the tree.

Garrick points at the large tree structure, making sure that Kristo is paying attention. "That's Halmin's church to Sutri, the goddess of nature. And see that woman with closed eyes by the blooming tree? That's Yuna, my mother-in-law."

Kristo looks at her and then down at Garrick from the horse. "Can I meet her?"

Garrick nods at Kristo's request, pulling the horse to a rail set up near a water trough. With help from Garrick, the half-elf comes down and the horse gets tied up. Putting a hand on Kristo's shoulder, Garrick guides Kristo underneath the shade of the church's branches and through the parting pews towards the woman in prayer.

7

ORDINARY

"WHAT'S THE CHURCH'S RECORD FOR CONTINUOUS prayer to a tree?" Garrick calls from behind Yuna to poke fun at her.

The woman turns around to take in Garrick's appearance, her eyes going over the man's scruffy chin. Wrinkles adorn the sides of her eyes, suggesting that she can usually be found smiling, which is what she's doing now. "Garrick! It's been months! I'm happy you're safe." The woman comes closer, putting her arms about the knight to give him a hug, which he gives back. Once they part, Yuna addresses the half-elf that had gotten out of the way for the two to greet one another. "Hello. Who might you be?"

Kristo has his eyes on Garrick, who gives a gentle pushing motion in the air to encourage the child to introduce himself. "I'm Kristo."

Yuna gives a slight bow of her head. "It is good to meet you, Kristo. All are welcome here. But what are you doing following this troublemaker around?"

Kristo looks at Garrick with a raised eyebrow. "Garrick brought me here to see Halmin. It's Mabel's hometown. I've always wanted to see it."

Yuna's smile turns to a serious demeanor, her focus now on Garrick. "Mabel? Is this another prank, Garrick? Or did you really find her?" The woman folds her arms across her chest, wanting an explanation, not finding the supposed joke funny.

Garrick shakes his head and briefly explains how he met Kristo, about Mabel, and what they've been doing since.

While the conversation goes on, the three walk out of the church to stand under a tree with elongated blood-red pods. Yuna puts out a hand, and a faint green mist swirls about it as pods are called to her grip one after another. The woman runs a finger about one end of each that flies to her. She then hands one to Kristo and one to Garrick.

The child looks up at the adults holding the pods in one hand while they speak, not understanding what is happening.

"So now I'm here to deliver the boy so he can have a home."

Yuna gives a nod and takes a second to process the information. The deep-seated sadness remains on Yuna's face. "So that's what happened to Mabel. . . . I didn't realize Effilnem was being used in such a way. What about her parents? They were taken too."

Garrick shakes his head. Then he flicks off the top of his pod, takes a drink, and wipes hips lips with his thumb. "I assumed they would have been with Mabel, but they weren't in the slave house where I found Kristo. I suspect they might have been put somewhere else, just like at the iron pits, but in truth I don't know."

Listening to the conversation, Kristo speaks up. "Mabel said she was taken from her mom and dad after a year of being in the iron pits. She doesn't . . . uh, didn't know where they went."

Yuna's shoulders sink at the news, clearly upset that Kristo can relate Mabel being separated from her parents without a drop in his voice. "Well, Garrick, this isn't exactly what Sera meant when she wrote about wanting a child, but I'm sure she'll take care of Kristo. If she doesn't, then I have an empty bed for him."

"Well, now that I'm back in town, you can rest assured that your bloodline will continue," Garrick says with a bit of sarcasm. "I was actually planning—"

"Garrick, I don't want to know. But are you sure the army doesn't need you back as soon as humanly possible?"

The exchange confuses Kristo. Instead of trying to follow along any longer, he flicks the top off his pod just as Garrick did and drinks from the long pod. Immediately, his tongue is hit with a bitter complexion with a nutty-sweet aftertaste, Kristo's face scrunches, and his throat gives out an involuntary noise much like a cat trying to get a hairball up.

Yuna offers to take the pod from Kristo, which he hands over immediately. "Nobody initially likes the juice from the teska, but you get used to it eventually. Why don't you have some of the Almenian grass sap to get the taste out, okay?" The woman motions to the grass beneath their feet.

Kristo breaks off and swallows some blades, getting the sweet flavor to cover up the horrendous taste of the pod.

Garrick finishes his drink and hands the pod back to Yuna. "It was nice seeing you. I'm going to be making a small roast tomorrow since Kristo wants to try my cooking, so why don't you stop by to have dinner with Sera and me?"

Yuna's eyes go wide for a second at the prospect, and then she composes herself. "I'd love to."

The knight takes his leave of Yuna and says to the boy, "Come along, Kristo. I'm going to introduce you to my wife."

With slow feet, Kristo follows Garrick. The child is sucking sap from his fingers as Garrick undoes his horse from the rail to walk on, waving goodbye to Yuna, who returns the gesture. As the two make their way through town, Kristo and Garrick pass apartment houses. Closer to the town's center, Garrick plucks from the branch of a house a bright-pink squishy ball that's translucent enough to see small black seeds inside. He offers it to Kristo. "Kessi fruit. It's super sweet and sticky, so eat slowly."

Then Garrick makes a sudden stop, staring down the row of buildings a little to the left at a dangling shop sign depicting a loaf of bread with a quill over it and the words "Marmuin Family Bakery and Literacy School." With a smile on his face, the man drops to one knee to look at the boy. "Kristo, I want you to do me a favor, okay? It's important."

Kristo nods, seeing Garrick acting excited.

"Okay, so Sera should be teaching classes right now since it's before noon. I want you to go in and tell her that your father wants to enroll you in classes and that he's outside. If she asks you to tell him to come inside, tell her that he insists she come outside to talk."

While the child understands the instructions, he doesn't understand the reasoning. "Do you not want to go inside to see Sera?"

Garrick shakes his head. "It's not that. It's . . ." Garrick's face turns a little to the side to find the right words. Then a smile spreads over his face. "It's because Sera will be very happy afterwards. Oh, and don't call her Sera. Call her Mrs. Marmuin."

"Okay."

Garrick pats Kristo on the shoulder. Standing up, he takes his helmet out of the empty ration sack on his horse, puts it on his head, walks next to the bakery window just out of sight, and turns around, his back to the front entrance. "All right, Kristo, go inside just as planned."

Kristo goes into the bakery, and a bell rings to signify his entry. Inside, a large open area to the front has been repurposed for classes. Here children, teenagers, and one woman in her late twenties with black hair sit in rows to face a blond woman that is reading a book to everyone. In the students' hands are sheets of parchment that evidently have the same words from the book so they can read along with the teacher.

Marking the edge of the room is a stone half-wall with a large wooden bench behind it for kneading dough and to act as a barrier to show where customers shouldn't go beyond. Over the back of the half-wall, there is a brick oven with wood piled in front for fuel. In the back, various containers and cabinetry hold all the required supplies for the shop. Far to the back right, a stairway leads to the housing section of the family business that no one is normally allowed up, as marked by a crate in front of it.

Kristo, having taken in everything, is getting stared at by all the students.

But the blond teacher with blue eyes shows a smile very much like Yuna's. The woman then speaks in a calm tone that peaks in odd places yet soothes one's ears. "Hello there. I don't think I've seen you in town before. Have you come for bread for your parents?"

Kristo's mind goes blank as he tries to remember what he's supposed to say with all the faces trained on him. "Uh . . ."

With the child drawing a blank, the teacher gets up, puts her book on the bakery counter, and kneels to look at the boy at his eye level. "Are you lost? Do you need any help?"

Looking at the woman's face up close, Kristo sees all the details that Garrick had told him earlier. And then he remembers. "No . . . my father wants to enroll me in classes here. He wants to talk to you outside."

Sera looks out the glass windows to see a man in chainmail and a helmet looking away from the building. Giving the half-elf a smile, she gets up to her feet and offers her hand for Kristo to take. "Let's go see your father then."

Kristo looks at the tall woman's hand and takes it, giving her a smile back.

Sera addresses her students. "Class, try to read the pages we just went over in your head. I will be right back." With Kristo in her charge, Sera opens the bakery door and confronts Garrick's back. "It's nice to meet you, sir. Your son tells me you want to have him learn how to read and write."

"Yes," Garrick says, still facing away from Sera, "I was hoping this place could offer him housing too."

At the sound of the man's familiar voice, the woman tilts her head.

Garrick takes off his helmet and turns around for Sera to see his face.

Stunned, Sera immediately drops Kristo's hand and places both of her hands together over her mouth. Garrick drops the reins of the horse and his helmet to open his arms for her. Without a need for words, the woman steps closer and wraps her arms around her husband. Leaning into him, Sera holds onto Garrick tightly, silent tears wetting her wide-smiling face. "I missed you." Garrick rubs her back in a calming manner and lays a long thought-filled kiss that has the weight of sleepless nights and desperate life-or-death moments behind it. Sera responds in kind, delivering her own hours of worry mixed with the pain of not having someone so special near for all the happy moments she's had in his absence.

The wordless gestures go on for some time until Garrick moves his arm to tell her it's time to break. But instead of fully letting go, he holds her about the waist with an arm out to Kristo. "Honey, I'd like to introduce you to Kristo. He is a curious and loving child that I'd like us to adopt."

In a hushed tone with a worried smile, Sera says, "Garrick, this isn't what I meant when I wrote you about wanting children."

Garrick's voice is calm with a bit of flame underneath. "I know. I have a few days' leave to help with that." He then rolls his head toward Kristo, wanting to change his wife's heavy gaze back to the child. "Kristo here was a friend of Mabel's. She watched over him, and I want to continue her kindness."

At the mention of Mabel, the woman's eyes sharpen as if to pose a question.

Garrick pats his wife on the back, ushering her forward. "It will take a while to explain. Why don't we go inside? Send your students out to play for the day while we discuss things."

The woman gives a short nod, goes inside, giving Kristo a warm smile while rubbing her head, and tells her students they have no more class for the day.

The knight ties his horse's reins to a low post outside the bakery, picks up his helmet, and places it under his arm.

A stream of kids soon rushes out of the bakery, yelling at one another in jubilation. Sera is inside talking to the young woman in the class that seems upset at the lesson getting cut short. Garrick then goes to Kristo, putting a hand on his back to tell him to go inside, which he does with the knight following him. Sera explains to the woman that, no, in fact the class wasn't let out to discuss a child's education and that it's about adoption with her home-from-war husband. Realizing her mistake, the black-haired woman apologies and soon leaves the bakery.

With just the three of them left in the shop, Sera picks up a few chairs, moving them into a small triangle, and all sit down. After an initially awkward air, Garrick starts explaining what's transpired over the course of meeting Kristo just as he did with Yuna. "So that's what happened to Mabel . . ." Garrick gives Sera a while to process the explanation before continuing to speak. "Yes, I want to honor her memory through Kristo, which is why I want us to adopt him."

Sera gives a warm turn of her lips with a crinkle in the corner of her eyes. "Would you like that Kristo? Garrick and I . . ." Mabel's words hesitate for a second as her eyes looks off to the side, then come back to Kristo. ". . . we were good friends of Mabel. We would like to take care of you in her absence."

Kristo's eyes search Sera's face, looking for any malice in her expression. He finds none, but instead senses sadness from the way she is presenting herself.

Not fully understanding, Garrick finds Kristo's expression odd, and he tries to be comforting. "There is no need to rush your decision. You can live with us here while you think about it, or you can stay at Yuna's if you'd like. Even if the answer is no, you'll be welcome here."

Kristo nods at the offer. "I'd, uh, like to stay here. Halmin seems very nice, better than Mabel described."

Garrick's and Sera's shoulders deflate, but after just a moment, they recover themselves.

Taking off his mail gloves, Garrick says, "I am going to change out of these clothes." He motions at Kristo. "Why don't you and Sera go to the butchery and pick up a round cut of beef? Make sure to get extra ice so it'll stay overnight for tomorrow."

With the idea of an expensive meal, Sera looks at Garrick as if he's being reckless.

"It's all right, Sera. I promised him a home-cooked meal. I'm only here for a short time too. Let's enjoy ourselves while we can." Garrick grabs a jingling pouch tied to his side and offers it to Kristo, who takes it.

Sera gets up and, in gentle humor of Garrick's shorter stature, tilts her head down to place a kiss on the top of his head. She casts a soft lingering eye at him and then turns to Kristo. With an outstretched hand, she says, "Come along. If you really like magic, then you'll love the butchery."

Interested and curious, the half-elf gets out of his seat and cautiously places his hand into Sera's.

Garrick waves a goodbye as the two walk towards the door, chiming as it opens.

Through the bakery's window, Kristo hesitates, looking back towards Garrick. The knight gives a gentle shooing motion and raises his voice to be heard through the building's walls. "Go on. You're safe here." Still, Kristo drags his feet. Garrick flicks his wrist for the child to go. The ex-slave nods and finally lets Sera guide him forward.

"Kristo?" she asks. "What was Mabel like when she was with you at Effilnem?"

The half-elf scrunches his eyebrows in thought. "She was nice. I'd ask her questions all the time about Halmin. She missed this place very much and always wanted the walls of our slave house to grow food. If we had that it, would have been a lot nicer. There wasn't much to eat."

Disturbed with the description, Sera clenches Kristo's hand for a second and Kristo raises his eyebrows at the woman. "It's nothing," she says. "Please continue." As the pair walk through town, many people greet Sera, who nods in return while trying to pay attention to the child's words.

"When the guards didn't give us much food, Mabel would give me a bit of her own. She would tell me she didn't have much of an appetite." The child then smiles as he remembers his friend. "But then when we were given the leftovers from feasts or on other days we had a lot of food, she'd eat so much that she would go right to sleep after. Mabel was funny like that."

Sera smiles, but her eyes seem vacant.

Kristo continues as the two round a corner and the butchery shop comes into view. "She was nice. She, uh, she really cared for people in the pits. Sometimes when I'm happy, it's strange it's like . . . it's like . . ." Kristo's shoulders go down. "I don't know."

Frowning, Sera looks down at Kristo and says, "Like she's still here?"

Kristo nods, sadness crossing his face now. "Yeah . . . I miss her a lot. I wish she didn't die protecting me."

Getting to the door, Sera pushes it open, and the wood slams into the wall with a loud bang. Startled, Kristo flinches. Sera recoils from the bang too, an embarrassed look on her face as she stammers out an explanation. "Sorry if I frightened you. I, uh . . . sometimes use too much force; it comes with being so big."

The thickly muscled, bald, and eyebrowless butcher listens to Sera's explanation for the loud entry, sighs, and then goes back to cutting the giblets out of a bird on a long work bench in the back of the shop. Soon finished, the butcher dunks his hands in a wash basin and then wipes them on a rag before attending to the pair. "Hello, Sera. Come for some chicken again?"

With an open hand down towards Kristo and a smile at the butcher, she shakes her head. "No, this time I would like a round cut to go on a spit."

"What's the occasion?" the butcher asks in surprise.

Sera wags two fingers at Kristo, who doesn't understand what she wants, and slowly places his other hand into Sera's. The mistake causes her to look down and snort once out of humor as she takes the purse from the boy while talking quietly. "I need Garrick's purse to purchase the meat." Sera offers a silver hexagon to the butcher who inspects it, seeing its fresh shine. "Garrick is back, and he brought this little man with him. Promised him a roast for his first full day in town."

The butcher pockets the silver. "I'll give you a fatter cut than normal since Garrick is in town. Just make sure some leftovers get back to me. Oh and," the butcher moves in to whisper to Sera, "it'd be best for Garrick to lie low while he's here. You know how the town is divided in its loyalties to either Lenfro or Brenan." After a tap of his nose, the warmly wrapped worker goes back to a stone door and opens it. Cool vapor pours out.

The half-elf is up on his tiptoes to look over the counter and see the fridge. "Sera? Why is everything so cold here?"

Sera smiles at the boy's curiosity Garrick described to her earlier. "I told you that you'd like this place. It's because of books."

Still unenlightened, Kristo just stares up at Sera.

"The butcher's cellar back there is kept cold by a couple of books whose pages are filled with glyphs. They take in mana from the world around them and then force it to go through a catalyst process described by a water weaver in the books."

Kristo looks like his brain is being assaulted by a mob of angry peasants.

Sera's eyes soften in understanding. "The books are like little water weavers, but they can take in mana to do only one thing, make the air cold."

Kristo is struck by inspiration. "Are there other glyph books?"

With a nod of encouragement, the woman brims with a teacher's pride in her inquisitive student. "Yes, in fact, we'll be roasting the beef with a set of fire glyph books tomorrow. You can see those in action yourself."

The sound of the stone door in the back opening interrupts the conversation as the butcher brings out a meaty leg with bone of a cow to carve. After chopping off a healthy chunk of meat, he brings over a book and flips through it. Then he takes a little crate from a stack by his workstation, puts it on his workbench, and drops the meat into it. From a nearby chest with a mound of ice, he uses a pick to carve chunks and tosses them around the meat. As the job is completed, the butcher brings his work out to the front counter for Sera. "Remember to bring me back some of Garrick's cooking."

Sera nods, amused with the butcher's insistence. "I'll be sure to tell him to save a cut for you." At a wave goodbye, she picks up the crate of meat to leave, asking Kristo to open the door and then follow her. On the walk back, Sera explains what the various fruits, vegetables, and leaves on the walls of the houses are. Every now and again, she leans down with the crate for Kristo to drop some vegetables he has picked for their dinner tomorrow.

Getting back to the familiar grassy row of buildings, Kristo goes to hold open the bakery door for Sera, who enters and places the cold crate of ingredients on the bakery counter across from Garrick.

He has changed clothing, now wearing brown trousers with a blue tunic, the designs of which are simple yet proper enough to display the status of a successful business owner. Leaning on the counter, he speaks to Sera in a teasing tone. "Where would I be without my strong giantess of a wife?"

"With your sense of humor, you'd probably be unmarried and without a bakery."

"Yeah, that seems about right." With an amused expression at Sera, Garrick takes the crate off the counter and puts it in the back of the wheat-scented shop and next to a few rags on the floor to soak up the ice that will inevitably melt.

In the front of the shop, Sera sees Kristo eyeing the bread in the baskets around the shop, especially curious about a pink loaf with semi-sharp seeds throughout it. "Kristo, you're free to have a loaf if you want. Just don't eat too much, or we won't have inventory to sell."

The prospect of having an entire loaf to himself overwhelms Kristo. Trying to figure out what loaf to try, he settles on a deep-purple, knot-styled bread that he takes to a seat and begins ripping some of it to eat.

With Kristo distracted by the bread loaf, Garrick and Sera exchange glances as they move towards the stairs at the back of their bakery. Garrick then calls to Kristo while he's eating as much as his stomach will allow. "Sera and I are going upstairs to . . . get your room ready. Why don't you go out and find some more kessi fruit so I can make a cake?"

Given an order, the child nods, turning his head to acknowledge Sera and Garrick. "I will do as you ask."

Both give looks at one another from Kristo's odd response, but when Garrick gives Sera a gentle pat on the back, they both continue going upstairs.

Kristo puts the remaining half-loaf of bread down on the bakery counter and goes outside with the jingle of a bell. In his previous life, there would be people around to watch what Kristo was doing with the pain of punishment hanging over him for doing the wrong thing. But here, there are no guards and no threats. People walk about, giving little thought to the half-elf as they pass by to continue their business. As he relaxes in the relative freedom, Kristo realizes just how green everything is here—the grass, the leaves that grow from the houses, the moss that dangles from outcropping support beams. During Kristo's examination of the area, Garrick's horse has made its way closer to the child and strikes, messing up the boy's hair with her lips. Smiling, he pets the mare and then spends the next couple of hours picking the watery pink fruits for Garrick's cooking. Not knowing how much the knight wanted, Kristo bustles about the town, filling the front of his tunic held up to make a basket of sorts. Once the load is considerably heavy, he makes his way back to the bakery, receiving odd glances from everyone he walks by.

At the bakery, Sera and Garrick have seats set up outside their shop, notably away from Garrick's mare. Sera is leaning into her husband, holding his hand while watching Kristo come back with a tunic full of fruit.

Sitting with his eyes closed and face up at the sky, Garrick feels his hand get squeezed. As he opens his eyes, he follows his wife's gaze to the child coming with all the fruit. Amused, Garrick chuckles and says, "Good work, farmer Kristo. Next time, get just a couple. It's my fault for not telling you how many I needed." He gently pushes Sera, so she understands to sit up for him to get up. As Garrick opens the door for Kristo into the bakery, he says, "There is a fruit crate near the bread bench. Go put the kessis in there. Be careful; they might smoosh."

Kristo nods and moves his feet over to the bench. Spotting the fruit crate that has various odd-shaped edibles in it, he gently unloads his shirt to drown them in a sea of pink squishy balls. With a lack of direction now, he looks about without a sense of what he's supposed to be doing. There are no tasks for him; there is no pain in his feet begging for a rest. Instead there is, nothing. The child's gaze moves around the shop once more and then rests on Garrick, who is back outside with Sera. Kristo's legs start moving, taking him outside to the pair who are talking about what happened in town since Garrick's absence.

Sera notices the child looking at her and her husband and calls to him in a caring tone. "What is it, Kristo? Do you need something?"

Kristo shakes his head. "No . . ."

Garrick flicks his wrist at the boy. "You don't need to serve us if that's what you're thinking."

"That's not it. I just don't know what to do."

Garrick nods in understanding, having been with the boy for a few days now. "Yeah, that feeling's normal, but that's for you to learn when you're older. For now, why don't you get used to the town? Walk about, enjoy yourself."

Not having any better ideas, Kristo nods.

Garrick relaxes back in his chair. "Just make sure you're back in the bakery by sunset."

The boy gives a long awkward look at Sera and Garrick while the knight's steed creeps up on Kristo again. But he leaves with wandering feet before the horse can do anything, causing her to give an annoyed huff. As Kristo goes off, he can hear Sera and Garrick talking about potential names for the horse next to them. Not knowing anything or anyone, Kritso gets lost in the landscape of flora-covered houses, his curious eyes taking everything in. Eventually his wandering leads him back to the church of Sutri, where he takes a seat in a front pew to examine the giant cherry tree in greater detail.

The few green-robed women working in the area pause to look at the boy. Yuna soon comes out and sits next to him, causing the remaining priestesses to go back to their duties. She gives the boy a pensive appraisal till the words of what she wants to say come to her. "Hello, Kristo. Would you like to learn more about the goddess that the town holds dear?"

The boy shuffles his feet and then nods, turning to listen to Yuna.

A soft smile appears on the priestess's face as she turns back to the cherry tree, tracing its length with her eyes. "Sutri is the goddess of rebirth and nature. Every day, things die, from growing old or from events beyond their control. Sutri takes what's left after the soul of each living thing departs and lets it become one with her grand creation of our garden world. The dead owl becomes fruit for the scholar to enjoy while reading. A mouse might dine upon a berry bush its whole life, and then on its death, it could become the energy that very same bush dines on in return. In this way, we are all connected. Sutri guards this process in her humble glory, and we as her servants ensure everyone in the town can experience that love."

Kristo has his eyebrows down to think about what Yuna could possibly be trying to say, but he does enjoy the words that are coming from her. It is almost as if they've been thought of or plucked carefully for years.

The aging women nods towards the giant flowering tree under the church's care. "The cherry tree was her first creation. When Sutri saw Axon mold the planets into being, she came to each world and wept, for Axon's creation was without soul. Our plane of existence was devoid of life and love. The tears that fell from the goddess hit our soil, causing a great cherry tree to bloom from the weight of her emotions. Petals that fell from the tree became the vegetation and life you see around you, and through Sutri's tender care, the gifts from her love spread across all continents. To her sadness, she found her creations, being born from emotion, did not share the immortality Sutri herself has. In her misery, she made it that the plants might use the energy of the dead to grow as proud and support new life."

Kristo is smiling from the idea of everything coming from a tree, the thought being an amazing fuel of imagination. "Is this that tree, Yuna?"

The aged woman gives Kristo a pat on the head. "No, child, the cherry tree born from Sutri's emotions is deep in the Elven Empire to the east. Under the love of its branches, the capital of Heshval stands guard over the goddess's creation with walls and houses sung from the tree's bark."

"Sung?"

"Yes," Yuna answers. "When a nature speaker casts magic, we refer to it as singing. We hear the tune of the plants around us, and our magic alters the song of the plants by adding our own notes to make it do what we want. It's strange, I know. The only people who can really understand are other mages. Imagine trying to describe what color is to a blind person."

Kristo makes a noise that sounds like he's processing everything that has been told to him.

Overhead, the sky is turning a soft shade of orange, suggesting night-fall soon to come. Yuna gently shakes Kristo's shoulder to rouse him from pondering. "Why don't we get you home, Kristo? It will be dark soon." Yuna stands, offering a hand to the half-elf who takes it to be led back through the grass passages between buildings. "There isn't a single kessi fruit about . . ." she says, perplexed. "Guess I'll grow some tomorrow."

Getting back to the bakery, Kristo sees candlelight flicking out through the glass of the shop and hears a faint sound of stringed instruments leaking out into the world. Closer to the window, Kristo can see Sera in a red dress, looking down while holding Garrick in a blue tunic, the pair slowly swaying with each other in the center of the bakery. The chairs inside have been moved to give the couple space. On the bakery counter, a model of a concert stage has shadowy figures expressing their emotions through their instruments.

Yuna smiles at the two and then pulls Kristo over to the side of the window. "Let's give them a moment more to enjoy themselves before we interrupt."

The half-elf does as Yuna asks, staying out of sight against the bakery wall with her but trying to peek his head around to gaze inside. "Yuna? Why is Sera so tall?"

Yuna looks out towards a set of hills by the setting sun. "Her father, or my husband, Theotis, is a half-giant. You know what a giant is, right?"

Kristo gives a quick nod but is still looking at the couple dancing. "Mabel used to tell stories about them."

Yuna hums at the thought. "Well, I met him when I was younger when I was . . . tending to the woods. One thing led to another, and I settled down here, and eventually we had three children, all of them inheriting a portion of his height."

Kristo turns his head to Yuna. "Where is Sera's dad now?"

Yuna gives a hush to Kristo as his tone has been getting louder, pulling him away from the window. She then talks in a lower tone to not disturb the couple inside the bakery. "Theotis? He's probably off in the woods right now having to advise his tribal chieftain on another matter that the man is too inept to deal with himself. The only reason Theotis is not chief is because he's half-blood. Still, the tribe requires him, and he is duty bound to help. Not that he doesn't try to steal a few moments for me. I do the same for him if I find myself with a free couple of days." Once the music emanating from the bakery stops, Yuna pats Kristo's back, motioning to the bakery door, and they enter with a jingle of the bell.

"I think you both lost something." Yuna turns the half-elf in her care loose towards Garrick.

Kristo walks towards Garrick halfway, as if waiting for orders.

Garrick turns to speak to Sera. "We didn't lose him, did we, honey? I set him on the town to terrorize it."

Sera gives Yuna a deeply content grin and then picks up a pink loaf of bread riddled with seeds to offer to her mother. Yuna takes it, reaches up to pat her daughter's cheek, and then pinches Sera's cheek with a wink. To Garrick with mock scolding, Yuna says, "I wouldn't put Kristo in the same boat as you. He's not going about trying to challenge people with a stick."

"You're right . . . I need to find a good stick for him to do that first."

Instantly, a veil of green wind comes about Yuna's finger as she wills a seed out from the pink bread in her arm and flings it at Garrick's head.

A grunt signifies a direct hit, making Garrick rub the point of impact. "All right, no stick."

Yuna gives a contented huff at Garrick and then smiles down at Kristo. "If you're good and help Garrick with the roast he has planned tomorrow, I'll tell you the story of the first animals." The old priestess gives Kristo an enthusiastic nod that the boy returns. Having Kristo's word of helping Garrick, Yuna takes her leave with a wave of her green misty hand that wills the wooden door open.

After her mother leaves, Sera locks the door, speaking to Kristo at the same time. "Kristo, it's time for be—" Sera stops herself short and looks towards Garrick. He slaps his forehead, getting an embarrassed expression from his wife, and then heads upstairs. She holds a long hum before she completes her sentence for Kristo, "It's time for beef inspection. I forgot to look it over, so we should do it now." Sera motions for the half-elf to come with her to the corner where they are storing the iced beef and examines the cut. While pointing her finger at various innocuous parts of the beef round, she glances over her shoulder several times until Garrick comes back downstairs. "There," Sera says, "I think all is okay. It's late, Kristo. Why don't you go with Garrick so he can show you your bedroom?"

Kristo nods, and he and Garrick go upstairs. On the second floor there is a large open space that has a dining table made of light-colored wood acting as the centerpiece with chairs pushed in neatly surrounding it. Walls here have decorations that depict various baking techniques, two cabinets to house dishes, and a hyper-realistic black-inked portrait of a family. There are six people in the portrait, three of which Kristo recognizes as Yuna, Sera, and Garrick. There is an incredibly tall man in the back of the group, then two other men along the sides of the group, each a tad taller than Sera. The background contains a grand tent with various stalls set up and people going around to enjoy their time.

Two doors, one on the opposite wall and one to the left of Kristo, are seamlessly crafted into the wood of the house. Garrick puts a hand on Kristo's shoulder to guide him to the dark-green door to the left, opening it for him. Inside, the room contains a dark oak dresser and bed, which has a wool pillow and quilted blanket on it. The room is devoid of any ornaments, save for a small mirror hung up near a window that looks out on the town. "Here you are, Kristo, your new room starting today. Sorry it's not more furnished. It was meant to be a guest room until today."

"There isn't any hay to sleep on?"

Garrick gives a puzzled expression to Kristo. After a few blinks, he shakes his head. "No, you're supposed to sleep on the bed." Garrick's hand gestures to it. "If you need anything, Sera and I will be in the other room. Have a good night, Kristo." With a final pat on the boy's back, Garrick exits and shuts the door.

Alone in the room, Kristo eyes it all over and then goes to the dresser. Reaching into his shirt, he produces the amulet of the moon that Garrick gave him. Tied to the chain is Lady Amelia's embroidered handkerchief, which Kristo holds up to look at in the moonlight from a window. After a pause he tucks the treasures away in the dresser and then tries to figure out how to best sleep on the bed.

8

MABEL'S GIFT

IN THE MORNING, KRISTO WAKES UP to a scent of fresh bread wafting through the crack between his door and the floor. He walks downstairs to the sight of Garrick in an apron standing behind the bakery counter, leaning over his countertop, and reading the same copied pages that a class of students are reading in the front of the shop. A few of the children are enjoying the bakery's bread for breakfast, along with kessi fruit in a basket by the shop entrance for the children to grab.

Hearing Kristo come downstairs, Garrick motions with one hand for the boy to join him and, with the other, puts a finger up to his lips to not disturb Sera's lesson. The half-elf comes over to the apron-wearing knight, who pulls up a chair for Kristo to see the pages. Garrick points to letters on the page with a flour-stained finger while whispering to Kristo about the sound they are supposed to make when spoken. Over the course of the next two hours, Kristo takes his lesson, occasionally having to keep track on his own while Garrick takes care of customers coming in.

Eventually Garrick goes back to grab the roast, bumping Kristo with his elbow to motion for the child to follow him to the backyard. A patch of flat stones is set up with a hand-turn metal spit over them with two metal spike holders. "You have to pay close attention so that my wife and her mother can enjoy some good roasts while I'm gone." Kristo gives a nod and watches as the knight takes the metal pole off its holder, sliding off one spike brace, and hands it to the child. "Hold it with the spikey end up."

Kristo does as asked, and Garrick adjusts the brace left on so it'll be close to the center once the roast is on it. Then he picks up the meat from the melting ice, forcing it lengthwise onto the skewer and down farther until it sinks into the brace. Garrick slides the second brace down into the meat, securing the brace to the pole and takes the pole from Kristo, placing it on the holders.

Garrick gives Kristo a pat on the back, pointing to his bakery's back door after. "Go inside and grab the two red books on a shelf above the flour barrel."

The boy goes inside, climbs on the flour crate, and then comes down with both books, taking them out to the knight.

"Okay, Kristo, here's where the magic is. The seasonings, the way you flavor your food, are just as important if not more so than how you cook your meals. The fat that comes from the meat, the way it interacts with the spices . . ." Garrick motions for Kristo to watch. The knight cuts the vegetables he gathered yesterday and then sets them aside. He concocts an oily mixture from another set of ingredients. All the while, Garrick's explanation of the intricacies of combination of flavors goes on.

The half-elf child attempts to absorb as much as possible from the master chef as the lecture continues. After half an hour, a dense fog sets over Kristo's mind from the overwhelming information being pumped into him.

"And so, we put the books open under the spit to radiate heat. Then place the side dishes to cook next to it once you think the meat will be done in about fifteen or twenty minutes. You might need even more time if you have hearty vegetables. Make sure you brush the meat with the oil mix every now and again, so it doesn't dry on the outside."

The pair have been taking turns cranking the meat, switching off when their arms get tired. Kristo, now at the spit, is vacantly blinking as the directions continue.

Garrick looks out to the forests behind the backyard from his resting place. After spotting something in a thicket of trees, he gets up. A flat motion of his hand indicates for Kristo to stay where he is as the knight investigates.

The half-elf sees Garrick pick up a sturdy stick, gauge its strength by smacking it into a tree, and then nod. The man returns, passing the child with a finger over his lips, and goes through his bakery's back door. He comes back with a hatchet. "Every boy should have a sturdy stick to practice fighting with." Garrick gives Kristo a wink and then starts crudely stripping wood from the stick, casting the shavings into the books under the roast to hide the evidence.

Kristo eyes Garrick's handiwork while cranking the spit and smiling in enthusiasm at the man's giddy nature about carving the stick.

"I'm not a great carver, but this should do." Garrick holds up a crude bark-stripped wooden stick that has been made barely comfortable for a child to hold at one end. "Go on and take it. Practicing with a stick when I was younger is probably one of the reasons I'm still alive." The half-elf takes the cruel mockery of a weapon as if he is receiving his first blade, while the knight takes over the spit. Focusing his attention at the roast, Garrick brushes some of the oil mix on it.

Kristo swings the weapon like it's a bat, but the power he's trying to put into the stick takes his body along with it. Blindly swinging his sword, the boy twirls in place with it and violently smacks Garrick on the side of his knee.

"Awwk!"

Kristo stops and drops his stick to go to the knight. "Garrick?"

The chef gets up from his slump to hop about, laughing at the pain that he knows is his own fault. "Ah, hah." Garrick bends to rub his knee and then starts to walk around, limping about. "Nice hit . . . just try to watch where you're swinging." Garrick walks to Kristo, patting his back to reassure him. "Why don't you go practice hitting a tree? That way you won't be swinging that thing around my legs."

Kristo nods and goes to the thicket of trees where Garrick found the stick. Loud cracking can be heard coming from his knee-slaying weapon as it smacks into the trees.

Sizzling soon comes from metal pans filled with vegetables near the open red books.

From inside the bakery, Sera says, "Garrick! My mother is here!"

Snapping a look at the half-elf in the trees, the knight shouts to the boy. "Kristo! Hide the stick!" Kristo looks about in a panic from the urgency in Garrick's voice and then flings the stick deep into the neighbor's backyard.

Sera and her mother come to see the roast, stepping outside as Yuna's hands gently guide floating chairs out of the shop and into the house's shadow. The two women look suspiciously at the two males in the backyard that are giving them forced friendly smiles. The priestess gives Garrick the firm glare of an experienced mother, knowing that something is wrong, but she just hasn't yet figured out what. "You boys didn't spike the food with some prank potion, did you?" The master chef gives her a sly smile. "No, but I should remember that for next time."

Yuna's right hand goes up to massage her brow, thoroughly disappointed in Garrick's response. Sera on the other hand has an amused face from Garrick's quip but smiles apologetically at her mother once Yuna turns her attention back to her daughter. "I don't see why you had to be attracted to such a churlish man. You could have been with that nice young apprenticing blacksmith, you know. He was such a well-mannered fellow."

"I know, but if I did that, then you wouldn't get free bread or invitations to roast dinners."

A loud chest-deflating huff from Yuna is heard even by Kristo off by the trees. "Yes, that much is true. I do enjoy the bread."

While Sera's mother laments her daughter's poor choices as a form of satire, Garrick motions for Kristo to come over. "There are planks of wood and table legs inside just to the right. Could you bring them out for Yuna to put together please?" While Kristo retrieves the wood, Garrick takes a pair of tongs and flips the books shut now that the food is finished. Kristo hands the first pieces to Yuna, who says, "Thank you, young man. That is very thoughtful of you." The boy smiles to Yuna and then goes back for the rest of the table.

Having all the pieces for the table outside now, Yuna waves a misty green hand at the planks, lifting them together and fusing all into one solid piece that stands firmly off the ground. Sera moves the chairs near the table. With every dish properly seasoned and cooked, Garrick calls for people to place the food out while he goes inside to get plates and utensils.

Kristo looks around without a clue as to what to do until Yuna instructs him to sit at the table. When he takes the seat on the end, Yuna smiles and says, "Good choice, Kristo."

Returning to lay out plates, Garrick sees Kristo sitting in the knight's seat and is about to open his mouth, but he catches a glare from Yuna. The two adults look at each other, one with a stern straight face and the other with confusion until Garrick suddenly understands the situation and then goes about setting up the rest of dinner.

As everything gets properly displayed, Kristo reaches over the table for some bread, but he gets his hand slapped by Yuna and promptly pulls it back. "Why is everyone slapping my hands?"

The old woman gives a stern voice. "I'll assume you weren't taught the rules of a table during your time as a slave."

Kristo pushes himself back in his chair at the mention of more rules, his eyes rolling up in disbelief of more unspoken, unknown boundaries.

"Don't take that attitude with me, mister, or I'll hang you up in a tree branch by your pants."

Kristo looks at her in surprise, his angular eyebrows scrunched together at such an outlandish threat.

Garrick and Sera carry over the spit to place the meat on a platter, taking off each bracer to then remove the rod. Garrick nods to Kristo mid-work. "She means it, Kristo. When I was younger, I challenged her to a duel. She said it's rude to challenge members of the nature god's coven to duels, but she accepted anyway. I was stuck in a tree for half a day."

Yuna gives a smirk, remembering that time. "Yes, you and your devilish friend Demio were constantly getting yourselves into trouble. Where is he, by the way?"

Garrick shakes his head. "I don't know. The last time I saw him was before I left for Plick's marshalling field."

Yuna looks at Garrick and nods sadly to him.

"I know that look, Yuna. He wouldn't be a loyalist; he's probably part of the northern army tasked with holding off the dragonbornes under Joc."

Yuna tilts her chin downward and casts her eyes on Kristo, who was trying to sneak food again. With a flick of her green windy hand, Yuna has the table grow a pole under Kristo's plate, putting it out of reach. "Now, you're supposed to wait for everyone to be seated before you take food. Then you're also supposed to wait until everyone gets food on their plate."

At learning yet another bit of silly information, the boy shakes his head in confusion, looking up at his plate. "But why?" he asks in genuine curiosity. "Why are there all these rules that make no sense?"

The adults try to figure out a way to explain it to a child. Once the meat is properly on the cutting board, Sera takes her seat by Kristo, leaving Garrick out at the end of everyone else. She speaks calmly and patiently, as if explaining to one of her students. "It's a show of respect and love, Kristo. It's saying that you'll stay hungry for a little while longer to ensure everyone is cared for and ready."

The half-elf takes a few moments and then nods.

Yuna and Garrick start passing around the food to load their plates. The platters eventually come round to Kristo, who mimics what everyone else is doing after his plate is lowered by Yuna. With a clap, Garrick stands up and begins carving the roast, setting meat down on everyone's plate.

Once he is done, Yuna puts her head down for a prayer, which the other two adults do as well, so the child does the same. "Thank you, Sutri, for providing the feast which we dine upon. May those not with us find in your bounty a meal just as extravagant as this wherever they may be."

The prayer is over, and silverware—even reserved Yuna's—moves with gusto from plate to mouth. Kristo soon understands the enthusiasm as he takes his first bite and is eagerly stuffing his face, which comes with another lesson from Yuna. The attention of the table soon turns to Garrick about his time in training and his deployments, the details of which he gives over reluctantly.

Kristo listens to the conversations that spring up from the three adults, and a smile spreads across his face as jokes and gentle scoldings are passed amongst everyone. The child butts in a few times, trying to interject a little of his own humor, and the adults indulge his attempts, even though only one of them is vaguely funny. By the time the sky bleeds orange, the four people around the table have talked themselves silly and now are playing a basic game involving dice that Sera helps Kristo learn. As darkness claims the sky, the leftovers are taken inside, and Yuna dismantles the table back into boards with a wave of her hand, floating the leftover wood back into the bakery.

Going inside for the night, the four continue their celebration by playing charades, using Sera's teaching area for seating. It's not until deep into the night that Yuna says her goodbyes. She gives Kristo an awkward first hug, which the boy melts into, and then she makes her way out of the store.

The two remaining adults are giving each other soft looks. Garrick gets up at long last, offering a hand to his wife. "Sera and I are going for a midnight stroll."

At first hesitant about leaving Kristo by himself at night, Sera just looks at the hand being offered to her, but her face turns to embarrassed flattery as she takes it to get up, linking her arm with Garrick's. "Kristo, you're free to do what you want, but don't light any fires or let the smoke spirits out of the oven. You can even have some extra cake if you want."

Kristo's eyebrows rise at hearing there are smoke spirits in Garrick's oven, and he walks towards the oven once he sees the couple has walked out of view of the window. His hand knocks on a lower compartment, and a light groan can be heard from inside. The boy blinks at the noise and flicks his head about, trying to see if Sera or Garrick is around. Seeing no one, he grabs the whole plate of cake and then goes upstairs to his room.

9

HOMEFRONT

THE SOUND OF SCRAPING CHAIRS AND hushed concern filter under the crack of Kristo's door, rousing the child from his slumber. He goes down the stairs to the bakery's front. Garrick is sitting back in a chair holding to his nose a bloody rag that is becoming more crimson. Sera moves swiftly to put a bit of leftover ice in a different rag and then place it on her husband's face, taking care of the previous one. Neither of them notices the child until he is right next to Garrick to inspect the knight's nose. "Hey, buddy." Garrick's pained expression leaves his face for a bit while he attempts to give the boy a smile. Sera is gently pulling away Garrick's hand while he is talking to apply the ice to his face. "What are you doing up? You want some cake? Sera and I are just tending to a fall I took while out walking."

Kristo takes a moment to think about what is happening and then shakes his head. "No, I had the rest of the cake."

Garrick's eyebrows rise in amusement at the statement, but Sera's expression is dark after hearing Garrick's explanation of the situation, quiet rage stirring on her face. Seeing his wife's expression, Garrick places a comforting hand on her forearm to let her know things will be fine.

Kristo moves to take a seat, observing the two in front of him. The child then shifts about, trying to figure a way to show his concern. "How did you fall?"

Garrick gives a little chuckle to ease the tension. "Oh, well, I tripped over a root that was jutting from a building and fell into the stonework."

After a bit of time, his nose dries, and he pats Sera's side. "Thank you, honey. I should be fine." Sera searches his eyes, running a wet cloth over Garrick's face to clean him before taking a seat next to the two. Her hand is repeatedly gripping the rags while looking over her husband, her eyes coming to rest on his blackening knuckles.

Garrick breaks the silence. "I would have liked a bit more cake."

Sera shakes her head at the attempted joke, putting a hand on her forehead before looking at Kristo. "Time for bed again." She gently pats the boy's shoulder, motioning to the stairs. "Garrick and I have to talk about his clumsiness."

Kristo looks at both adults, knowing that something is wrong, but doesn't argue. Going to his room, he closes the door and then lies on the floor, putting his ear to its crack.

"Garrick," Sera says with worry in her tone, "what are we going to do? They said they saw you walking through town in your uniform when you came here. Halmin is neutral by decree of the reeve, but that doesn't mean—"

"Honey, I know about the decree from the town's official," he says with an undertone of worry as well. "I'm sorry that you and Kristo are caught up in this. I'll leave by tomorrow or the day after. I just want to ensure Kristo is happy here; then I can leave. You both shouldn't be bothered by my choices."

Sera's voice trembles slightly with her husband's words. "What if you are attacked again while you're here? Or what if they come after Kristo and me when you leave since they know you're a rebel? And if you do go back to war . . . what happens if . . ."

Kristo doesn't hear anything so assumes they are talking lower, and he gently opens his door to hear.

"We can't worry over everything that might happen to us," Garrick says. "We would be immobilized by our own fear. We'll prepare for the worst. If they try anything more violent than just a beating, well, I'll be wearing my sword around the town from now on. It may piss them off, but that's the best I can do. . . . As for the war . . . I have to go back eventually. We've lost too many to the inquisitors and the laws here; Brenan can't be allowed to continue the way that he's going. What world would it leave us if no one were to stand up to his rule? I must fight." There is gentle shuffling with another pause between words.

"I know . . . I know," Sera says. "I love you. Just . . . please be safe."

Kristo hears footsteps on the stairs and quietly closes his door and dives for his bed.

The next day, Kristo does the same as last morning, coming down for his lessons. Now however, some students are missing from the class, leaving a good number of empty seats for Kristo to be able to sit down and listen to Sera read a story about an owlbear searching for its family. Garrick is behind the counter, bruises on his face and his gifted blade on his hip. Baking goes as usual until class lets out, and most of the children run off like bullets to the door. A few stay behind an extra moment to buy bread for their families before they leave.

Kristo is eyeing the door, which Sera notices. She chews her lip in contemplation and then speaks. "When class lets out, you are free to do whatever you want, Kristo. Just make sure that your room is clean before you leave."

The half-elf runs up to his room, then back down the stairs, and out the door. Looking back through the bakery window, he sees Sera rubbing her head and then getting up to help Garrick with the baking.

Out and about, Kristo sees the kids of the town playing with each other or helping run their families' businesses. His legs fidget in place, his eyes looking at the center of the bakery where he had seen Garrick with a bloody nose. He looks out to the rest of town and begins wandering down streets. Finding a yellow, fat fruit on a house, he plucks it to eat while scratching his head now and again. His eyes are drawn to the yellows and reds of people's clothing, eyeing anyone with those two colors.

Finding little to do, the child wanders off to the church of Sutri. Under the bows of the combined branches, Kristo takes a seat, just looking around at the trees and sung wood that makes the church.

An hour later, Yuna returns to the church and finds Kristo sitting in the church's garden, chewing on some fat blades of grass. "Hello, little one. I was busy with regrowing the fruits around the town. One of the sisters told me you were here."

Kristo gets up from the ground to look at her. "It's okay. I was enjoying the grass." He scratches at his eyebrow, attempting to think.

"What's wrong? If you have something to say, you can say it to me. I am here for you, my child." As Kristo continues to hesitate, Yuna lets her hand flow with green light. Out of a pocket of her dress, a seed is flung into the earth. Before the child's eyes, a little tree grows and hangs to one side as a pale-yellow fruit grows, weighing it down. Yuna motions for the child to grab it, and once he does, the tree sucks down into the soil and the seed returns from the earth to her pocket.

Kristo eyes the fruit in his hand and then lets his arms fall to his sides. "I want to know about the war and how I was let go."

Yuna's tone is full of patience, and it even has a happy tune to it from the child's curiosity. "I figured you'd want to know something like that. But why are you asking me? Garrick rescued you from Effilnem. Why would you not ask him?"

Kristo explains what happened last night.

Yuna motions over to the pews, all of which have freshly grown moss on them, for them to sit down. "I see; you don't want them knowing you were listening in. It will be our secret. They are nice to want to let you have what little childhood you have left, but it seems you already know more about the cruelty of the world than you should at your age." Her hand gently rubs Kristo's head while the child eats the fruit. Yuna then speaks while looking over the branches of the cherry tree. "The answer to your question goes back around twenty years. King Brenan Vanari was newly recognized by the pantheon leaders after the death of the old king, Polic Winterbloom. With Brenan's crowning, he brought reforms to the kingdom's prison system. The worst of the worst—murderers, rapists, and those that would steal grand amounts—would be sentenced to work for the rest of their lives. Somewhere along the line, prisons were slowly redone as well. Instead of being brought to a local facility, prisoners were transferred to labor houses to be worked to the bone for the length of their sentence."

Yuna nods to herself. "Many, including myself, agreed with these reforms. Those that have wronged others must be punished. Their labor would be used for the benefit of our kingdom. It seemed just. The problem came from laws being enforced in an increasingly strict manner. Guards were under orders to capture people for even the lowest crimes. People from all over the kingdom were finding themselves without relatives. Vandalism, a crime that once brought only a community service sentence, could land you in a labor house for twenty years. Naturally some guards refused to follow such orders, so Brenan passed a law that made it illegal for them to question the king's decrees, so many more people were taken and sent off to the prison houses. Your friend Mabel was one such individual, swept up by the system thirteen years ago. She was just a child too, but her whole family was reported for stealing books from the town library. At that point, trials were still in place, but they were a poor attempt to hide the fact people were being shipped off for their labor, a thin veil that everyone saw through. I was there for the sentencing of Mabel's family. They were the first lot of people to be sent away from Halmin." Yuna shakes her head remorsefully in remembrance. "I didn't know what to do. As a local figurehead I had to attend. As someone who lived in Halmin, I was outraged. Yet nothing could be done. The inquisitors were at the height of their power. Raising my hand would mean the destruction of all I hold dear."

Kristo blinks down at the grass under his feet. Yuna moves her hand to rub his back. "Only two years ago did someone stand up to the king; that man was Lenfro Strixwi. He is a noble from northeast of Asmeria and was set to become the minister of war in Brenan's court. Believing Brenan's orders to be a violation of rights, Lenfro refused to sentence people according to the king's laws after inheriting his lordly status from the passing of his mother. Lenfro soon found a small force march on his land holdings to seize him and his property. To everyone's surprise, Lenfro beat back the force, and the resulting violence led him to form the restoration rebellion. People of the country are now torn between which side to take. While the king's laws were cruel and unfair, he is still the king recognized by the pantheon to be a divine ruler. Not only that, but his army is also more put together than Lenfro's. Neighbors' opinions vary here, childhood friendships were sullied, business deals cracked, and the occasional brawl occurs at the tavern now. Those that join the king's cause are either loyal to the crown and its noble backers or frightened of what might happen to them if the rebellion loses. Those that back Lenfro are fighting for what they believe to be a just system and to ensure the future is a free world. They wish to see Brenan ousted from power due to his tyrannical rule."

Kristo has been staring at Yuna since she started rubbing his back, just listening to her explanation, and knows which side she now supports.

"So Garrick being attacked last night . . . Halmin, by decree of our reeve, is a neutral place. No army may take station at it, but supplies can be requested and delivered to either army that asks for them without question. It must be this way. If Halmin took sides, we would be the first target for assault. We are centrally located, grow most of the kingdom's food, and have no walls to speak of. It is due to these things that Halmin has both a vibrant loyalist population and a large number of rebel backers. Garrick walked alone into town with a rebel uniform. There is safety in numbers when an army camps in a town. No one wants to feel the rage of a full force of soldiers. But if there is just one . . . let's say an ant is only a threat because of the colony behind it."

Kristo is staring at the pit of the fruit in his hand, going over everything in his head. "Do you think he should leave?"

Yuna gives him a hug to the side. "My heart wishes he could stay, but I know he must leave. The world may be an unforgiving place at times, wanting to kick you when all you want to do is be happy or do the right thing. To give into every challenge of your peace and ideals means you will never have either. However, even Garrick knows that if he overstays it won't matter; he can't stand up to every loyalist in town. Some fights you can't win."

Yuna gives a sigh and then shakes her head about the situation. "Garrick knew what he was doing, as did every able man from Halmin when the decree came around that they were being summoned for war. Garrick chose his side willingly, and he knew what it meant. He'd be killing the very people he grew up with; those on the opposite side knew this as well. I wager he also knows his presence here is causing a lot of pain for those that have lost family members to rebel soldiers."

"But I don't understand . . . he has to leave to go back to the army . . . yet he should stay here at the same time?" Kristo's eyebrows are scrunching together from the confusion of the circumstance.

Yuna lets the child go and offers to walk with Kristo by a movement of her hand. He follows Yuna, who moves through the back lawn of her church where the housing place of the churchwomen resides. Going past this, the pair walk through the side yards of a few houses to end up on a grassy street looking across at a naked field. Children from the school are playing tag, a few boys are playing soldier with sticks, and a couple of the younger girls are pretending to have a tea party. "A child like you should be out here, making friends. Your whole life was torn away from you without your asking. Garrick knows that too, and seeing Mabel dead . . . I imagine it brought back all the memories of his younger days through a new lens. He stays for now because he wants to make sure you are going to have a good life."

A shake comes from Kristo's head at the level of kindness that is being brought forth to him, his voice on the verge of breaking. "But why? I don't understand. First Mabel, now Garrick. Why are people . . . why are they . . . they are going through terrible things for me? What makes them different from the guards that watched over me? Those men didn't care, and they were there throughout my whole life!"

Yuna maintains a gentle smile for the boy, putting a hand on his back. "I can't answer why it is you, but I can answer the why it is someone *like* you. Even if you never met Mabel and Garrick found you, he would have taken you in."

Kristo shakes his head once more, not understanding what Yuna is saying.

Yuna slowly moves down, taking a seat on the grass to talk. "Your name, Kristo. What does it mean?"

Kristo plops on the ground to join Yuna. "It doesn't have a meaning; it's just my name."

Yuna then gives a nod to his answer. "You are right. But at the same time, it holds meaning for those around us. To me, Kristo means a young boy that is wise beyond his years from enduring the scorn of society around him. He asks questions that no other child would ask based on seeing that ugliness. To Sera, Kristo means the child her husband brought home from a war that has left her with an empty home. It is also the continuation of the spirit of a childhood friend." Yuna dips her head in thought and then turns to Kristo. "And to Garrick . . . well . . . Kristo means everything he and his comrades are fighting for—a new future for everyone that will bring back a just order to the world where people can be happy and proud they live in it. You are the hope behind all the killing."

Kristo is staring into Yuna's face, examining it to find the meaning in what is being told to him. "What about the guards or Mabel?"

Yuna gives Kristo a wink and then a pinch of his cheek. "I can't do all the thinking for you. What do you think your name means?"

Kristo looks at the ground to play around with the grass as he thinks about the question.

Before he can answer, a few kids notice Yuna is sitting outside and yell to their friends, causing them all to swarm the priestess.

"Mother Yuna! Please grow some fruit for us!" one says.

Another one calls at the mage. "Can you grow a tree with a vine swing for us?"

The swarm of younglings wind up surrounding Kristo as well.

While Yuna is taking care of the various requests from the children around her, a black-haired girl looks down at Kristo. "Hi, I'm Bree. You're the teacher's new kid, right?"

Surprised to be talked to by someone he doesn't know, Kristo raises his eyebrows. "Yes, I'm Kristo, just Kristo. I don't have a last name."

Bree looks at Kristo with a sad expression and then her expression lightens. "Maybe you'll earn one, like my dad. His last name is Ironlung. He's a guard here in town."

Kristo's face saddens a bit as he hears there are guards here. "Oh . . . there are slaves here in Halmin too?"

Bree shakes her head and thanks Yuna for a piece of fruit from the tree she's been growing. "No, Halmin doesn't have slaves. My dad guards the town and farms to make sure no monsters or bandits try to hurt people. He's very good at his job too. He thinks he's going to be promoted soon."

Kristo is glad to learn the guards have a different purpose here in Halmin than he experienced before. He starts to get up from the ground, and Bree offers an arm to help him. "Thanks. Your dad sounds nice to want to protect the town from monsters."

Bree gives a prideful nod at Kristo. "Yup! When I turn sixteen, I'm going to try to become a guard just like him. You get put under apprenticeship for forever, but it's worth it."

"I guess there are good guards out there too," Kristo says, scratching his eyebrow. "Garrick was teaching me how to swing a stick. He carved it for me to resemble a sword. It should still be in the backyard somewhere. Do you want to find it and practice?"

The offer makes Bree bounce a little. "Yes! That sounds awesome. Could we find another stick and have Garrick carve it so we could practice together like the older kids?"

Kristo gives a shrug and then motions for Bree to follow as he makes his way back to the bakery. "I don't see why he would say no. Unless he's busy baking or cooking. . . . He gets really excited at the chance to cook for some reason."

"Of course he does! He's the best cook in Halmin, even above the tavern chef. I'm not sure why you call him Garrick though, he's your papa now."

Kristo chews his lip at the thought. "He's not my papa."

Bree scrunches her eyebrows in confusion. "What do you mean?"

"He offered to be my papa, but I just . . . I didn't accept."

Kristo turns the corner to the bakery to look at a newly set-up water and feeding trough for the horse tied outside. Next to her, Sera and Garrick sit in chairs discussing a possible name for the hair-loving mare, finally deciding on Pilosus.

The adults' attention turns to the children as they strut up with a "wanting something" air about them. Garrick looks at them with a smile as he drinks from a wooden cup. Sera addresses the pair. "Hello, Kristo. Making friends with Miss Bree?"

Kristo nods at Sera. "Yup, we were hoping to get fighting lessons from Garrick using sticks."

Sera raises her eyebrows at the idea, turning with a "we'll talk about this later" look at her husband, his bruised face justifying no excuses in her mind.

Garrick shrugs, finishes his cup, and gets out of his chair. "Sure, better to teach it to a pair. We'll go to the backyard." Bree and Kristo exchange smiles, thrilled with the idea of learning swordplay, and follow Garrick with a bounce to their steps. In the backyard, Kristo runs off to find his stick in the neighbor's yard and then comes back with it and another one that he manages to find. Garrick shows them the basic stances and maneuvers, and the children follow his instructions. Kristo ends up with a few marks on his arms from Bree's executions, but she emerges scar free.

Once the sun starts to hang low, Garrick calls off the training, motioning for the two children to get in the house. "I think that's enough for today. You two head inside and get cleaned up. I'm going to start preparing dinner. Bree, you are welcome to stay if you think your parents won't mind."

Bree gives Kristo a happy slap on the arm in affirmation, but he winces from her hitting a tender spot. "You're lucky, living with the best chef. My mom makes a good shepherd's pie, but that's about it. She tries hard, though."

Kristo goes inside to the wash basin to clean his face and hands with a washcloth, making space for Bree after he's done. "I think I'm lucky too." Kristo looks over at Garrick placing a few cuts of meat onto a cast-iron skillet, and they begin sizzling with no flame under it. He then looks outside the bakery window to see Sera with a student that didn't come to class, having him read a book in the chair next to her as she helps him along.

Bree looks at the way Kristo is eyeing the adults and then nudges his side softly. "Whatcha thinking about?"

"Yuna was talking about how everyone sees each other differently, how we all mean something different to others."

Bree scratches her head and nods. "I think I know what she means but . . . why does it matter?"

"What?"

Bree shrugs and leans against the wash counter behind her. "I mean why does knowing what other people think of you matter? You're going to be yourself anyway, right?"

Kristo's eyebrows furrow at the thought, attempting to come up with an answer, but no words come to him.

Bree squints at him in amusement and curiosity as she watches his brows move. "You think too much. Keep moving your eyebrows like that, and they may fall off."

Kristo's expression cracks, and then he shakes his head. "You want to play Shakers? It's a dice game I was taught the other day." With a nod from

Bree, Kristo goes off to get the dice, and the pair wind up at the kitchen table playing until dinner is ready.

A few sizzling pans are set down on the table on cooling rocks, and plates are passed around. Sera comes inside with the student and offers him a place at the table across from Bree and Kristo as she introduces him. "Kristo and Bree, this is Hile. Hile, Kristo and Bree." The brown-haired lanky kid gives a smile to Kristo. With the new people at the table, the meal is eaten slowly from everyone talking and getting acquainted. Conversation lightens up when Garrick offers to make some sweets for dessert.

Soon Sera and the three kids are all rolling dice while the smell of Almenian sweet grass and kessi fruit fills the air. The sun finally sets outside, and the baked treat is happily consumed. Sera fills Hile's and Bree's arms with biscuits, and as they move toward the door, Sera nudges Kristo to see the guests outside. In silence, the three children stand awkwardly for a moment.

Then Bree speaks. "I know an even better game than the dice one we played earlier. It's called Stable Masters. It's a board game about making the most profitable stable. I can grab it next time."

Kristo scratches his eyebrow, wondering what a board game is. "A game that involves boards seems kind of heavy."

Hile shakes his head in amusement. "What? It's played on a thick piece of dyed animal hide, usually cut into a square. Did you really think Bree was talking about a game played with big pieces of wood?"

Kristo shrugs at Hile's comment. "I've never played a board game. I thought it'd be played with boards."

Bree giggles at the idea. "Hile, don't mind Kristo. He thinks way too much." Bree then motions down the street and looks at Hile. "I live down this way. I'm going to get going now—EEEHHHAAAAA!" As Bree suddenly shouts and shoots her hands to the top of her head, her biscuits all drop to the ground. Garrick's horse is standing behind her and flapping its gums around on Bree's hair, making a mess of it.

Kristo and Hile are laughing and pointing at what's happening when the bakery door slams open. The boys jump in fear at the bang. Garrick, wild eyed and trying to figure out what's happening, has his hand on the pommel of his longsword. Seeing the horse, Garrick sighs in relief and relaxes his expression. "Pilosus, knock it off. You have to ask to eat the children first."

Bree ducks and moves away from the horse, trying to fix her hair so it lies correctly. "You don't actually feed your horse people, do you?"

"Horses don't eat people," Hile says. "They eat grass and apples and other things like that."

Garrick hides a smile and speaks sternly to the kids. "Well, we don't normally feed her people. Just kids who stay out late or skip their class-work. She must have realized the time and was—"

"Garrick!" Sera yells from the bakery. "You leave those kids alone right now! They're too young to tell you're joking!"

Temporarily silenced, Garrick then addresses Bree and Hile. "Have a good night. Don't let the horses bite."

From inside the bakery, a piece of bread flies out and hits Garrick in the back. He feigns to be horribly injured, turning around to go inside. "Ah, oh, my kidney! My sensitive kidney!" The door shuts, but the children clearly hear Garrick. "I'm going to get you back for that!"

"What are you doing?" Sera says. "You deserved everything you got."

"Bahhrhhhhhaaa!"

"Garrick!"

Laughter replaces the words, and then hushed voices fade to quiet with the kids standing about, looking at each other.

Hile breaks the silence. "I remember my parents telling me once that the Marmuin family is a bunch of weirdos, but I never really understood what they meant."

Bree finishes getting her hair straight and then looks down at her bis-cuits strewn across the grass, a disappointed look on her face. "Those were my favorite."

Hile offers a few to Bree from his arm.

The girl lights up again. "Thanks!" Bree tucks the sweet treats securely in her arm and then speaks. "The Marmuins are nice people, even if they're weird. I've got to get home; I'll see you guys."

Kristo speaks before Bree turns away. "I'd like to see the board game you were talking about tomorrow."

Bree nods. "I'll bring it over. Have a good night," she says and then starts walking off.

Hile says goodbye to Kristo and leaves, commenting about how he lives in the same direction.

Kristo takes a moment to pet Pilosus. "Try not to eat anyone, okay?" Then he goes inside.

Garrick and Sera are sitting on the floor against a wall with a knocked-over chair in front of them. Sera has her head leaning against Garrick's shoulder, the knight's arm holding her affectionately. Garrick gives her a kiss on the head and then moves his body as he tells Sera they should get up, but she doesn't move, staring off out the window as she holds her husband. "Just a bit longer . . ."

Garrick gives a happy sigh and adjusts his arms to hold her more comfortably. "All right . . ." He looks up at Kristo, speaking to him. "Did you have a good day today?"

The child nods. "Yes. I asked Bree to bring over her board game tomorrow, and she said she would."

Sera nuzzles Garrick's shoulder so she can look up at Kristo as she talks to him. "Good. It's nice that you're making friends. We'll have to have Garrick cook you both a nice meal tomorrow." Sera's tone is off, as if she's not really talking to Kristo.

Garrick turns his head to look at Sera who meets his eyes.

"Won't you, Garrick?" Sera's expression is stern yet loving, indicating he can't say no.

Seeing his wife's expression, he turns his head to look outside as Sera continues to stare at him. After a long moment, Garrick turns back to look at his wife. "One more day . . ."

Getting what she wanted, Sera moves her head into Garrick's chest and gives a deep contented smile.

Kristo looks at the pair with his eyes going back and forth between their faces. He saw couples sit like this before against the wall of his prison house, and his lips form a smile in seeing Garrick and Sera doing the same thing. "I'm going to go to sleep. Have a good night."

Both wish him a good night but stay on the floor, watching the half-elf wander up the stairs to bed.

Going to his room, Kristo is all smiles and stays up for a little while, looking out his window at the night sky. His expression slowly turns to a frown as he realizes he's staring up at the same night sky he used to look at with Mabel. "I wish you were here, but I hope you're happy if you really are up in heaven."

10

HATE AND LOVE

"HAVE YOU EVER LOOKED AT THE stars and wondered if the world truly cares for you? The goddess Sutri . . ." Yuna is standing at the head of her congregation and behind a podium grown out of the roots of a cherry tree. Before her are members of the town with a notable problem she is addressing. The seats near the middle aisle are empty with people having moved over to the far left or far right of the moss-covered benches. Occasional glares of disdain are sent from one side to the other side of the aisle.

Kristo, along with Garrick and Sera, are sitting near the front, having gotten to church early.

Yuna notices what her congregation is doing to one another, and with an abrupt slamming of her sermon book, she gathers the attention of her flock. "The way you all are behaving is nothing short of a horde of children."

Everyone's face turns confused or angry as the people gaze upon the aging woman.

"Your neighbors are not your enemy; the war has not come to Halmin. How will any of you function outside of this church if you require the services of another who holds a different opinion? Will you sacrifice your need for soap and commodities if the general store denies you service? Will you let your family go without meat if the farmers refuse to sell to the butcher or if the butcher refuses to sell to you? Where will your horses be stabled? Your nails and hinges shaped? Who will teach your children?"

Yuna for a moment puts her eyes on Sera and then casts them back to scan her flock.

"Do any of you want bloodshed here in our town?" Yuna lets the question sink into everyone, holding their silent attention. "Because if you do, we are heading down the right path. Every soldier in this war is fighting out of fear and hope. Fear that the king will punish us all for the actions of Lenfro and his soldiers and the hope that if we stay loyal to his ideals, we may prosper under his guidance. There is the fear of our freedoms being crushed under a new wave of law and the hope that enough force will push the king's hand back. I am not here to debate which is right, but I am going to tell you that if you give into these tidal waves of emotion, we will all be lost to the ocean before any army comes."

At being chastised the men and women of the town are all silently thinking, looking at one another to see what their loved ones' thoughts are as they collect their own.

"You are all free for the rest of the day. Take the time to think about what kind of future you want." Yuna motions towards the back of the church and waves her hand with a green wind to part the branches, opening a passage so people can leave.

As the crowds get up to go, Garrick leads both Sera and Kristo up to Yuna. "Yuna, you didn't have to do this for—"

The priestess snaps her fingers in anger. "You think this is about you? The town has been slowly turning on itself for the year you've been gone. Your being here is just hurrying the process along. At this rate, we're going to have more than what happened to your face on our hands."

Yuna's words halt Garrick in his approach, but Kristo doesn't seem to care, walking right up to the woman who puts a hand on his head, looking at him.

"Garrick, you are here for all the right reasons, but the town can't handle your presence. My words can do only so much to lessen the tension of the town, and I fear having a rebel here is pushing beyond what even I can mend. Kristo is safe, you have seen to it; there is no reason to tarry."

Sera, behind Garrick, comes to his side to press her weight onto him.

Garrick looks over at her with a nod. "I promised one more day. I will leave tomorrow."

Yuna sighs, her shoulders falling as she turns to look at the cherry tree that one of the sisters of the church is tending. "I wish the world were a better place. Raising a child in the wake of such times . . . your parents would have been exceptionally proud of you."

Garrick stands for a long moment, feeling his wife's comfort next to him. "Come, Kristo. Sera and I were planning on getting you clothes today."

Yuna looks down at Kristo with pursed lips. She comes down to give him a hug and then tilts her head to tell him to go.

The child moves to follow Sera and Garrick.

When the three get close to the parting branches, Yuna says, "You're always in my prayers, Garrick. Should the worst come to pass, I know Sutri will accept you into her garden."

The knight stops before the exit and turns back to her. "I made a promise that I'd plant a tree in her honor for getting me through a battle. . . . I'd like your help with it."

Yuna nods to Garrick and then turns her eyes to the side with thought. "I'll read to see which tree would be appropriate and come by later."

For a moment, they stare at each other until Garrick breaks eye contact to join Sera and Kristo outside the church. Sera goes to Garrick and curls her arm through his, a pained smile on her face as she looks down at him. "We still have now. Let's take Kristo for his clothes. There's time for a few more good memories here."

Having had his fill of sadness for the day, Garrick takes a deep breath. He grabs a squishy pink ball from a nearby vine, bites into it, and motions forward with it for them to get moving. Following the pair of adults, Kristo is trying to figure out how to properly do so, switching between behind and to the side. It's not until Sera extends her hand to him that Kristo knows where he's supposed to be, taking it as he walks next to them.

A few turns through the town's grassy streets and vibrant flora puts them at the tailor, whose building has a giant spool of thread and threaded needle made out of wood with vines as the thread. Garrick motions for Kristo to go inside. "Go on and hurry in. You can have your pick of new clothes. What you have on must be itchy by now."

Getting the go-ahead, Kristo opens the door, looking about at the various shelves of clothing and going over to the section of blue tunics and trousers.

Soon an elven man carrying a pile of clothes approaches Kristo, peering down at the child. "Anything happen to catch your eye, little half-elf?"

Inside, Sera takes a seat on a bench in the shop by the door. Garrick sits next to her, and soon Sera's head is resting on his shoulder, looking at Kristo. "He's such a sweet boy but very aloof for his age."

Garrick's arm moves about his wife's waist to hold her. "Yes . . . he's had a rough childhood. I doubt he had time to learn more than how to be a servant. He'll do well here. This generation of kids has a great soul to them, unlike ours."

Sera lets her eyes look up and shakes her head. "No, our generation is great too. It's full of strong men willing to risk everything for their families' and neighbors' sake."

Garrick smiles, looking at Kristo grab a pair of trousers to hold up to the elf helping the child pick out clothes. "Your family is blessed with the ability to speak so well."

Sera shakes her head once more from Garrick's words. "No, *our* family is."

Garrick's chest rises and falls with his breath, looking down at his feet. "How many memories have I stolen from the people I've killed? Days out, cakes eaten, feasts enjoyed, sermons hea—"

"You aren't at fault," Sera says, moving her hand to her husband's free one and tenderly holding it. "Those men chose what they believed in. You aren't wrong for having different opinions."

It's now Garrick's turn to shake his head. "But there is a difference between killing a man and debating his ideals."

"Sometimes there isn't. This war is proof of that. Those men chose their side. They are courageous and honorable, just as you are. The fault is with not them but their leaders—the ones spreading the message that their cause is righteous. The truth at some point has gotten lost."

Garrick's shoulders slump. "That doesn't make what I'm doing any easier."

Sera's head nuzzles into him as she sees Kristo has moved on to picking out tunics now. "You wouldn't be my husband if killing was something you could do without thought. The death at your hands is awful, but you are making a better world, even if half the town hates you for it. I will still be with you."

"I wish I could never be apart from you, but I know I must leave. The caravan is no place for you, though, nor is it for Kristo."

Sera perks at the thought, sitting up and looking at her husband who is watching her face. "Why not? It isn't difficult to cook a meal or to fetch water as needed."

Garrick looks at his wife, his eyes flicking between both of hers with his head shaking. "Because I don't wish you to be. A stray fireball or arrow could easily kill either of you. An attack on the baggage train could have you in the middle of an ambush. A disease from the wounded could pass through camp. Besides, what of the children here? As their teacher, you hold a portion of their future in your hands."

"The children can be taught after I get back," Sera rebuts quietly to ensure they don't disturb the shopkeeper or Kristo. "Why is it fine for you to risk your life, but when it comes to me, it's a no? I could easily argue that the town needs its dedicated baker back. A mage could easily overpower your line and end you and your fellow soldiers, and I'm just supposed to deal with that?"

As Garrick is about to respond, Kristo is escorted to the front counter to pay for his clothes, picking out some socks from the display built into it. Garrick gives Sera a silent look, letting her know that they'll talk about it later. He goes up to pay, looking over all the items that Kristo is getting— a few pairs of brown trousers, blue tunics, socks, and an apron. Looking over the items, Garrick is a bit puzzled. But then, moving his arms and legs to inspect himself, he notices his clothes are the same that Kristo has selected. The knight takes a moment to center himself before addressing the shopkeeper. "He'll also need a pair of leather boots, maybe a half size bigger than he is for room to grow."

Kristo looks down at Garrick's feet and then back up at the knight's face.

The elf nods, taking Kristo to the back of the store to find boots for him.

After the two return with proper footwear, Garrick counts out the silver needed, puts it into the hand of the elf, and then picks up the clothes. "Time to go, Kristo. There is a part of town I'd like to show you."

Outside, Sera looks over the clothes in Garrick's arm, giving him a knowing smile. Garrick adjusts his arms and then starts walking toward the northwest part of the town. Within a few turns, Sera knows where they are going and takes the front, motioning for Kristo to walk in front of Garrick with her. Knowing what Sera is trying to do, Garrick shakes his head, following them with eyes that soak in their every movement. Rounding their final corner, they are at an open-ended street that leads to the forest. Along the sides in front of houses are various stalls set up with self-sizzling pans or heat books, depending on what's being served. Around each of the stalls, the herbs or spices for cooking dangle from the little shop fronts or grow near them. The entire street here is dedicated to these shops, and where it ends, workers are growing a new house.

Garrick gives a call ahead. "Go and pick out whatever you want,

The child goes ahead of Sera, looks back with a wide smile, and runs forward to look at everything being prepared, attracted to the stalls by the wonderful smells coming from them. Sera looks back and waits for Garrick to catch up and then walks alongside him, giving him a playful nudge. "Keep this up, and you'll be spoiling him rotten. I wanted that to be me."

Garrick looks at his wife out the side of his eyes. "Who says I am spoiling just him?"

Sera cracks a smile, pushing her arm through his to be closer to him. "You know what I want then."

With a knowing gaze, Garrick escorts his wife to a stall near the end of the street while Kristo, at another stall, is pointing at a plethora of meat skewers that are being stuffed into a polished box. Looking at the store's menu carved on a wooden board, Garrick speaks to the woman wrapped up in a stained apron. "We'll take two cucumber logs and a pitcher of Redthorn."

The woman reaches under her station to open a chest that causes frosty air to flow out of it. "It'll be right up." Having placed their order, Garrick and Sera turn to see Kristo running to them. The adults wait patiently, knowing Kristo is going to ask for something. "Yes, Kristo? Running from killer bees?" Garrick has an amused curl at the side of his lips as Sera pushes at her husband's side to tell him to stop. "What do you need?"

Hearing about killer bees raises one of Kristo's brows in worry. "There are killer bees here?"

Wearing a sly grin, Garrick says, "We—"

"No," Sera interrupts with a nudge to her husband, "Garrick is just being his trouble-starting self again."

Kristo takes a moment to look at Garrick and then speaks up again. "The cook said I need money for the food."

Without question, Garrick sticks his fingers into the sack on his side, pulls out a few coins, and deposits them into the child's hands. "This should be more than enough."

With a smile on his face, Kristo runs back to the stall.

"Were we like that at his age, running everywhere and requesting things without a thank-you?" Garrick looks up at his wife with a curious eye.

Sera looks down slightly at him in return. "I think we were worse than that. We'd get into so much trouble." She gives a pained smile at the thought. "He's been through a lot; we should just let him have what he wants for now." Sera turns back to wait for her food. When it comes, Kristo is running back to her and Garrick, several small boxes in his arms. Sera and Garrick look at each other with amused expressions from the amount of food Kristo has bought.

Garrick says, "In the future, Kristo, buy just enough food so you won't be hungry anymore after eating it."

"You don't want to share?"

Sera kneels and puts a hand on Kristo's shoulder. "Of course, we want to share. We just didn't know that's what you were doing, or else we would have had you order less. We bought our own favorite food to share with you too." Sera gives a wide-eyed, uncertain look at Garrick from all the food and then starts directing Kristo back home, walking with him.

When they all get back, Bree is waiting outside, petting Pilosus on the side. As judged by its devious eyes, the horse is biding its time before striking. Seeing Kristo, Bree waves to him and then picks up her board game from a chair nearby, coming up to the half-elf. "Good of you to finally show up to your own house."

Kristo gives Bree a few blinks and then nods down at all of the skewer boxes in his arms. "We were out at church and then got food. We can share if you want."

Garrick walks by the kids and grabs the house key off his belt to unlock the door, holding Kristo's clothes in one arm while he swings the door open.

Bree smiles to Kristo after being ushered in by Garrick. "Food is a pretty good apology for making me wait so long."

Garrick is nodding along comically to the conversation but stops himself once he finds Sera is looking at him with raised eyebrows.

"Kristo," Sera says, "put the food on the table and then go upstairs to change into your new clothes. What you're wearing is filthy. Don't forget to wash your face too."

Kristo nods, puts the food down, and heads upstairs. When he comes back down in his new, clean clothes, the board game is already unpacked, and he takes a seat at the table.

Sera passes the food around to everyone. After cutting into her cucumber log to reveal it filled with spiced meat, she says, "So how do we play, Bree?"

After a long explanation of the game, they play a practice game where everyone's cards are shown so Bree can explain the basic rules and fundamental strategy of Stable Masters. With everyone getting their fill of the food, they begin to settle into the game to trade and build their fortunes. After their third game, Bree looks outside to see it getting late and decides it's time to clean up the board. "Thanks for having me over. I'd stay a little longer, but I have to fetch water for the house before nighttime comes."

Kristo gives Bree a smile and gets up to see her to the door. "If you have the time tomorrow, I'd like to see what other games you have."

Bree smiles back and nods. "Sure. We should invite Hile too. He loves board games."

Kristo immediately nods. "Yes. I can't wait to see his face when I beat him at Stable Masters."

"You didn't even win one of the games we played," Bree scoffs playfully.

Kristo just shrugs it off. "I just had bad luck. I'll make sure you and Hile remember my stable name forever. The Great Horseshoe will be a legendary stable one day."

Bree chortles at him and then motions that she's leaving. "Bye, Kristo. I'll see if Hile can stay after class tomorrow."

Having witnessed the interaction while Sera and Garrick were cleaning up dinner, she keeps her voice low while talking to Garrick in a lightly approving tone. "I can't tell if you're a good or bad influence on Kristo."

"I think most people would view saving a child in a war and giving him a home as being a good influence."

"True, but then again, most people aren't telling that same kid that they feed bad children to their horses."

Garrick shoots Sera a wink, starting to clean out the skewer boxes so they can return them tomorrow. "So now it's a bad thing to tell the truth?"

Sera scoffs, finishing her work on the table with an amused smile on her face.

Kristo comes back to the table, sitting down to snack on the remaining meat. Seeing Sera and Garrick have cleaned up for him, he asks, "Is there anything I can do to help?"

Sera comes over after drying off a dish Garrick had scrubbed in the wash basin and places a hand on Kristo's shoulder. "Hun, you're fine. You don't owe Garrick or me anything for us taking care of you. It's what we want to do. Just relax."

Kristo shakes his head. "What if I want to help you both then?"

Sera thinks this over while Garrick sets down the rag he's using to scrub the dishes and dries his hands. Going over to one of the higher shelves on the wall, he reaches up and pulls down a leather book with a clasp. "Here's what you can do, Kristo. You can make and memorize the recipes in this book." Garrick places the book in front of Kristo, opening it to show off the plethora of recipes inside it with little illustrations to go with them. Garrick puts a hand over the image of an herb-wrapped fish. "These recipes have been passed down for years from my great-great-grandparents to me. I took the time to write what my father remembered, and he took the time to draw all the pictures in here."

Despite feeling the importance of being shown the book, Kristo shakes his head. "But I can't read."

"I know, which is why you have to promise me you'll take the lessons from Sera seriously while I'm gone."

Kristo looks up at Garrick to see him looking into his eyes, waiting for him to respond. "When you come back, I'll cook you a roast to celebrate."

Garrick bites his tongue and then forces a smile. "I can't wait to try it." Then he slowly closes the book, putting it up on a lower shelf to leave it within arm's reach for Kristo. Going over to his wife, who has finished with the dishes, Garrick places an arm about her waist. "It's time for bed, honey . . ."

Sera gently picks up an already dry plate to run over with her cloth. "I wish it wasn't. The days are passing too quickly . . ."

Garrick places his second hand on her hip as well. "I know."

Sera turns her head to look into Garrick's eyes, soaking them in for as long as she can. She then turns her head a little further to look at Kristo. "Kristo, sweetie, it's time for bed for you too. Run along upstairs."

Kristo gets up from his chair and makes his way to bed, leaving both adults staring at one another in the kitchen. After some time, footsteps are heard climbing the stairs together as the couple makes the long journey to their bedroom.

11

No Good Deed

WHEN MORNING FINALLY ARRIVES, NO ONE in the house wants to move. Each breath is done in a painstaking manner to let these moments linger forever. Eventually, though, it must end. As Garrick gets out of bed, the weight of the world reaches his shoulders as he goes about getting his chainmail and blade ready. Everyone meets in the kitchen for a breakfast that is cooked silently, the cracking of eggs against a skillet being the only noise in the bakery. Garrick clinks heavily as he takes a seat next to Sera, who begins portioning out the food to everyone.

Garrick speaks first, breaking the silence. "I won't be wearing my colors until I get a decent way towards Effilnem. That way, people will have a harder time identifying my loyalty on the road." Sera just nods. Kristo is cutting the same egg over and over again while looking at Garrick.

Once their heavy meal is done, Garrick goes outside to load Pilosus with all his gear, getting rations from the bakery and stuffing his yellow tunic into a sack on the mare's side.

The shadow of a large creature flying overhead from the north catches Garrick's eyes, and he turns to inspect it. The figure becomes clearer—a black winged horse with a rider clad in red is flying in circles searching for a place to land, getting lower as it does. The rider, while getting closer to the ground, spots Garrick and takes his steed down to land and turns into a run to him.

Garrick immediately brings his hand to his longsword as the flying soldier lands near him.

"Garrick? Is that you? It's been forever!"

Eyes opening wider, Garrick takes in the sight of his childhood friend—a man with long, black hair and deep-brown eyes, leaner and taller than Garrick. "Demio, I'm surprised to see you. . . . You're a winged-horse rider?"

The man gives a proud nod coupled with a pat of his steed. "Yup, but my official station is scout. On the side, I also deliver letters of importance." Demio then nods at Garrick's horse. "What's been happening with you? I haven't heard from you for about a year now."

"I've been knighted for my actions at Effilnem. We lost the city, but Lord Tengress saw my work to save my fellow soldiers. I'm to be given the falcon crest on my shield soon."

Demio comes closer and gives his friend a proud pat on the shoulder. "That's wonderful. The army is starting to recognize how good you are with a sword." Despite Demio's happiness for his friend, his face then turns to a frown. "Still, we lost Effilnem. How did that even happen? I'm not looking forward to reporting that to General Nirkin."

Garrick continues the ruse. "They came upon us so suddenly it was hard to tell what was happening. Come to find out, only a few days prior, Lord Bushan's army was devastated at Kurin's Retreat. The rebels pushed their advantage right into Effilnem."

Demio puts his hand on his head to brush back his hair in a disbelieving stroke. "Dear gods, the southern campaign is in shambles."

Garrick gives a sympathetic nod and then gestures at Demio. "What are you doing here?"

"I'm here to check out the state of the town. I'm the first scout to arrive."

"What?" Garrick blinks in an unbelieving manner. "I thought Halmin was supposed to stay neutral."

Demio gives a pained expression. "It was supposed to, but our army has recently gotten wind of rebel soldiers coming here. With how badly you say the southern campaign is going, it wouldn't be too much of a stretch to say the rebels might claim Halmin to starve us out. General Nirkin has ordered us to march south and take hold of this town before anything more sinister happens. From what it sounds like, he couldn't have picked a better time. Our dragonborne friends from the badlands are holding that bastard Joc Strixwi at bay in the north. From what I hear, they're doing more than just holding him at bay. They're kicking him across the northern front. All it took was a little help with the orcs, and now we have an incredible ally. It's hard to believe one noble house can put up such a fight. If we win, the Strixwi branch will be ruined."

Demio scratches his bulbous nose. "The rumors are true too; they can breathe fire or acid from their mouths at will. Horrifying stuff, but also cripplingly fascinating to watch."

Garrick raises his eyebrows, looking about the place. "Well, the conquest sounds as if it's been going well for Nirkin's forces. I'd be jealous, but I'm just happy we haven't lost. But tell me, how is Laina doing? I've been in town for only two days, so I haven't had the chance to see her."

Demio smiles from ear to ear. "She's pregnant, six months gone by now, and we've had letters going back and forth about the name."

Garrick gives another nod, noticing out of the corner of his eyes a few other riders are starting to trickle in over the town. "Why don't you bring her over? I can get you both some bread and a meal going."

Demio nods, motioning away from Garrick. "Sure, I'll bring her over later tonight. For now, I've got to get everything squared away. You take it easy until then, Garrick. You can tell me how you escaped Effilnem later." He gets back up onto his winged horse, riding it on the ground to move through the town.

Once his friend is out of sight, Garrick bursts back through the front door of his bakery, startling both Sera and Kristo. "Both of you, we're leaving. The loyalist army is coming to occupy Halmin. Grab food and we're gone."

Sera scrambles to fill a basket with bread. Kristo, on the other hand, is shaking his head at what's happening.

Noticing Kristo, Garrick goes over to him and puts a hand on his shoulder, coming down to eye level with him. "Hey, you're going to be safe so long as you're with us. Get some water plus whatever you think is valuable and carry it."

With wide, nervous eyes, Kristo nods at Garrick and then parts from him to do as suggested.

The knight then goes back outside to finish his work with Pilosus, getting her ready to move out. When everyone's tasks are finished, they meet out front with Garrick. "We're going south. We'll most likely be spotted by a flier if we take a normal route out, so we'll stick to alleys and then cut through farmland. When we get to the wheat fields, we'll stay there until nightfall."

Kristo and Sera nod to Garrick, who pulls on Pilosus's reins and leads everyone out of town. More than a few townspeople eye them going through the area with provisions for their journey. All remain silent, even those with anger in their eyes. As the family nears the edge of town, fewer fliers are overhead. When at last there are only two scouts in the sky, Garrick urges his family forward into the farmlands just outside of Halmin. With a moderated pace, he makes it look like they are just farmers from on high, even taking off his chainmail to throw under the hides on Pilosus. Every now and again when an on-patrol winged horse comes by, Garrick commands both Sera and Kristo to start picking the farmland clean of weeds.

At the slow pace, the family eventually gets past the first farm and into the wheat fields where they all begin walking until they are just near the southward edge. "We're going to wait here. Then when it gets dark, we are going to march until the forest covers us so the fliers can't peer in." Garrick looks to Sera and Kristo and then sits down, still holding Pilosus's reins. The other two soon find their own patch of soil to call their own and sit, waiting for the blackness to creep overhead. The occasional scout flies a patrol route over town, but neither horse nor rider catches them biding their time below.

When the stars come out and the sliver of moon in the sky sheds its pale beauty on the world, the family begins moving again. Their pace is hurried as they attempt to take full advantage of the protective darkness. Kristo begins slowing and teetering in his steps, causing Garrick to grab him and lift him up onto the back of Pilosus. When they get to the forest's embrace, past the saplings trying to retake the forest's old glory, they begin to slow their speed. The cover of the trees gives the family shelter from eyes flying overhead. Having the worst behind them, Kristo starts dozing on the horse, leaning forward to embrace the mare's neck. Darkness takes over the family's sight as the trees block out more of the moon's embrace the farther in they get.

As Sera breaks a loaf of bread from the basket she is carrying, Garrick notices the shape of a small symphony hall in it. "You didn't need to bring that. It will grow heavy." Garrick motions to it with a piece of his pink bread. Sera shakes her head, gently brushing Kristo's hair behind his ear as he has fallen into a light sleep. "My arms will hold. When you were gone, the memories that came to me were mostly of us dancing at festivals and in our home after we bought this." Sera is looking down at the little symphony hall, her expression full of past smiles.

Garrick nods to himself, squinting forward to see in what remains of the light being shed on the forest floor. "I remember. My favorite memories are the family parties. People eating and enjoying one another; those memories wouldn't have been possible without you."

Sera moves to the side of Garrick now and leans into his arm for a few steps. Catching his attention, she moves the little stage and shows his family's cookbook to him before covering it once more. "Those events wouldn't have been half as good without you cooking for them. They equally required you to be there."

Garrick gives a pained smile, looking at the basket for a second longer and then stares forward to guide his family. "I don't suppose you have my knives and rolling pin in there too?"

"I only had the one basket. Sorry."

Her husband gives an amused huff at her comment, his pained smile turning to a failed one. "I'm sorry, Sera. I'm sorry for all of it. I thought I could change the world, and instead I caused it to come down on us. What right did a man like me have in trying to impose his will on the world, trying to move it towards something he thought was better? All I get is bloodshed for my attempts."

Sera puts an arm around Garrick's waist to stop his movements. Having him feel her weight, she then places her basket several steps into the woods. Coming back, she takes Kristo down from Pilosus. "He's quite heavy, but luckily, he's short for his age. We'd die from exhaustion trying to march all night."

Garrick looks at his wife's silhouette in the blackness and then follows her, tying Pilosus up to a sturdy tree branch. The couple then seat themselves against a tree, Kristo's head nestled into Sera's lap.

"You've nothing to be ashamed of or sorry for, Garrick. The world as it is now is a pale version of what it could be. For you to dream and wish for better is a great thing. The men who fight next to you have the same thought. Even your leader Lenfro believes so. As a noble, he had no reason to betray the king. Lenfro's life was set, yet he turned on the king. Lenfro knew there were many people suffering from Brenan's rule. How many children like Kristo are out there? How many people like Mabel are suffering through years of slavery? How many of your lives would you be willing to sacrifice to make it stop?" Sera is stroking Kristo's hair as he falls deeper into sleep.

"All of them. My life is nothing compared to the good that would come. But it is not my life that I'm afraid of sacrificing. I'm afraid of sacrificing the lives that make the world worth it."

Sera moves her head upon Garrick's shoulder, seemingly ready for rest. "I am also afraid for you. I was afraid every day you were out with the army. I am afraid now, and in a few days, I will be afraid of what my new life with the military convoy will bring, but that fear doesn't mean we should stop doing what is right."

Garrick's head slowly turns to kiss the top of Sera's, with him staring down at Kristo in her lap. "What of Kristo? His life deserves to be a happy one. We would be putting him at risk. He deserves to have parents that can give him a peaceful life. We would be throwing him in harm's way."

Sera nods into Garrick's shoulder. "Do you think that's what he would want?"

Garrick shakes his head, thinking the question too far out there. "He's too young to know what would be good for him."

Sera's eyes come back from staring off into the woods to look down at the half-elf in her lap. "His choice of clothes seems to say otherwise."

"Any animal would idolize whoever saved it from the life it once had if it was as harsh as his."

Sera moves up from Garrick's shoulder and puts a hand on his cheek to have him turn to look her in the eyes. "Never speak like that again. We are in the mess we are in now because people viewed one another as mere animals. I won't have you doing the same. You are better than that."

Garrick stares into Sera's eyes, his gaze showing a hint of deep worry. "He deserves to have peace, Sera. I can't give it to him, not with what I have to do."

Sera shakes her head at Garrick now. "True, you can't. But you can give him love, and you can give him values. You can show him the type of man to be to make the world know peace, even if it's forgotten what it truly looks like."

Garrick's head turns to look at Kristo again with a light smile. "Your family really does have a gift for speaking."

Satisfied, Sera lays her head on Garrick's shoulder once again. "*Our* family."

Garrick nods. "Yes, *our* family."

12

RETURN TO CHAINS

W HEN MORNING ARRIVES, GARRICK CRACKS HIS eyes open to see wasps buzzing about his family's impromptu rest site. Next to his horse is a woman dressed in an outfit of furs and leather with hair tied about a deer's shed antler. Beside her is a slender girl dressed in the same manner that is about three inches taller than Kristo. Garrick eyes a wasp upon his knee and then looks at the woman that is soothing his horse. "Good morning. My family and I mean no harm to your forest. I am Garrick Marmuin; my wife is Sera. She is the daughter of Yuna."

The woman in furs raises her eyebrow to look at Sera, causing Garrick to nudge her.

Sera rouses from her sleep and is immediately struck by the sight of the wasps, turning only her eyes to look at the woman. "Hello, Tender," she says, seeing the woman is scrutinizing the details of Sera's face.

"Does Yuna uphold her end of the bargain?"

Sera gives a gentle nod, and the wasps about the family scatter about the wilderness, leaving Kristo to look at everything with curious eyes till Sera responds. "Yes, the town is lush with vegetation, and the houses are sung from wood. Branches of living trees even spring from them. Every new building that goes up honors her deal with you." Sera takes her eyes off the tender for a moment to witness what seems to be the shifting of vines behind some trees.

The tender then gives a nod. "She honors the pact with the forest, not with me. All of you may leave and move through without incident. Tell Yuna she owes me a favor for staying a few hungry owlbears from eating her daughter's family." The tender pats Pilosus on the side and then moves past the three as if they aren't there anymore, going deeper into the woods with her little look-alike until they are out of view.

Garrick sighs in relief, his eyes moving to Kristo. "We're lucky Sera is here."

Kristo's tilts his head in confusion.

"Forest tenders have a pension for not liking soldiers, or any men, for that matter."

Kristo blinks at the idea and then gets up with his caregivers, moving on with them. The sun mercifully rains on the forest floor through the parting leaves, and the family is able to trek once more with sound footing. Along their march, they pass bread and water around to whoever needs it, stopping only once along a stream for Pilosus to fill herself. Garrick takes his chainmail from Pilosus's back and puts it on once more.

By the time the sun begins to set that evening, the travelers are in an area where the trees have been thinned out from lumber workers' clear-cutting. A reddish landscape flows into view, the soil underneath everyone's feet becoming looser. Large, dominating outcroppings of sandstone appear just at the edge of their vison, and as they make their way through the forest's thinning, the city of Effilnem greets them a short march away. The tents of Lenfro's army surround the walls of the city, and upon the great sandstone tower of Effilnem waves a yellow banner, depicting a white winged horse in flight for all to witness.

Garrick looks up at Kristo who is once again in Pilosus's saddle. "This isn't how I wanted to show you Effilnem. I was hoping to bring you on a trip back after the war is over for you to see how the city functions during peace . . . but it seems . . ." Garrick notices that Kristo isn't paying attention to him. Following the child's gaze, Garrick spies a rock with a silverish streak flowing down the center that Kristo is staring at. "We'll have to purchase that plot of land to ensure her grave isn't disturbed." Kristo flicks his eyes down to Garrick, the two looking at each other for a moment with understanding setting into the lines of each other's face. After taking to heart one another's expressions, the party moves once more.

Midnight soon arrives as the trio reaches the outer encampment of Effilnem. Two guards on watch shift their torches at the tired party coming to join their ranks. Getting closer, a tan man in padded armor hails the group and goes to Garrick. "You, sir, what's your business?" The man casts a raised brow over the three and then aims his expression back at Garrick.

Garrick points up at the banner of Effilnem's tower. "I'm Sir Garrick Marmuin, and I have a message for Lord Lenfro about the loyalists seizing Halmin."

"Horse sh—," the man flicks his gaze to Sera and Kristo for a second, "spit. The hunger agreement prevents either side from occupying the town. Where are your colors? Why aren't you wearing them?"

Garrick pulls his overtunic out from Pilosus's saddlebags, showing it to the guard. "I wasn't wearing it because I was in Halmin as the town was being occupied. Would you wear the colors of a rebel alone against an encroaching army?"

The guard murmurs to himself and then shakes his torch at Effilnem's gate, which has been repaired to its former glory. "Right to Lenfro. Then we'll know if you're up to funny business."

With a thankful nod to the guard that just grunts and shoos them all forward, Garrick leads Sera, Kristo, and Pilosus through the camp, bringing them to Effilnem's walls where the gates are cranked open. Once through, they trudge up the streets and conspicuous bends of the keep, arriving at the open-air garden of Lord Tengress.

Entering the lush area, Sera looks at everything like it was some sort of field trip. "Do you think the lord here copied my mother?"

Garrick waves his hand to dismiss the idea, moving through the garden to the second set of oak doors. "No, just because Yuna holds the title of grand gardener doesn't mean every garden takes inspiration from her. That being said . . . a lot of plants from the town are here. Do you think the magic community used to take stock of her work before the war? A town of edible plants everywhere must have attracted the attention of mages at the Rose Keep. They are too observant there."

Sera nods, plucks a teska pod from a tree, and then takes a knife from Pilosus's side to cut it open for herself. "I'm willing to wager that a mage passed through the town at some point and stumbled on her work. It would be reasonable to assume that the Rose heard of her work. Even a passing caravan would let rumors fly. Then there are all the new residents that came in . . ."

Garrick nods in understanding. "Still, she can't be attributed to every garden."

Sera smiles slyly, knowing she'll strike him down with her next words.

Garrick knows the look and seems to be yielding defeat already.

"You're right, especially not one that was clearly grown by a nature mage just like herself, growing the same plants as she does, and with it being done in a lord's garden, which is most likely tended by a well-informed mage in the lord's court."

Kristo looks down at Sera and Garrick, shaking his head. "It's tended by Lord Tengress; Lady Amelia told me."

Sera raises her brow.

Garrick tilts his head, his voice tinged with pride. "Kristo had the honor of running into the little lady of the house while I was being knighted."

Sera mouths a realization and then looks at the door that is up a few short steps. She takes Pilosus's reins from Garrick. With no water or food trough in sight, this place was clearly not designed to hold horses; nonetheless, Sera ties the mare to a nearby tree.

Garrick helps Kristo down from the horse and goes to the oak doors to open them. The space inside is like the rest of Effilnem with the walls and floors made from the same reddish-tan stone. The large difference comes from the grandeur of the interior's designs and furniture. Detailed columns proudly support the weight of overhead rooms. On the floor are rugs with gold tassels and tapestry so interwoven that the fingers that made them could not have been human. Along the walls, deep oak cabinets line the entryway, their glass faces lavishly displaying various party needs. Racks for coats and cloaks can be seen in a room that has been left open, the storage space so filled with things that the idea of hordes of nobles popping out at any second from one of the adjoining rooms isn't a faraway thought.

This was not the case, however, and in the dead of night, this noble place is home only to the sounds of the family's footsteps and a bell that rings off in a room to the right of the front door. Soon an old dwarf wearing a sleeping gown wanders out of the room, with a nose so large that one would think it to be a joke. A candle burns in his hands brilliant enough to illuminate most of the hall. The dwarf mutters to himself, going to the door to greet the family. With the candle coming closer, Kristo shields his eyes from the bright flame. The dwarf looks over Garrick and hums to himself. "Mmm, Marmuin. I never forget a face or a name, not of a knight or noble anyways. All the lords are sleeping, as are any other decent folk you might be here to see. Come back in the morning."

Garrick motions behind the short man to let him through. "We have urgent news for Lenfro."

The dwarf guffaws. "No one comes to this place in the middle of the night with anything less than so-called urgent news. What makes your news so urgent it can't wait till morning?"

Garrick tilts his head at the dwarf and raises his eyebrows at the dwarf's dour demeanor. "Halmin is under control of a loyalist army."

"Oh." Shifting in place, the dwarf's eyes flick about the room until he nods. "I'll give word to Lord Lenfro right away. If you would wait in the library, that would be most appreciated." The dwarf turns and makes his way through the entrance area to a circular staircase, stopping for a moment to use his candle to light another one on the wall before continuing.

Garrick motions for Sera and Kristo to follow him, taking to the left side of the entryway and walking down to where an open arch is cut into the stone. Past the arch is a lounge with upholstered chairs and a wooden bench featuring thick padding. Along the walls are a plethora of shelves filled with books and trophies alike that reach to the curved ceiling of the chamber. Sera makes her way to the room's fireplace, placing a few logs in it to light. Kristo finds himself drawn to a wall in the back corner that has a map of the world sung from the stonework, the light of the fire showing how intricate its details are. Garrick keeps himself near the entryway, waiting for Lenfro's arrival.

It is not long until Lenfro makes his appearance, the blond man wearing simple yellow tunic and trousers, far beneath his station, for these small hours of the night. A bald man with a long red beard in similar clothes accompanies him, and Kristo immediately recognizes the man as the knight that had woken him up on the day he met Amelia.

Lenfro, his face lined with discomfort and fatigue, still looks attentive through his squinting eyes, which dart about to take stock of who else is in the room.

Garrick puts his hand over his chest to salute his lord, waiting for his acknowledgement.

Lenfro waves a hand, giving him leave to relax. "Tell me, Garrick, what news could a newly appointed knight bring that would cause him to wake his lord from slumber?"

"News of treachery and broken promises." Garrick looks at Lenfro, whose blue eyes are waiting for the rest of his explanation. "Halmin has been laid claim to by General Nirkin from the north."

Lenfro places a hand upon his brow, rubbing it as if to cause the frustration and malcontent to leave his mind. "Your proof, Garrick?"

Garrick shuffles in place. "I have nothing but my word and my loved ones, who I had come with me to avoid backlash from loyalists. I watched as flying scouts came into town and didn't stay long after their initial landing."

Lenfro nods in understanding. Then he turns his head to speak to the red-bearded man next to him. "Call on Luken and Quiv. Make sure the steward has a round of teska pods ready, and get the maps from my room."

The knight salutes Lenfro and then goes off.

Lenfro rubs his eyes. Approaching the fire, he nods to Sera who is tending it. "Thank you, Lady Marmuin. I will need your husband for the next few days. Take the child and find chambers in the keep. You both will be cared for under my good graces."

Sera nods in affirmation, going to Kristo to guide him out of the room.

Once the two are gone, Lenfro's arm beckons Garrick to come to the fireplace. "Garrick, I know Halmin is your hometown. I need your expertise on its defenses. Topography, the layout of its streets, any details you can give me."

In the hallway, Sera and Kristo run into the dwarf, who has a knife in hand and a satchel over his shoulder. Sera waves her hand at him.

The dwarf stops to address her. "Yes, Lady Marmuin?"

Sera hesitates a moment at hearing the title. "I'm hoping you could show Kristo and me to unoccupied quarters."

The dwarf motions for the pair to follow him. Making their way to the staircase, they climb to the next floor and enter through the intersecting hallways to a door by a glass window looking into Lord Tengress's garden. The dwarf indicates a room on the right. "You all may rest here."

Sera opens the door to the small room and its furnishings worth well more than everything in the bakery she and Garrick left behind. Across the room along the wall are three single-sized beds and various amenities for each. Sera looks down at the dwarf, giving a grateful nod. "Thank you."

The dwarf gives a short bow and moves past to attend to his other duties.

Kristo has already moved into the room and is examining everything in it with twitching eyebrows. His eyes are moving over every piece of opulence with a mix of anger and sadness. Sera, catching his expression, comes into the room, shutting the door behind her. She takes a seat on one of the beds and addresses Kristo who is staring at himself in a full-body mirror, putting a hand against the glass. "What are you thinking about, Kristo?"

The child looks to Sera in the mirror and examines the carving of the wood frame that holds the mirror up. "The whole time I lived in Effilnem, neither Mabel nor I had a bed. . . . This room has three. . . . An unused room . . . has three . . ."

Sera's face saddens at hearing his thought. "The world isn't fair in its distribution of wealth. Nor is it fair in its distribution of responsibilities or pain." Sera looks at the child again, trying to see if he understands.

Kristo has turned to look at Sera and is scanning her face for meaning. "Mabel never had a chance to even get her own freedom, to be with Temury. This place . . . Birkin explained it runs on the ore we mined. What right did the Tengresses have in taking . . . no . . . stealing our time? Was it for this? A room that they'd never use filled with . . ."

Sera gets up from the bed as Kristo's face is beginning to contort in on itself, the child looking at the walls of the room. Her arms envelope Kristo in a deep hug, petting his hair. Kristo in response to such an act lets his arms dangle, frustration still in the creases of his face. Sera talks, still trying to calm him. "Your life was awful, but it isn't the case anymore. You have every right to be angry, but anger to the point of resenting the world around you will do nothing but lead you to hate it."

Kristo shakes his head at her words. "The world deserves it."

Sera leans back out of the hug to look into Kristo's eyes. "No, just as you didn't deserve to be a slave, the world doesn't deserve your anger. Only a select few are truly responsible for the situation you were in. Being angry at everyone will just cause more bitterness."

Kristo pushes, moving free of Sera to sit on one of the beds. "Aren't the Tengresses to blame for the slave pit?"

Sera nods, but her tone is a cautious one. "Yes, they engaged in it, but we don't know if it was willingly." Examining Kristo's expression, Sera continues. "Did you enjoy meeting Amelia here?"

Kristo raises his eyebrows at the question. "Yes."

Sera gives a slow nod to this. "Was she nice to you?"

Kristo tilts his head in thought and nods after a moment.

Watching the boy puzzle everything out puts a gentle smile on Sera's face, one tinged with pride. "Why Garrick and Lord Lenfro fight isn't to harm the people responsible for your imprisonment, Kristo. It is to change the way the world thinks about slavery. You wouldn't want to harm Lady Amelia, in that same way Garrick doesn't want to harm the loyalists."

Kristo shakes his head. "People are still dying, and they are still fighting with the loyalists."

The truth of his statement causes Sera to pause, purse her lips, nod, then continue. "Yes, the reality of the war is that it was caused by arguments and disagreements that did nothing to figure out whose opinion was correct. Asmeria and its inhabitants were, for the most part, living luxurious lives compared to the rest of the world's peasantry if the story of the loyalists is to be believed. The slave class, or jailed class, made this possible. Not having to pay people more than what they need to eat and drink brought the prices down on goods across the kingdom. Many people had access to more free time and materials than before." Sera now goes to sit on the bed with Kristo and turns her body towards his to speak.

"Most people agreed with such a punishment for those with the worst crimes, and . . . perhaps they are right. That area is still under debate. The problem came when the king started decreeing that punishments be stricter. Some nobles immediately saw the king's plan, knowing what it was for. More slaves meant more resources; more resources meant the country could export more. Exporting more meant the king could make more in taxes, as could any noble or high merchant who decided to go along with it. Lenfro and a few other nobles thought this a breach of the nobility's duty to safeguard the citizens as the nobility itself was now the leading cause of suffering. Debates spiraled out of control, and nobles that refused to comply were imprisoned. These debates still happen, except instead of using thoughts and carefully pointed arguments, they employ fireballs and spearheads."

Being given the long explanation, Kristo stares off, scratching his eyebrow. "What does this have to do with Amelia, and why does it matter? The people here still caused everyone I was friends with to live terrible lives compared to Halmin."

Sera gives a little sigh, patting Kristo's shoulder. "Amelia and her family were in the wake of the king's new laws and the punishment for not obeying his decrees. While the family did nothing that we know of to combat the king's ideals, they were still the victims of his wants and desires, just not as much as anyone else. On top of that, Amelia is a child; she can't be held responsible for the actions of her father or mother since she never had a choice to begin with. Wishing harm upon her is cruel and unjust. The actions of her parents are up for debate, depending on how willing they were. To get justice, proper justice, you have to look at the facts and all sides of a situation, or else you'll be throwing someone into the fire that didn't deserve it."

Kristo shifts on the bed, his eyes on the floor now, being quiet for a while. "The Tengresses . . . still allowed this to happen. They could have fought back like Lenfro. They chose not to. There was fighting in the streets outside my slave house. People died for their lack of . . . of . . ." Kristo stumbles over his words, trying to figure out the right word to use.

"I believe the word you want is *will*." Sera nods with Kristo's statement, unable to deny it.

Kristo frowns with a furrowed brow but eventually nods and looks up at Sera again. "Not only that, but they also didn't see us as people, or else they wouldn't have allowed the slave houses. I don't think Lady Amelia is to blame, but her parents are."

Sera, tilts her head. "If that's what you believe, I won't fight you on it. The only thing you have to think about now is, if you decide to break a window or burn this place down, are you indirectly harming Amelia? Let's say the worst punishment is delivered to her parents. Lady Amelia would still inherit this estate, as well as the title of lord of Effilnem."

Kristo looks about the room. "I . . . get it."

The tall woman smiles across from him. "It's okay to be angry. Just remember that your anger has to be directed at those that deserve it."

The door to the room swings open to reveal Garrick, having come back from his own long explanations to the war council. The knight rubs his face and starts undoing the buckles of his armor while talking. "You have to make sure your anger is also backed by enough reason if you're going to act on it, and that it's proportional."

From her husband continuing the conversation Sera was having privately with Kristo in their room, she shoots Garrick a confused look.

He shrugs. "I managed to hear the last bit of your words through the door."

Sera gives Kristo a pat on the head, then gets up to go to her own bed. "I think that's enough pondering for you today, Kristo. I imagine Garrick is very tired and wants some sleep." Sera turns to look at her husband as he is about to say something, but the expression in the eyes of her down-tilted head clearly shows how he is supposed to act.

Now in his tunic and trousers, Garrick looks at his bed. "I'm going to sleep for at least two days. The feathers of this must be so nice and fluffy." He then falls onto it, making short work of getting under the covers.

Sera then says to Kristo, "You heard him, bedtime."

13

AGAPE

WHEN MORNING COMES, GARRICK IS SUMMONED out of the room by the same dwarf from the evening for cavalry training. Having slept for only a scant couple of hours, Garrick is fumbling about, muttering angry nothings before finally leaving. With all the noise, Sera and Kristo decide after a look to one another to find breakfast. Passing out of their doorway, Kristo's gaze is drawn left to the courtyard where he can see Lady Amelia sitting at a tea table with her attending knight accompanying her for breakfast. Examining the little ritual for a second, Kristo turns back to Sera and quickly catches up behind her. Once down the spiral stairs, Sera follows her nose to where she thinks the kitchen is.

Kristo looks at her walk off and shrugs, going out to the courtyard through the heavy doors. Outside, Kristo goes over to Amelia's table. The knight Reginauld is eyeing the boy, but Amelia is paying him no mind, just accepting Kristo's presence. Kristo stands in front of the table until the time passing forces one of the three to speak, that one being Amelia. "Yes, Kristo?"

His eyes flick about, as if insinuating there might be some other ritual he must complete before sitting. "Would you mind if I sit and eat with you?"

Lady Amelia nods but then tilts her chin as if asking a question. "I would not, but it's typical for someone in possession of a lady's favor to show it before speaking to her after an absence." Amelia's voice drops as she then gives Kristo a lightly disappointed tone. "That, or he apologizes for losing it."

Kristo's eyebrows rise as he was right about there being some other ritual he must attend to. "What's a favor?"

Amelia closes her eyes for a moment and then opens them, speaking in a disapproving tone. "It's what I gave you as proof of our bond . . ."

Kristo scratches his eyebrow. He stands there thinking before giving a loud "Oh!" Putting his hand down the neck of his shirt, he then shows off the napkin tied around the necklace he is wearing. "I wouldn't lose it. It's one of my most favorite things."

A choking noise comes from Reginauld, who hits his chest, placing his teacup back on its saucer.

Amelia coughs and reaches for her teacup to hide whatever emotion she was feeling. Once composed, she offers the seat to the left of her. "You are welcome to sit at my table any time then, Kristo."

Not knowing why he was getting such a reaction, Kristo takes his seat, waiting on Amelia. Once offered tea, the little ritual that happened a few days prior repeats, but with Kristo acting more like a proper gentleman.

Once everyone is enjoying their meal, Kristo speaks up. "Do you ever wonder why there are things we have to do before we eat?"

Amelia tilts her head at the question. "What do you mean?"

Kristo adjusts his seating, holding his teacup a little awkwardly in his hand. "When I was eating in Halmin, we had to wait for everyone to get their food as a sign that we'd be hungry a little longer to ensure everyone had enough food. Here at this table, it seems . . . not needed?"

Amelia almost immediately responds. "My father told me once that our little rituals are what separates humanity from beasts."

Kristo blinks at the idea. "What do you think, Lady Amelia?"

Amelia's puffy appearance deflates, causing a crease of her brow to appear on her face. Her expression is deep in thought for some time, not upset, but contemplative as she fiddles with her sandy-blond hair. "I think that someone's willingness to comply or not comply with rituals like teatime or waiting for people to get everything on their plates allows others to figure out what kind of person he or she is, but I also agree with my father."

Kristo nods to her statement, wanting her to continue. "Do you think that if someone didn't want to engage in a ritual that it would be rude or mean?"

Amelia examines Kristo's face for a hint of judgment or hook digging into her but finds only innocence. "Not necessarily, it would depend on the circumstance. For example, when I met you, I thought you uneducated in manners and annoyed from being hungry. However, if someone like a merchant's son came in and did what you did, then I would consider him a menace." Amelia adjusts in her seat to grab the fruit dish at the table to scoop some onto her plate. "Why the odd questions, Kristo?"

Kristo gives his own shifting motion in his seat now as he racks his brain. "Do you think that people refusing to be slaves is also rude or mean?"

The new line of question causes Amelia to sit up straight, casting concerned eyes at Reginauld before she speaks. "No, I don't think so. Just as much as I enjoy leaving the castle, I would imagine other people would like the freedom to live the lives of their choosing. The manner of freeing was incredibly violent, however, and caused a good deal of people to lose their lives and valuables."

The former slave quietly crunches a cracker and continues to think, staring off at the teapot as he finds his words. "Do you believe that fighting is wrong when it's done for freedom? The people that were hurt, do you think their pain was worth it for us?"

From hearing the word *us*, Amelia's head droops a little as she realizes just whom she is talking to; her eyes are staring at her teacup that she is repeatedly clenching her fingers around. Reginauld, eyeing the two of them, leans forward in his chair. Amelia catches his glances and takes her hand off her teacup to give a gentle wave of dismissal that causes Reginauld to rest back but not relax. "I can't tell you if it was right or wrong, but I don't think your people had a choice. I can't begin to imagine the rage your people felt after years of labor. Perhaps in the same manner an executioner uses a blade, violence is justice for the enslaved, regardless of who it affects so long as it results in freedom. I know for now all I can hope for is that the blade falls on the truly deserving and is not to be used as its own means of terror."

After hearing this, Kristo takes a couple of minutes to process what was said. As he does, a group of rebel knights walk out of the keep, through the garden, and out to the rest of town. Kristo eyes the men, looking them over with nothing short of admiration in his eyes. When they leave, he goes back to staring at the teapot. "I don't understand. We weren't made free by other slaves. We were made free by people like the ones who you said were caught in the violence, by the people who were already free. No matter what I'm told, I can't understand how they are willing to give up their amazing lives for someone they haven't met. They might even hate us once they've gotten to know us."

Amelia puts a hand on Kristo's to express her sympathy.

The small act brings Kristo's eyes to Amelia's, and they scan hers.

"I . . . I don't know, Kristo. Maybe they are hopeful. I know many of the people enslaved here were horrid people. I know that my father sorted the slave houses based on a person's crime. Perhaps you didn't get to see the truly awful side of things because your crime wasn't that bad."

Kristo shakes his head. "Still bad enough to be enslaved for life."

The children break their gazes to stare down at their tea, letting time pass while Reginauld watches them. After the baked goods run low, Kristo and Amelia sit in a long silence. After a few minutes Kristo finally goes to speak, but as he does the doors of the keep open with a bang, revealing Sera, whose eyes immediately lock on Kristo.

Carrying a picnic basket and a blanket, Sera marches over to Kristo in a bit of motherly rage. Sera puts a relieved hand on her forehead, then gives a curtsey to Amelia. "My Lady, if you would excuse Kristo and me."

Lady Amelia gives a nod and watches with raised eyebrows as Sera grips Kristo's ear to pull him out of his seat, causing Reginauld to give an amused smile.

Kristo gives grunts of pain and confused objections the whole way to the outer gate of the courtyard until they are out of earshot of the little noble.

Sera talks with a hushed angry tone. "What are you doing, Kristo? I thought you were following me to get breakfast. You have to tell me if you're going to wander off."

Once Sera releases his ear, Kristo is rubbing it and shaking his head, confused. Matching Sera's hushed tone, he says, "I didn't know that. How was I supposed to know that? Back at Halmin, I was told to wander off and explore."

Sera rubs her head again, groaning in memory of the previous conversation. "From now on, you have to ask permission. I was worried sick, clambering all over the keep to find you. Who knows how many nobles I might have embarrassed myself in front of." Sera shakes her head and motions towards the keep's winding trail to town with the basket of food. "I figured you'd want to watch Garrick's training, given how much you liked training with Bree."

Kristo gives a nod, and the pair start making their way out of the red-stone city to where the soldiers are practicing. The child keeps an arm's length away from Sera. Reaching their destination, they find a prime piece of land to watch Garrick take rounds on Pilosus, trying to get his lance through small dangling metal rings set up on various holding posts. Attending squires are ensuring the rings are put back up after each knight's charge. After Garrick's fourth attempt, the red-bearded knight rides up alongside him and points out Sera and Kristo with his lance. Garrick rides over, dismounts Pilosus, and sits on the ground with them. An attending squire then comes over to pull Pilosus to water and food.

Sera leans into Garrick, offering him a piece of meat from the basket. "You looked rather dashing out there, Sir Garrick."

With Sera's underlying tone, coupled with her subtle rubbing of his back, Garrick flicks his eyes at Kristo and then back at his wife. "I have good reason to try my hardest out there, Lady Sera."

Kristo, who is eating and watching the knights practice their cavalry charges, doesn't notice as Garrick and Sera adjust themselves so that she is lying with her head on Garrick's lap while he plays with her hair.

With everyone enjoying their picnic and entertainment, the basket empties of food with squires occasionally offering water to the family. Kristo looks at the running boys and young men with a tilt of his head. "Why are they running water? Isn't that the job of a slave?"

Garrick raises a confused brow, shaking his head. "No, they are apprenticing knights. In return for the knights teaching them, they do basic tasks for them." Kristo nods to himself while the two adults watch.

Practically smelling what Kristo's brain is cooking, Sera taps Garrick's chest and motions her head at the child.

Getting the point, Garrick speaks up to Kristo. "After the war, Halmin will need more food for all the people coming back. It was starting to attract a lot of moving families. The town will need another baker."

Kristo scrunches his eyebrows. "But the war would have to be over first."

Sera gives a sigh at Kristo's words, rubbing her forehead. "Kristo, why—"

Garrick cuts her off by putting a hand on her stomach and then speaks over her. "Kristo, I know what is on your mind. We'll talk later, after my training."

Kristo looks back at Garrick, who has his face slightly turned, eyeing Kristo with a clear yes being the only answer the boy can give. The child gives an obligated nod to Garrick, who in turn gives a curt drop of his chin.

Sera, clearly upset with the outcome of the conversation, taps Garrick's chest to stare up at him once Kristo has looked away again. Seeing he's in trouble, Garrick rubs the back of his neck. "I need to get back for sword training." He starts to move, but Sera keeps her head on her husband's lap until her message has clearly sunk into him. When at last Sera releases her prisoner, she sits up and watches as he goes off to a circle of knights that are wielding wooden swords. Sera the whole while is staring at Kristo, examining his blue clothes and leather boots for a moment before getting up. "I'm going to go back to the keep, Kristo. You're free to either stay here or come with me."

Kristo gives a nod, looking back at her. "I'm going to stay here and watch."

Sera then puts a worried hand on her head, messing with her braid before patting Kristo's head. "Be good for the knights." She grabs the basket next to Kristo and turns, leaving the boy to watch the knights and squires go about their training. Kristo sits there on his little slice of the world, watching everything. Sword play turns into proper shield use, which turns into armor study until the knights finish off with command lessons where they are taking turns shouting orders to the squires that are pretending to be soldiers under their command. When the sun begins to set over the desert, the men start to feel the chill in the air, causing the training session to break.

Garrick turns over Pilosus to be put under the care of one of the attending squires and thanks the young man. Then the knight turns to look at Kristo. After a moment of contemplation, Garrick goes to the boy and motions for Kristo to follow him. "Come along," he says sternly, but the man's hard look doesn't seem to be directed at the child.

Kristo notices the sternness, getting up to follow Garrick.

The two return to the city, but instead of Garrick taking the boy back to the keep, they walk down the main road for a time. City life here hasn't returned to normal, but there are still a good number of people walking about. Businesses have started to open their doors once more, and food stall workers have started selling to the occasional passersby again.

The noises are quite familiar to Kristo, but now being able to see what causes them has him looking around. The child watches as adults are going about business and kids are attempting to play with one another, despite the occupation. Garrick guides the boy to a food stall, purchasing enough smoked meats and cheese for them both while the master of the stall looks scornfully at Garrick.

"You know," Garrick says to Kristo, who is still enamored by the bustling city streets, "there is a place we can go where we'd see everything here all at once."

Kristo turns his head to Garrick who is tilting his head at the keep's main tower. The boy's eyes light and shift to Garrick to see if he's serious.

Garrick ruffles Kristo's hair and takes his food in a tied-up cloth. The pair make their way up the winding road to the keep and inside its heavy doors. The hallway having light and voices spilling into it from the library due to plans still being drawn. Upon walking up to the second story, they hear soft crying coming from one of the rooms to their left.

"Garrick?" Kristo asks, looking up at Garrick, "What is—"

"Leave it be, Kristo."

With questions still causing his eyebrows to move, Kristo follows Garrick up to the second staircase leading to the tower. At the top, Garrick opens the hatch door, and a yellow-tunicked guard that was looking out on the city turns to them. He shoots the pair a questioning gaze, noticing the yellow tunic on Garrick.

"I'm Sir Garrick Marmuin," the knight says and motions for the man to relax. "Let us have the tower for an hour."

The guard on post shrugs his shoulders at being told what to do from a knight. "Break time, I suppose."

Given the guard's nonchalance, Garrick can't help but smile as the man goes down the staircase. Up here, there is a small table with a few chairs around it. Lying on the ground is a pole and a few flags of various colors meant for signaling. Garrick places the food on the table; they sit down and begin their supper.

After finishing his meal, Kristo is up and looking around at the city in the fading light of the sun. Eventually his eyes settle on his old slave house, and he peers into the corner where he used to sleep.

Noticing the unremarkable building of the boy's gaze, Garrick says, "Something interesting down there?"

Kristo nods, pointing to the spot he's staring at. "I used to sleep right there."

Garrick's eyebrows come together in a furrow, trying to see where he's pointing, using his own finger to guide his vison. "That's where we first met then."

Kristo nods again. "I'm happy to have met you . . . yet sad for the reason."

Garrick's eyes close as he breathes a heavy sigh. "Kristo . . . about you wanting to become a squire. I won't allow you to. There is no reason why you should have to fight, not at your age, not without having had a life first." He opens his eyes.

Kristo looks directly at Garrick. "I want to fight because I'm going to have a good life. I don't know if there are other people like me out there, but if there are, they deserve to have the life I've had the past couple of days."

Rubbing his lower face and the beginnings of a beard, Garrick says, "Yes, but not at the sacrifice of your own. You can't throw your life into something like war at such a young age. You deserve peace and friends, a chance to grow."

"Don't you deserve the same?"

The innocence of such a question strikes Garrick, who turns his eyes away to look at the dying sun. "Everyone does, but it's not possible for everyone in the world right now. It's my duty as an adult to guide you and the rest of your generation on the right path, even if it means fighting. It's my . . . obligation to the future generations that forces me to act. You will have the same obligation when you are older."

Kristo shakes his head, not accepting Garrick's argument. "If that's how you feel, then I feel the need to fight for everyone that might still be living how I was."

It's now Garrick's turn to shake his head, turning to look out on the city that's being covered in growing shadows. The plinking of piano keys starts to fill the air with the same tune Kristo heard when fireballs rocked the keep. Garrick's head turns to look at the source of the music and sees Lady Amelia playing a piano underneath a gazebo, surrounded by hedges in the rear courtyard. Next to her are two people, a tall blond man in expensive clothes and a woman wearing a regal dress and a wig. Both are intently listening to what Amelia is playing, not regarding any-thing else in the world as worth their time. Soon the man moves over to a section hidden by a flower bush and comes back with a violin, adding his music to Amelia's.

Garrick looks at Kristo, who has moved next to him to watch Lady Amelia. "Kristo, I won't let you be involved in the combat. How about cooking and cleaning for the soldiers? You'd still be helping the army, and it's a job that is important. Then, when we take Halmin, you'll stay there with Sera. She'll need your help running the bakery and the school."

"Hmm. The army is going to Halmin?"

"We have to," Garrick says reluctantly yet firmly. "The rebel armies and the eastern half of Asmeria would starve if we don't go."

Kristo is still eyeing Amelia, his ears soaking in the notes she's playing. "I hope we don't hurt anyone who doesn't deserve it."

Garrick gives a simple pat on Kristo's back, leaning in his chair to also watch Amelia below. "I hope so as well."

14

THE GROWING CHOIR

THE NEXT MORNING, KRISTO AND SERA approach the army camp to get their assignments. They are told to help the chefs and attend to the wounded as needs arise. Their day is full of meal preparation and cooking.

Garrick, once again, spends the day training with his fellow knights. From the time the family gets up from bed to when they lie back down, music is heard from the rear courtyard.

This is how three days pass, but on the fourth morning, the family wakes to no music playing. The keep is left with the sounds of preparations coming from the first-floor library.

On this morning, the attending dwarf knocks on the family's door.

Garrick greets him. "Good morning."

The dwarf, who has a somber face, produces a note for Garrick to read.

As the knight's eyes scan the paper, his face turns into a frown, and he looks back at Kristo who is putting on his boots. Garrick gives the dwarf a nod and closes the door, looking back at Sera sitting on her bed who is giving him a questioning gaze. Instead of speaking, Garrick hands the note to Sera to read while he grabs his gear.

Kristo now looks at the note in Sera's hand and goes to sit next to her. "What does it say?"

Sera gives a huff and then forces a smile on her face, pulling Kristo into a side hug. "It says that you've been doing such a good job as an assistant that you've been given today off. Why don't you spend some time with Amelia?"

Kristo nods with a smile and leaves the room.

Garrick watches him go and then slides his chainmail on and adjusts his belt. "Do you think she will appreciate his company?"

Sera helps her husband adjust his gear. "I don't know. It'd be better than her being alone with that knight, though. He barely talks."

After a moment of consideration, Garrick nods in agreement. "Even if she yells and takes her anger out on him, Kristo is a strong boy; he can take it. And his being there is better than her being alone."

Sera pats her husband's side and then goes to sit on her bed again. "Someday, he won't have to be." She inspects Garrick as he puts his sword on his hip. "Do you want me to go with you?"

Garrick's response is short, but not out of anger. "No, absolutely not."

Sera leans forward, her hands knitted together in her lap as a reaction to Garrick's voice. "Then perhaps I can—"

"Sera, you don't have to do anything," Garrick says, taking a seat beside her and cupping her hands with his. "I love you, and I don't want you to witness this. You shouldn't have to, and I don't want you to feel any sort of responsibility for me having to do this."

Sera nestles her head into Garrick's shoulder, quietly denying his will. "You are my responsibility, just as I am yours. We both guide each other; I am also to blame for the responsibilities you bear. Don't deny me trying to help you find peace with your station. Let's walk and talk tonight. We can even be silent if that's your wish."

Garrick moves his head to the side to place a kiss on top of Sera's head and then whispers just for her. "How could I ever say no?"

Sera presses her side into Garrick, not caring about the rough feel of his mail. He holds her for a long while until bells begin tolling. At the sound, he rises from his wife and gives her a dutiful nod, which is returned. Then he leaves, making his way out of the keep and down to the center of the city.

The market is flooded with people surrounding a stone slab that has been raised from the earth. On it, a headsman's block, raised from stone, sits in the center of the slab. Benches made of stone adorn the left side, while on the right there is a table with its own bench. Garrick and a few other men in armor push themselves through the crowd to sit upon the benches, waiting for the grim event to begin. From the bench, Garrick looks at the crowd, finding numerous wiry men in ill-fitting rebel tunics in their ranks alongside women in rags.

Beyond, coming down the road from the keep, is a small procession of twenty soldiers surrounding two people. At their front is Lenfro, dressed in a fine yellow tunic, embroidered around the edges to show his import. As the entourage draws closer, the soldiers push aside the crowding people, forcing their way to the impromptu stage. Lenfro makes his way up, carrying various papers under his left arm and takes his place sitting at the bench with the table in front of it. The two people then take their grand stage. Lord Tengress is the first to calmly climb and then offers aid to Lady Tengress, whose chest is heaving with such fright that even those in the far back of the crowd can see it move.

The accompanying soldiers take their places around the raised block of stone, posing a barrier between themselves and the trial about to commence. As the couple stand in front of the guillotine, Lenfro comes beside them, holding a piece of paper, reading it aloud for all to hear. "Here commences the trial of Lord Vincent Tengress and Lady Penelope Tengress. They stand accused of robbing many a man and woman of their liberties far beyond what the extent of the law should have permitted, in some cases, overlooking purposeful wrong persecutions in order to increase the industry of Effilnem and their other land holdings. Do the accused understand the charges?"

Lord Tengress looks at his wife with a single nod and then speaks for the crowd to hear. "We do."

Lenfro nods at the response, continuing. "How does the accused plead?"

Lord Tengress stares at his wife and then back up at his keep. "Guilty . . . for myself," Lady Tengress's voice cracks and tears begin to flow, "innocent for my wife."

At Lord Tengress's claim, the crowd roars, justice being called from every throat via exclamations of anger.

Lenfro motions his arms for the crowd to calm down. "The purpose of this congregation is now to determine Lady Tengress's guilt or lack thereof." He approaches the bench of attending knights. "You all have been called today to act upon your honor, to bear witness to this trial, and to judge accordingly. Your allegiance to our cause of rebellion is to be forgotten while you sit upon this bench. Your intrinsic nature and striving virtue of station are to be put above all else. Does each of you understand? If so, please say 'I do' or remove yourself from the bench."

As one, the assembled knights speak loudly and with clarity, "I do," to be heard throughout the market.

Lenfro returns to his desk, rifling through papers to produce evidence. Taking one letter, he hands it to Lord Tengress. "Do you recognize this letter?"

Flicking his eyes over it, Lord Tengress nods and says, "Yes, it is a letter from an appointed judge in Green Hill stating that a quota for prisoners has been filled. It also details their arrival date."

"Where was this letter retrieved from?"

Lord Tengress shuffles in place. "It could only have been retrieved from the desk in my study. However, I have already stated my own guilt. This letter does not prove my wife to be guilty of anything."

Lenfro shakes his head. "This single letter is enough to prove both your and your wife's guilt."

"B—"

"Lady Tengress," Lenfro says, cutting Vincent off, "would you mind recalling the vows you were told to recite by the priestess that ordained your wedding, the words every man and woman in the kingdom of Asmeria recite before being bound to one another?"

With more rapid breathing, Lady Tengress recites, "For this life . . . I take you Vincent to be my partner and love. In this life . . . I promise to both nurture and guide you upon the path of virtue. . . . Should you stumble, I shall catch you. Should you fall, I shall help you to walk once more. In our love, I understand that your soul is in my keeping, and I am to see that it be free of weeds and tangled growth. My actions and words shall be tools, meant to ensure your path leads to the glory of heaven."

From her words, the knights stir, understanding the accusation Lenfro is putting forth. The crowd too is silent, making audible the stifled crying of Lady Tengress.

Lenfro nods. "Lord Tengress, there is no reasonable way you can ever say that you have not sought your wife's counsel or comfort in the actions you have taken. This is true, is it not?"

Clearly distraught, Lord Tengress looks about, trying to think of a way out of this line of accusation. "Yes," he shouts with intensity. "However my actions are my own! She cannot claim guilt for the things I've done or the orders I have given!"

Lenfro shakes his head. "No, her very vows are meant to keep you from the actions you have taken. What you have done is evil, against the very nature of freedom given to every soul on this earth. You yourself admitted to seeking counsel with your wife, and your wife's vows were clearly meant to keep you from taking such actions in this life. Your wife is your partner and keeper, the one person meant to keep you in check. Your actions clearly indicate that she supported your endeavors, or at the very least did not try to stop them."

Lady Tengress has her hands covering her face, rubbing the tears from them. Lord Tengress has balled fists and is shaking his head, his brow straining to find some way to convince the counsel to adjudicate in favor of his wife.

Lord Lenfro waits for one of them to speak, but neither does, so he approaches the bench of knights. "The decision on Lady Penelope Tengress's guilt is left for you twenty to decide; the evidence and arguments have been laid quite plainly for all to hear. The sentence, if she is found guilty, shall match her husband's. You will have time to think about this trial, four hours, until the bells toll three." Lord Lenfro looks directly at each knight in turn and then returns to the bench at his desk, waiting for the counsel to make their decision. On his face is a whisper of a smile, lightly smug in its corners.

The knights stir uncomfortably as they consider the charge and guilt of the woman, none of them taking the potential sentencing lightly. The sun moves higher in the sky, and squires run water to everyone on the stage, letting them cool themselves.

When the bells of the city strike three, Lenfro rises from his desk to approach the bench of knights. "Let us hear what you, men of honor, have to say about Lady Tengress's fate." Lenfro motions to the first on the left of the bench, going down the line.

"Guilty" is spoken from every set of lips.

In the beginning of the second row, Garrick calls out, "Guilty, with pardon."

The other knights on the bench stare at Garrick with curiosity.

Lenfro, as well as the Tengresses, have raised brows at such a decree, and Lenfro's whispering smile changes to a stern grimace. The lord's waving hand instructs Garrick to step forward from the bench.

Garrick takes the stage, looking out to a bloodthirsty crowd.

Lenfro goes to Garrick's side. "State your name and where you hail from."

"I am Sir Garrick Marmuin of Halmin," he says loudly for all in the crowd to hear.

"On what grounds do you state the accused found guilty should receive pardon?"

"Lady Tengress is under accusation of being a loving and supportive wife, willing to give her husband respite from the world he inhabits. While it could be true that she lent aid to his dealings, she does not have firm responsibility for Lord Tengress's actions."

"It is as you say. Lady Tengress clearly has failed her duty as keeper of Lord Tengress's affairs, and Lord Tengress has even admitted to seeking her counsel. How do you not believe her to be just as guilty?"

Garrick closes his eyes to breathe and then looks out on the crowd. "This implication means that every man's wife, child, and relative is responsible for the actions of one another. The desire of freedom for all is the foundation of our very rebellion. One cannot have freedom without personal liberty, and with that comes personal responsibility. The ultimate guilt of these dealings lies with Lord Tengress. Thus, he is the only one that should forfeit his life to justice's will. If this sentence were to be carried out on Lady Tengress, then that means all our own wives are equally responsible for the lives we knights and soldiers have taken due to their support of our choices and moralities."

Lord Lenfro looks down at the ground in contemplation, his brow seeming to crease with anger. The lord then calms himself, looking at Garrick again. "You still claim guilty. Do you not wish to see those that violate the freedoms of humanity be punished?"

Garrick looks at Lenfro and then at the Tengresses before addressing the crowd. "I would see her punished, but not executed. Her crimes do not warrant such a sentence."

Lord Lenfro raises his chin at the statement. "What would you consider a proper sentence?"

"She should be stricken from all noble and land-holding titles and made unable to inherit anything. She should also be barred from all noble courts. Inheritance of anything from the death of Lord Tengress meant to go to her should be adjusted by him now."

Lenfro raises an eyebrow at the thought, looking at Lady Tengress.

The proposed idea causes the crowd to murmur, taking in the new suggestion.

"I would add," Lord Lenfro says, "that Lady Tengress shall be branded, should the counsel of knights find this proposed sentencing to be just."

Lord Tengress closes his eyes with his shoulders slouching, but when he opens them, he seems to have found peace in the arrangement.

Lenfro's expression grows angrier as he approaches the bench of knights, leaving Garrick to stand. "Upon hearing this new suggestion, what say you?" Lenfro gestures to the first knight.

"Guilty, with pardon."

Each knight in turn repeats the same, most of them looking at Garrick with silent approval.

At the final knight agreeing with Garrick's proposal, Lenfro nods from the decision made, turning his back on the knights to approach his own bench. "So it shall be. All Asmerian courts shall receive news of now Penelope Tengress's sentence."

Lord Lenfro is furiously writing on a piece of parchment and then moves to center stage to speak to the crowd. "Now shall commence the execution of Lord Vincent Tengress, his claim of guilt heard clearly by all that bear witness here today. Sir Garrick, escort the prisoner to the block."

Garrick stares wide-eyed and with lips slightly sucked in, looking from Lord Lenfro to Lord Tengress.

Lord Tengress gives a nod to Garrick, signifying both his gratitude and acceptance of his fate.

Lenfro curtly motions to the block. "Do as required, executioner."

Garrick turns to eye Lord Lenfro and, at seeing his demeanor, does as asked.

Before Garrick reaches Lord Tengress, he straightens himself up like a proper noble and walks to the block, kneeling to lay his head over the crescent cut into it. "I am ever grateful to you, Sir Garrick. Wherever my soul is sent, I shall speak of you there in the highest regard. My wife shall live, and my daughter shall continue to have a mother because of you."

Unable to bear looking at Lord Tengress, Garrick stares off to the side as he approaches the block.

Lenfro goes to the other side of Lord Tengress. "Do you have any final words to be heard by this body of knights? Your wife can no longer inherit your or any estate."

"I would leave all that I own to my daughter, Amelia, given my wife can no longer inherit. Amelia shall be guided by Sir Reginauld, her attending knight until she reaches maturity. My brothers shall have no claim, other than minor titles of governance already given. While I do understand my wife has to forgo all land and titles, I would beg the court to allow my accrued wealth to purchase a small home for her so that she may not suffer homelessness."

The knights nod in agreement.

Noting their consent, Lord Lenfro looks down at his fellow lord. "Your request shall be granted," he says, and then, "Sir Garrick, draw your sword."

Garrick's hand goes to the hilt of his gifted blade, drawing it. His eyes roam the blade, as if to question it, and then takes an overhead swinging stance. Garrick's fingers fidget, furling and unfurling about the leather handle, awaiting the order to execute the father of Kristo's friend, eyeing a clean spot of his neck to make things quick.

Lenfro puts his right arm in the air, getting ready to give the order. "May your soul find peace in the afterlife, my kin." Lenfro drops his arm quickly.

Garrick screams in anger, bringing his blade down on the lord's neck.

15

FOR TOMORROW

Kristo and Amelia are both sitting in the back courtyard underneath the gazebo that was only a short day prior filled with the sound of a violin. Now it lies silent in a case nearby. Kristo is sitting in a chair to watch Amelia, who is absentmindedly plinking away at her piano. Reginauld is here, but away from them both, sitting on the steps of the gazebo as if on guard. Righteous yelling from the city invades the courtyard, causing Amelia to plant her elbows on the keys and bury her face in her hands.

Kristo and Reginauld are both looking at Amelia.

A hard breath comes from her mouth, and she straightens herself in her seat to read a sheet of music. Amelia then starts playing, an empty expression on her face as she leads a duet featuring no partner.

Where the song is supposed to end, Amelia continues it, repeating from the beginning, allowing neither of the two next to her to speak. If they attempt to say anything, she slams the next set of keys to silence them. This wordless exchange goes on until the door to the courtyard is shoved open. Penelope, looking from its arch towards Amelia, then runs to her, pulling up her skirt to run. The wig on her head is disheveled and falls off from the action, letting her tied-up, sandy-blond hair show to the world. Her arms fling open as she nears Amelia, surrounding her daughter in a hug.

Amelia turns in her grip to hug her back, sadness and relief on both of their faces. "Mother . . . I'm happy you're here. . . . Father . . . is he . . . ?"

Penelope shakes her head, hugging her daughter tighter. "Your father . . . he . . . isn't with us any longer."

While this interaction is happening, a small group of Asmerian rebels, accompanied by a knight, comes into the courtyard, keeping a respectful distance to allow mother and child to speak to one another.

"Amelia, I love you so, so much." Penelope pulls back from the embrace just enough so she can look down at Amelia.

As she looks up at her mother, Amelia's gaze runs over her mother's right cheek, which has a deep burn in it in the shape of a hand. "Father's idea worked . . . you're alive. Your face, why is it burned?"

Penelope shakes her head once more and then sits on the bench to tell Amelia what happened.

"You're not allowed to be here?"

Penelope nods wiping her eyes with her fingers. "No, your father . . . we will hold his ceremony within the week. I'm to have a house in the city, but I can't be here after the arrangements go through. He deserves the finest burial, fit for a great man." Penelope sniffles while nodding to herself. "Yes, we will fill the halls with his favorite things. Make sure no one ever harms his portrait, Amelia. He'll live forever through us."

Amelia can do nothing but nod, listening to her mother's words.

The rebels, seeing that Penelope is safe within the keep, are ushered to leave by their accompanying knight. As they depart, Garrick comes through the doorway, spying Kristo sitting and observing everything as usual. "Kristo!"

The child looks at Garrick, coming over to him. "Leave Amelia and her mother alone for now, Kristo. They need time."

The two pass through the doorway and go upstairs back to their room. Inside, Sera is tidying the place, making sure everything is in order as it was when the family arrived. She looks at Garrick, who gives a small shake of his head. He then takes a seat on his bed and tells the two about what happened down at the trial and execution.

Hearing Garrick's explanation, Sera sits beside her husband, offering her hand in his lap for him to hold. "Lenfro was that cold?"

Garrick takes his wife's hand, running his thumb along her fingers, examining them. "Yes, it's as if he punished my spoken judgment. I did what I thought was right, as any man should. Is that not the point of this?"

Garrick shakes his yellow tunic, pinching it at the winged horse. Then he lets it go, looking at Kristo and then at his wife. "I'm not sure what Lenfro fights for, but now I'm sure it's not for what's right. That just seems to be an effect . . . sometimes."

Horns are blown from around the walls of the city, ensuring that everyone in and outside the city can hear their blaring. Kristo, not knowing what they're for, goes to the window in the hall to look at the soldier blowing into one on the keep's wall.

Garrick nods at the bedroom floor and then looks at Sera. "It's a good thing you were cleaning. We're to leave tomorrow; that's the mustering horn."

Sera gives her husband a gentle smile, pushing her weight into him before getting up and tugging at her husband's hand to have him follow. On a dresser is the small concert stage, which she picks up and holds to her chest. "We certainly can't leave this place without a good dance. We are considered nobility now, even if it's minor, and I've always dreamed of dancing in a great hall."

The grim demeanor on Garrick's face cracks into a hint of a smile. "No, I suppose we can't. Where should we dance, Lady Marmuin?"

Sera pulls her hand from Garrick's and places it on his cheek. "There's a nice banquet hall attached to the first floor. It's a shame there hasn't been any dancing with the music that's been playing. I think we should remedy that, Sir Marmuin."

Garrick nods and strips off his armor to his yellow tunic. When he reaches to grab his sword once more, his hand stops as he examines the engraved scabbard. His uncertain eyes move along it length, and he refuses to take it. His hand coming back to hold Sera's waist as he makes for them to leave the room. "Let us be off."

Kristo, outside the room, looks up at the pair.

Sera gives a pat to Kristo's head and motions off down the hall. "Why don't you go to the library, Kristo? I heard the brown mage that fixed the city likes to spend his time there."

Kristo darts off, leaving the two adults to smile at his running.

"He's such a silly boy sometimes," Sera says.

Garrick cracks a full smile now. "Yes, but wise beyond his years. You should have heard the way he spoke on the tower."

Sera nudges Garrick's arm, leading him on a slow walk downstairs to the banquet hall. She places the concert stage on a long table running across the side of the room and then touches a rune for it to play. Garrick moves across the room to the other side of an embroidered carpet and bows at his wife. Sera in response curtseys to him, and they both move to one another. They come together in the center of the room under the candlelit chandeliers and then give way to the moving of each other's bodies. As they turn and sway, they are looking into one another's eyes.

Garrick gives a weak smile. "I'm sorry for you having to go through this, Sera. You shouldn't have to be here with me."

She shakes her head while looking slightly down at Garrick. "I am exactly where I want to be. You shouldn't have to go through this alone."

Garrick lets go of the troubled look plaguing his face. "You deserved a grander wedding than the one that we planned before I left for training."

"Yes, we both did, but I don't regret it. I already thought of us as being together when we were courting. You did promise to get me something to remind us of our bond, though."

"Yes, I did," Garrick admits with a sheepish laugh. "I actually bought a necklace from a silversmith, but I gave it to Kristo when I asked him to come with me to Halmin."

Amused, Sera's look tells Garrick his actions are instantly forgivable. "Then you gave me Kristo."

While the dancing continues, a curious knight pops his head into the banquet hall. "Am I intruding, or is there perhaps room for more people?"

"It's your ball, sweetie," Garrick whispers. "What would you like?"

"Bring as many as you'd like," Sera says to the knight in the entryway. "I'd say we all deserve a dance."

The knight nods appreciatively. "You are quite generous, Lady Marmuin." He gives a bow and then leaves as quickly as he appeared.

Garrick gives Sera a kiss, which is easily reciprocated. "Lady Marmuin, the hostess of the grandest of balls."

Sera gives a small laugh at the thought, continuing the dance with her husband.

A few minutes later, the knight returns with a brown-haired woman, escorted on his arm. They both give a polite nod to Garrick and Sera and then take each other in their arms to dance alongside the couple. As time passes, more knights and lords come in with their wives or mistresses, filling the hall with the sound of footsteps. Lenfro himself has come too, overseeing such a get-together and altering the small concert stage with his red glowing hand so it plays louder over the conversations and footsteps.

Garrick and Sera are relaxing in chairs near the walls where stained glass is glowing under the setting sun. Each of them is leaning on one another as they watch the noblemen and women sway to forget about their worries for the night.

A tall bald man with a long red beard sits next to them, accompanied by a small blond woman with a deep smile. "This is a wonderful little party, Sir Marmuin. I do have to say, though, you forgot all the refreshments."

"I'm so sorry, Kendir. The casks of wine were delayed on the road."

Kendir gives an amused smile, patting the woman next to him on the knee. "You know, Garrick, I've overheard the other knights talking about your adoptive son and your actions at the trial today. They approve, almost as if in jealousy. They've taken to calling you Garrick the Noble."

Before Garrick can respond, Sera, a tad flustered by how amusing Kendir thinks the knights' reaction is, says, "Perhaps my husband has been putting his fellow knights to shame. A room full of people born into stature and power, yet the only one with a moniker of nobleness is a man born into a family of bakers. Perhaps a title isn't what defines one's morals."

The woman next to Kendir giggles.

Kendir also finds Sera humorous. "You mistake my intentions. I'm not here to make fun of your husband, Lady Marmuin; I'm here to tell him that even Lenfro finds his actions laudable. He and I were just discussing you before we found you hosting this little party."

Glancing at his wife, doubt shadowing his face, Garrick straightens it and says, "What were you discussing about me? From the way you're talking, it's as if I'm being a nuisance."

"No, quite the opposite. As it stands right now, you're mildly famous. We would like to make it more so, to attract the people of the rebellion towards an ideal. Asmeria, regardless of the outcome of this war, will have to do its fair share of healing. We believe that by adding a figurehead to the cause it will allow for an easier transition for the commoners."

Sera and Garrick look in confusion at one another.

Then Garrick speaks. "I understand I might have drawn attention to myself, but I doubt I can rally the masses in the manner you want."

Kendir shakes his head. "You think too little of yourself. You calmed a bloodthirsty crowd and opened their eyes to mercy. Not many people can do that, you know. There are rumors flying about that this war is between nobles vying for power. This simply isn't true, but rumors do need to be combated. We could share your story, make it public. A simple man who was promoted to knighthood after displays of valor and kind-heartedness. It would certainly boost morale and recruitment."

Garrick takes a moment to think, leaning back in his chair, and then nods. "All right, do what you have to with my image."

Sera gently slaps her husband's arm.

"Not now," Garrick mouths.

Kendir gives Garrick a pat on his back and a nod. "It's decided then. If you would excuse us both, I think we should get a bit more dancing in. Your little stage is a wonderful bit of magic." He rises from his chair, taking his lady's hand to escort her to the dance floor.

"You don't even know what you agreed to," Sera says.

Garrick shuffles in his seat to face his wife, taking one of her hands in both of his and kissing it. "You are right; I don't know what I'm getting into."

"Then why accept?" she asks sternly. "Your image is on the line."

Garrick stares at Sera's hand for a while and then up at her face. "Do you think my image will matter at the end of our lives when we are judged before heaven? Kristo, he wanted to become a squire because he thought about all the other people that could be living the life he is. Regardless of what becomes of my name, if using it makes it so we are even a fraction closer to ending other people's soulless days, then it is worth it."

Sera's expression softens, and she moves her hand to cup Garrick's cheek. "Maybe Kendir will have you teach lessons on how to become a more upstanding person. Since when have you been so good at speaking?"

Garrick shrugs, moving himself back to resting against his wife. "I don't know. I suppose it just runs in *our* family."

Sera relaxes into a smile at Garrick's stress of *our*.

After watching the other couples dancing for a while, Garrick stands and offers a hand down at Sera. "Another dance, Lady Marmuin?"

Sera nods, taking his hand with exaggerated grace. "Of course, Sir Garrick the Noble."

Garrick shakes his head at his wife's teasing, coming together with her to start dancing. "That is quite the mouthful. Maybe you could come up with a better title?"

Sera gives a lighthearted laugh, looking down at her husband. "I thought you didn't care about your image."

"Touché."

16

THE MARCH

A T THE CRACK OF DAWN, THE horns blare through the city once more. Hearing its call, soldiers and the rebel army's new recruits pack to join the main camp outside of Effilnem. Having brought little with them, Sera, Garrick, and Kristo are lending their aid to the cooks, ensuring that everything is stowed away on carts properly. As they are doing such, a blond squire guiding Pilosus finds Garrick and hands her off to him along with a letter. Garrick leans against Pilosus's side, rubbing her neck while reading the letter and then dismisses the squire.

The knight moves to Sera, helping her load a crate of heavy cooking equipment, kissing her on the shoulder once it's loaded. "Got to go. Lenfro wants me clopping around camp and helping people who need an extra hand."

Sera looks down at her husband, petting his cheek, and then picks up a crate filled with heat books with his help. "I think you're already doing that."

Garrick gives a reluctant dip of his head to her point. "It's more about being seen than anything else. I'll see you and Kristo when we break for the night."

While they are talking, a detachment of scouts trot by, heading forward through the sand to the tree line.

Garrick then goes to his horse, mounts her, and slowly rides around camp to see if anyone needs aid. Sera and Kristo continue to work with the chefs until everything is packed and ready to go. Once the other members of the army are ready to move, a horn sounds through the caravan with a flag lifted at the front as the march begins. Wagon wheels creak, horses beat their feet, and people walk alongside. Rebels with spears line the sides of the caravan to ensure safety for the families, while other regiments stay in formation between wagon trains.

On the march, Kristo is told to sit on the wagon he helped load so as to not slow down the pace. Sera walks behind, carrying a satchel on her side with her concert stage and Garrick's recipe book inside. During the march, she rubs the satchel absentmindedly with a smile. After a few hours, the tree line is pierced, giving the army relief from the sun with the shade of the forest. The road through isn't wide enough for the army to continue its normal formation, so soldiers walk between trees, giving way to the forest kings that tower over the area.

In the late afternoon, the marching stops, and camp is set up for the evening. Sera and Kristo help the chefs prepare the meal and are soon chopping up potatoes together, using the back of the wagon as a prep station. The same black-haired elf as before, Venitria, is summoning water from the sky around her to pour into barrels. The streams forming from her weavings are heavier than in the desert, forcing her to rest now and then, using the time to distribute the water herself, floating jugs around by a veil of water underneath each one.

After the potatoes are done, Kristo moves to sit by the elf to watch her summon and then distribute her water.

Venitria looks down at the child and then floats a cup over to him, filling the inside. "Hello, little half-thing. You're looking better than before. You're not quite as ghoulish as I last remember, but you could still use a bath."

Seeing that Venitria is forming a ball, Kristo holds his breath as the water splashes all over him, sucking any grime off his body before it is drawn out through his collar to be tossed aside.

"Where is your caretaker, half-thing?"

Kristo gives a shrug. "He's supposed to be helping everyone. His wife, Sera, is over there." Kristo points at the tall woman still helping the chefs.

Venitria looks at her for a moment and then returns to her work, doling out water to those who need it. "Is his name Garrick by chance?"

Kristo nods.

Venitria relaxes. "He's a good man indeed. People speak of him highly."

Kristo shrugs. "He's nice. He cooked me a roast when we got to Halmin and gives me lots of food."

Venitria looks amused. "Niceness isn't decided by the amount of food on your plate, half-thing."

"He cares for me, about my future. He didn't want me to join the squires. He said I should have a chance to grow first."

Venitria hums to herself. "That is a long future indeed to think about, by his standards at least. It is good to hear him take such a stance."

Kristo shakes his head. "I wish he would have let me. What is the difference between being a slave or under someone's care? Your decisions still aren't your own."

"Life is full of tedious tos and fros," Venitria says refilling Kristo's cup. "You'll find before long there are only a few decisions that really matter. You are too young to know what's good for you, still a sapling, prone to drinking from tainted waters, despite the wisdom behind your words."

"I don't know what you mean."

"Exactly."

Sera, looks over to Kristo and, seeing that he's in good company, takes out the tent from the wagon, starting to set it up. Garrick soon returns, placing a hand on Sera's shoulder, helping her raise the tent. From a look of concern and searching on his face, Sera smiles and points off to where Kristo is, causing the worry to leave Garrick's mind. With the tent pitched, Garrick and Sera join the food line.

Venitria, still with Kristo, gestures to Sera. "That woman has the blood of giants in her, does she not?"

"Yes, she is a quarter-giant."

A chef comes by with a meal for Venitria, who thanks him and then sits a length away from Kristo to enjoy it. "Your caretaker keeps strange company, but most humans are inclined to. You and I are doomed to keep sane company, unfortunately."

Kristo raises an eyebrow. "What do you mean?"

Venitria offers a bit of bread, which the half-elf takes. "The years play a painful tune, young one. Keep with mortals, and you shall incur a few scars. You yourself are mortal but will live long enough to recount many close friends. Those that live with you, elves and dwarfs, will be weathered by many seasons. Humans think us recluse, but it simply isn't true. The friends we keep are our own kin because they stay above the grass longer."

Kristo looks about the caravan with sadness in his eyes, paying attention to those interacting with one another. "Why tell me this?"

"Because that is our life," Venitria says, pointing to the bread he's eating. "The quicker it is understood, the easier things will be for you. You march in a caravan heading to war. Not all of those you speak to will be able to do so once its journey ends, and the reality that you might outlive those around you is closer at hand than you'd ever like to believe."

Kristo looks to her, speaking between bites of bread. "Elves really are sad. I'm happy I'm only half of one."

Venitria relaxes onto one side, eating with one arm while the other props her head up. "I just want that lesson to set in. I am sorry that what I'm trying to teach you is dour, but it is my duty. Those ears of yours are pointed; we are kin. Those graced by the woods will always look out for one another." Venitria keeps her eyes on Kristo until she feels her words have set in. Then she flicks her head towards the food line. "Garrick and his wife are close to being served. Join them, little one. We can talk another time if you'd like. I've a job to attend to."

Kristo gets up from the ground, patting himself clean. "I enjoy talking to you, even if it's about sad stuff. Hopefully you'll be one of the sane people I unfortunately end up around."

"Who knows?" Venitria says with a smirk. "Maybe I will. Keep yourself safe, little half-thing," and she shoos the child away.

Kristo joins Garrick and Sera, the knight putting a hand on Kristo's shoulder.

As the night drifts by, the camp flickers in yellow light from torches held by rebels keeping watch. Morning eventually comes, causing the process of yesterday's packing to be repeated. The army soon marches, eventually passing a tree that has full white flowers filling its branches. It's only a little after noon when the army stops, causing people to look at each other, muttering about what could be causing the delay.

Kristo stands on the wagon behind the chef driving it to try to see what's going on ahead, his head bobbing about trying to peer through the trees.

Sera walks to the front of the wagon, attempting to look ahead as well. "What do you see, Kristo?"

"Hmm. . . . Oh! I see Garrick! He's riding back here."

Confused, Sera looks up to Kristo, but soon enough Garrick rides Pilosus around the wagon to her, offering his hand to help her up, his face stern. "Sera, we need you at the front." Still confused, Sera nods to Garrick and gets up on Pilosus, holding her husband to stay stable. Garrick then turns Pilosus around and looks at Kristo. "Stay somewhere safe, preferably hidden. We'll be back."

Kristo gives an expression of concern and then moves some of the cookware.

Garrick rides off with Sera, weaving through a few trees, and past the caravan to the front where Lenfro is speaking to the tender, the nature mother, who, with her brown horse, is blocking the road. Her daughter is nowhere to be seen. Discussion is underway debating the use of the road when Garrick turns Pilosus to the side to display Sera to the tender.

The woman puts her hand up to Lenfro to cut him off mid-sentence. "I've heard far enough from someone who would burn the forest to accomplish his goal of killing. Let she who would honor the forest speak."

Clearly annoyed, Lenfro relents, falling silent.

Sera looks at everything happening with a bit of confusion and then speaks. "Hello, Tender. Good to see you are well."

The woman's expression doesn't change.

Sera clears her throat. "This army moving through the forest means the area no harm. While the men may hunt and collect wood, they do not claim more than is needed."

The tender shakes her head. "This army was let in once, and once did they set a neutral place of gathering on fire. Why should these men of destruction be allowed back into Sutri's embrace?"

Sera moves her hand to her hair, brushing it back out. "Boars and owlbears also leave destruction in their path, yet the forest still stands. Sutri teaches rebirth. From the death of the trees, there is a chance for an even more beautiful grove to be tended."

The tender shakes her head, pointing at Sera. "Are you saying the destruction is to be repeated?"

Sera pats Garrick's back and dismounts Pilosus to approach the tender, showing that she is unarmed. "It is a possibility, but this army fights against those who would violate the natural free will of every person. The opposing—"

"Humanity gave up most of their natural instincts when developing society. The freedom of those bound by chains is the difference of only a few links from the chain society sets upon everyone as a condition for living in harmony with each other."

"Your ideals would be better shared by a society of freer-thinking individuals then, which is what we are working towards. The next generation of tenders cannot come from only the tenders themselves. If the loyalists would have their way, authority by title would be the only thing that mattered."

The tender takes a few steps back and forth to think about what has been said. Sizing up the caravan, she points off in the direction of the bend. "Your army may pass but may not take more than what is needed. You and your beasts will camp in what is left of Kurin's Retreat since you are so close to it."

Clearly angered by the statement, Lenfro dismounts from his horse. "That's not acceptable! We will be open to ambush from every direction should the loyalists attack!"

"Yes, you burned the forest. Now reap the protection it offers you, lest I tell the blights you do not belong here."

Lord Lenfro looks back towards his men and caravan, eyeing his knights and soldiers and weighing his options. He paces back and forth at the offer, his hands on his hips and his head shaking until he comes back in front of the tender. "We can't possibly fight two enemies, especially not the guardians of the forest. . . . We accept the proposal."

The tender moves to the side, offering her arm out to the rest of the road with her horse willingly following her footsteps. "Then make your way to your bed, dogs."

Lenfro, given no choice, bows to the tender and gets back on his horse, riding close to Garrick and the other knights. "Inform the sergeants we are resting in the open tonight. Tell them to establish double watches. Scouts have already reported indications of activity in the forest but haven't seen any people. This deal reeks, but we can't afford our supply lines to be cut. We also don't know if we'd be given safe passage out the way we came. If any of you happen to see any of the stone singers or nature weavers, tell them to report to me. Go."

The knights go off, except for Garrick who comes to collect Sera, offering her a hand up onto Pilosus.

The tender looks up at Sera, eyeing her and Garrick. "You both will be safe. The woods are alive. And tell Yuna I still have her antler should she want it."

Sera shakes her head at the tender. "She left your ranks years ago; she doesn't belong to it any longer."

The tender moves to her horse, which bows to let her on. "She left the ranks, but she will never not be one of us. Her grand garden is proof of that."

Sera searches the tender's eyes and then pats Garrick's back to let him know she is ready to ride. On the way back, they hear knights informing soldiers of the news, causing people to talk in whispers and watch their surroundings. When the two arrive back at the cooking wagon, Garrick lets Sera down and then goes about his duty, informing members of the caravan.

Sera looks inside the wagon, spying under some canvas a child-shaped lump with light-brown eyes staring at her. "That's a good spot. But come out; we're safe for now."

Kristo crawls out and sits on a bench. "What happened?"

As Sera responds, the caravan starts moving once more, taking a slower pace than before. Soldiers are moving about the wagon train, no longer walking in formed regiments, and instead, are offering increased protection to the supplies. "We are to rest in a very dangerous location. I want you to figure out a good hiding spot again when we get there. If anything happens, go to it."

Kristo gives an understanding nod to Sera and observes the soldiers going about their business. With everyone watching the trees, the army marches towards its campsite for the night. The grim grey-and-white ash field soon comes into view near the front of the caravan. Soldiers enter the dead area, their yellow colors in stark contrast to their black-and-white surroundings. Soon more men flood the tree line to scout the area until finally the mages make their way to the center of the clearing. Two men in chainmail wearing brown armbands have their hands out, brown mist falling from them as they force their will into the earth. Thick low walls of grey stone are pulled into the air, causing the dead debris to fall off. On more than one occasion, a forgotten body is dredged up from the ground, causing a few people to look away in disgust as the corpses are moved for a proper burial.

The wagon train has already started moving in, and tents are set up on areas of the ground where nature weavers have managed to clear the ash. The culinary wagon is the first to be unloaded, taking refuge behind the low curved wall that the brown mages are erecting for defense. Kristo and Sera help their wagon while the knights ride in with Lenfro to talk to the green mages clearing the ash. Pointing to the tree line, the mages nod and abandon their work to load archers into the tops of trees, giving them platforms to rest on. Evening is soon setting in, and meals are being passed around, thanks to the hard efforts of the chefs.

Closed lips hold a silence as the sun falls behind the trees. The brown mages have just finished their low wall, and spearmen take positions behind it, holding their weapons out to deter any charge. Ash has discolored their clothing and boots, with the men finding no way to be rid of it in such an environment. The convoy's grim surroundings deaden any hope of the people quartered here to show mirth. Sera and Kristo sit noiselessly on their wagon, scanning the tree line through squinting eyes for movement as a weak moon overtakes the sky.

Not wanting to speak loudly, Kristo comes to sit closer to Sera so he can whisper. "Where's Garrick?"

Sera puts her arms around him, kissing the top of his head. "He's out there protecting us. Now shush."

17

REAP

THE MOON CREEPS OVERHEAD. THE MEN defending the walls whisper to one another and crane their necks to see any sign of movement. People murmur about seeing things in the ash, which catches wind all the way to where Sera and Kristo are. A frantic runner can be heard going through the tents, moving like a ghoul in the night with his ash-covered body. Silence falls once more; then a blinding white light at the center of camp is shot straight into the air, the flare illuminating the camp's surroundings.

With the newfound brightness, the rebels take stock of their encampment, all their eyes drawn to the east, where the moonlight was blocked by the trees. Hundreds of red-tunic men, covered in ash and grime, are crawling like rats to the rebels' position, having already made it three-quarters of the way there when they are revealed by the light. Exposed, the attackers scream the roar of a murderous beast, letting their will be known as they rise from the ash like the dead to charge the rebel fortifications. The rebels at the east wall look at the sight in terror until one of their ranks screams back, steadying his spear. The rest of the men yell in both terror and resolve to live, releasing their fears. From the eastern woods a horn is sounded, unleashing streaking balls of fire and arrows onto the rebel position.

Sera and Kristo are still on the chef's wagon as squires run about the encampment with shields up, relaying orders through high voices. "Take cover! Swordsmen! To the east wall!" Sera is standing on the cart and, at the orders, yanks Kristo by the collar off the wagon. "Under the wagon! Under the wagon!" Kristo crawls his way under, followed by Sera, who covers Kristo with her body. Both Sera and Kristo watch as men and women scramble for any sort of cover as the arrows start falling. Just a short distance away, Sera and Kristo witness a young, black-haired woman with a medical band crawl under her own wagon. As she is looking about, the area becomes violently yellow, the balls of fire coming down from the sky. One fireball lands with an ear-rending explosion on the far end of the medical woman's cart, causing wood to blow high into the sky, falling to be strewn about the camp. The cart then slumps backward without its rear wheels.

Plights of agony surge through the camp as the explosions rock its inhabitants, the woman under the nearby cart included in the choir. Her left leg is gouged by the broken cart, pinning her in place. Her eyes search for help. Finding Sera as she is trying to claw out from her hiding spot, the woman extends her hands out, reaching for Sera, despite the distance. "Help me! Please, gods above, help me!"

For a moment, Sera looks down at Kristo and then at the woman again. "Kristo . . . I need you to stay here."

Kristo clutches Sera's dress. "No! No! No! You can't! I don't want you to!"

Sera immediately grabs Kristo's hands, trying to get them off. "Kristo! I have to! She'll die!"

The young boy looks at the medical woman yelling at them and her gored leg. Shaking his head, he lets go.

Sera crawls out from under the cart, looking up at the sky as another flare is sent into it. Not seeing a volley coming in, she scrambles across the ash to get to the broken cart, immediately being grabbed by her ankle by the medical woman.

"It's in my leg! If you pull me out, I'll bleed to death. This is a medical cart. Find a potion!" The woman lets go of Sera and points at a destroyed crate. Sounds of blades on metal ring from the east wall as Sera rushes to the broken crate, rummaging through shattered vials and hay finding only a few left intact. Horns erupt from the tree line once more, causing rebel squires to call for cover again. In a panic, Sera crawls under the woman's wagon as a rain of arrows and thunderous explosions fall around the camp. The woman then nods at Sera as she can see the potions. "Take the top off and put some of my blood in it." Sera nods, coming over to the woman's impaled leg, and places the vial by the wound to get her blood.

Sera offers the vial to the woman's lips, but she grabs it and smacks the cart on top of her. "I need this moved off of me so I can crawl out." Sera looks at the wagon and then at Kristo, who has been watching everything without blinking. "Kristo. I need help. Come do this and then right back under that wagon."

Kristo's chest is heaving at the thought, panic clearly written all over his face.

Sera calls to him again. "Kristo! This lady helped free you! Help her!"

Slow nods, then faster ones come from Kristo as he centers himself, pounding the ground with one fist. Yelling to the world, Kristo comes running out from under his cover to the back of the cart where Sera joins him. "Now!" As they both pick up the wagon as much as they can, the medical woman is lifted by the wood in her leg and then drops as her leg comes sliding off it. Stifling a scream, she crawls forward and drinks the potion. Immediately, the blood-flowing wound knits together as she crawls her way through ash to the chef's wagon.

Sera and Kristo make their way under the wagon with her. The medical woman grabs them both, shaking them. "Thank you, oh, thank you!" The woman wipes her eyes, causing ash to coat her face. "I still have a piece of wood in my leg, but there are bigger problems. The soldiers need the potions on the east wall. If those soldiers don't get the potions, we could lose the night."

For a minute, nothing else is said as another rain of arrows comes down. Kristo starts moving out but is dragged back under the cart by Sera. "You're staying here. I'm going." Kristo looks at her with fiery compassion but is silenced by Sera pushing him softly on the arm. "You'll have your time. . . . Stay safe." With that, Sera moves from the wagon, returning to the crate of potion to salvage as many intact vials as she can, and then darts off to the eastern wall.

Fighting along the wall has resulted in scores of loyalist bodies piled on the outside of the fortifications. Flares dominate the sky to illuminate everything in a pale-white glow. To continue the fight, the loyalist army treads on the bodies of their dead to climb the low east wall, and the rebels pull their spears back to defend the landing. Rebel archers hiding up in the trees are taking shots at the backs of the loyalists, cutting their numbers before they can even get to the encampment in the open field.

When Sera arrives at the assault, men are being dragged back from the front lines with cracked ribs and dented helmets. Alchemists and white mages are healing the wounded who are then told to get up and fight again. Seeing Sera with the potions in her arms, attending women mob her, grabbing her supply and using them to heal the injured men. With her arms now empty, Sera runs back to the medical cart to fetch more potions.

During the fighting, the rebel knights and cavalry are waiting in the woods, their horses stamping at the ground in anticipation as Lenfro walks his stallion back and forth across their formed line. Garrick is keeping Pilosus steady underneath him in the formation as he watches the battle unfold, the grip on his lance repeatedly loosening then tightening. Pilosus' back hoof is occasionally stamping the ground, causing her new bard to clink in similar readiness to Garrick.

From out of the woods, a rider in a black cloak and a purple armband comes to Lenfro. "My Lord, there have been no sightings of enemy cavalry or their winged-horse riders by any of the men."

Lenfro points to the defenses. "Take your men and have them cast illusions to make it look like we have more spearmen defending the other parts of the wall. We can't leave the east wall to the horde any longer. We are attacking."

The rider nods and then bolts into the woods.

Lenfro turns to face his men, his plate armor shimmering under the pale light. "The loyalists dared to grab Halmin, and in a few days, we will dare to unfurl their grip! But tonight is the night that decides everything! We took Effilnem by destroying the bastard Bushan's army here, and we will destroy the hound Nirkin's forces here as well. Liberation of our great kingdom will come from your hands! The future of Asmeria is in the strength of your arms tonight! Ride men!" Lenfro turns his horse around, pointing forward at the enemy, his hand surrounded by a fire that would immolate a normal man. Turning back to them, he says, "No manner of defense will stop you! Leave nothing but shattered shields and broken rings! You are hell on earth!" The lord tightens his legs on his horse, causing it to charge. "For Asmeria!"

Fueled by his lord's words, Garrick screams into the night, forcing Pilosus to sprint forward over the field of the dead. Each rider lets out a similar cry for blood, letting it be known they aim to add more bodies to the ash. Clouds of ash kick into the air from the force of hooves. Horns sound from the forest, causing arrows to rain on the horsemen who raise their wooden shields to protect their faces, the barding protecting their steeds. The night sky becomes a streak of red and yellow, balls of fire being flung at the charging regiment and coming down with a horrible heat. The balls explode on collision with their targets, horse and man alike being blown apart and trampled by determined riders. The loyalists that were charging the eastern wall are attempting to tighten their ranks, fear ripe in the eyes and actions of the foot soldiers as they try to get spears ready.

Lenfro, in front of his charging men, lets go of his reins, fire dripping from his hands onto the ash below and sticking to whatever it touches. Raising his hands, Lenfro urges his stallion directly into the throng of men who push and shove at their line trying to avoid being trampled. The lord's hands roar with flames, cascading the fires of hell over the loyalists surrounding him. Wails of torment from the flame arise by all in the clearing. Some raise halberds, trying to hook Lenfro from his mount, but his flames engulf those men, sending them screaming to their grave.

Garrick, watching the deeds of his lord in front of him, picks a man and lets his lance fall into position. With death chiseled on his face, he roars once more in both determination and sorrow as his weapon pierces the chest of the man and kills him. Garrick lets go of his lance from the weight and urges Pilosus to ram deeper into the formation, trampling the bodies of men that are in her wake. He reaches for his sword, draws it, and swings at the necks of those below him, blood flying through the air. The knight soon emerges on the other side of the loyalist formation; his fellow cavalrymen ram through in the same fashion behind him. They gallop a short way beyond and regroup, turning in the field, waiting to reform for a second charge, weapons at the ready.

Another signal call from the loyalist army sends its men into full retreat. Before the cavalry unit can reform, Lenfro is charging them down. "Kill the craven! Don't let them regroup!" While giving the orders, Lenfro is burning as many men as he can catch in his flames.

Kendir charges to continue the assault.

Garrick drives Pilosus forward, and his fellow knights join him, slaughter the only goal of their unit now.

All loyalist foot soldiers are fleeing. Their archers on the forest floor send a last volley before also turning to run. The rebel horsemen giving chase to free the enemy of their heads.

Rebels along the eastern wall collapse from relief of the assault being over, and the attending nurses get a share of respite too. Despite the clamor being over, flares are still being sent overhead to give people sight of what's happening.

But all is not over. Yelling from the west wall causes all eyes to see a loyalist charge closing in. The riders storm through the ash, wielding swords and torches, ready to break the west wall's thin force. In a panic, the rebel soldiers at the wall close their ranks together as men from the north and south walls come to reinforce them.

Kristo, who is still under the cart, looks towards the shouting coming from behind him, eyeing the wall where rebels are yelling orders to one another, squires relaying them along the line. When the cavalry hits the low wall, more than a few horses are skewered, throwing their riders into the encampment as the horses' legs break against the grey stone. Those that do land after the jump, crash into the spearmen with the long points having scraped against the horses' armor. In moments, the camp is flooded with the loyalist cavalry. Swinging blades from the horsemen kill rebels and squires alike.

A stout dwarf with a red beard and an embroidered tunic over his plate mail shouts at his fellow riders. "Burn the wagons! Starve the dogs who would side with killers!"

The horsemen spread out amongst the camp and throw their torches on the rebels' supplies. The dwarf giving orders has the same red flames to his hands as Lenfro and slashes them through the air as he relays orders. The dwarf moves about the camp, dousing in flame anyone who would dare interrupt the riders' work.

One such rider bears down on Kristo's wagon, tossing a torch into the back to ignite the packing hay inside. The dry fuel ignites immediately. Kristo soon feels the heat on his back, and he looks for somewhere safe to crawl. The medical woman near him grabs him by the arm, pointing him towards the east where rebel soldiers are charging to save their supplies and men. The two look at each other for a moment, crawl out from under the cart, and run towards the formation, going past burning crates and other wagons that shed a flicking light to the area.

Kristo is running as fast as possible, but the medical woman limps behind, unable to keep up. Having shown herself to the world, she is yelling pleas to the gods to help her reach the rebel line, tears streaming from her eyes. Kristo looks back at her. A horseman has the woman in his sights and snaps his reins to turn the horse in her direction. He brings his sword up, ready to reap the woman's soul as his horse shoots into a gallop. Kristo motions back at the woman, his hands pushing down towards the ground. "Behind you! Get down! Get down!" The medical woman turns her head and sees a wave of rebels coming around Kristo to wash over the western campsite, his sight being blocked.

The horseman swings at where the woman was and attempts to slow and turn his horse. But as he is turning, a spearman at the front of the rebel's wave skewers him along the waist just below the breastplate, dismounting him from the horse. The line of men passes over the medical woman to drive the rest of the horsemen out, the shouting of orders going with them.

Kristo walks back, looking around for anything dangerous. He approaches the medical woman's body, which is on the ground in a crumpled ball. He kneels and pushes her side, turning her over.

Looking at the night sky now, the woman is alive, with no marks of wounds on her body, but her mind has gone to other places. She doesn't register Kristo as being there. Her breath catches in her chest, and she struggles to breathe. The boy places his hands on hers and relaxes to sit on the ash. Cries of victory ring through the camp. Finally, the eyes of the woman flicker with fear. "I'm alive?"

Kristo nods, squeezing the hand of the stranger. "You are."

The woman moves her hands to her face, covering it and slowly sliding them down. A heavy breath streams from her nose.

"You're very lucky to be alive. We should celebrate with some kessi fruit."

"What's kessi fruit?"

"It's a pink fruit, very sweet. I first had it in Halmin. I figured everyone knows about it and has tried it. When we get there, I'll make sure you have some. There's even space to move into the town if you like the fruit and bread there."

The medical woman nods her head and relaxes herself fully on the ground. "Yeah . . . yeah, I might like that. Do they have teska pods?"

"As many as you can drink. I think they're pretty awful, though."

18

HEAVEN'S GATE

WHILE THE LACK OF LOYALIST ACTIVITY suggests the assault is over, those by the walls are keeping their eyes open for attacks after what happened to the supplies. The sun begins to rise from the east. Fires around camp go out one by one as Venitria is summoning great balls of water to throw upon them. The rebel cavalry is feeding back into the ashland at a trot, wiping blood from their swords after a successful hunt. When at last the soldiers begin to relax, the tiredness from combat and the late night hits all at once. Despite the hour and the field of dead around them, those that are living close their eyes for a restless slumber amid the crying of those that have lost loved ones.

Sera is walking about the tents and burnt wagons, searching. "Kristo! Kristo?" Getting back to the cart where she left Kristo and the medical woman, she looks at the smoldering wood with wide eyes. She grabs a piece of wood, propping up the cart's remains to look under. Her breath catches from seeing the absence of bodies. Sera puts a hand over her heart and continues to move through the camp, shouting his name. After a few minutes, she spies two hands waving above a ruined tent.

Kristo gets up to show himself. "Sera!"

With a quickness in her step, Sera goes to the boy waving at her, running a bit at the end to wrap her arms about Kristo in a tight hug.

Returning the gesture, he lets out a little grunt from the strength of the embrace. Released, Kristo motions towards the medical woman resting against an unburnt crate. "This is Iva."

"Thank you for keeping Kristo safe."

"It's the other way around," Iva says. "I would have been dead twice over if not for the both of you. I owe you and Kristo more than I could ever give."

"No," Sera says. "You've given so much by being here and helping the army. You owe us nothing. Is the wood still in your leg?"

Iva nods.

Sera offer her arms to Iva. "We should get you to the medical tents."

With Sera's help, Iva pulls herself up and leans her weight into the tall woman, and the two women and Kristo go to the medical tents. There, Sera gives Iva to one of the attending women. As Iva limps off to be treated, she casts a grateful glance over her shoulder at Sera and Kristo.

"We should get some sleep," Sera says. "Let's see if our tent still exists." She offers her hand to Kristo, which he takes with no hesitation, and the two walk through the ruined camp to where the cooks are staying.

After Sera and Kristo reconstruct their veil against the world, Garrick comes to the tent thoroughly spent with his legs barely carrying him. Sera, who has just finished patching a hole in the tent, sees her husband walking up. Her breath stops at the sight of blood along Garrick's right side, staining his tunic. His legs are similarly splattered, his trousers a mix of red and black from the night's work. Sera slaps the tent. "Kristo! Go fetch water." When Kristo emerges and sees Garrick, the boy runs to him. A tired smile comes from Garrick, who bends to hug Kristo, picking him up off the ground a few inches. "Good to see you, buddy."

Sera puts her arms around both of them, and when they part, she puts her hand on Kristo's head, looking him in the eye. "Go to Venitria and bring a bucket of water back, sweetie. She's right over there." Sera pats Kristo's back, pointing at the female elf who is half-asleep but still producing water for those of the camp.

Stepping over some ruined crates, Kristo makes his way to Venitria.

Garrick watches his wife, looking over all the grime on her face and dress. His hand caresses her cheek, trying to wipe off a smudge of black, but he ends up dirtying her face more.

Sera turns her head to look at him with curiosity, finding Garrick frowning at his hand. She leans into Garrick's side, putting her hand into the one he's staring at and tugging him towards the tent. "Come. Rest and tell me what's on your mind."

Garrick lets himself be led inside the tent to rest upon the hides, and Sera lies beside him. His eyes catch an extra set of clothes, which are free of the ash around the camp.

Sera pats them and then touches Garrick's side. "I cleaned them as best as I could. I can't let the rebel beacon look anything less. You can have them after you've bathed."

Putting his hand on a splatter of blood on the bottom of her dress, he quickly checks under for any cuts.

"I'm fine, Garrick," she says while rubbing his shoulder. "The blood is from Iva, a medical woman Kristo and I saved. After, I went to run potions for the east wall." While Sera continues to recount her night, Garrick looks away, not making eye contact.

A little bit after her story ends, they hear water splashing outside. Sera opens the tent flap to see Kristo with a frightened look and one of his two buckets of water spilled on the ground. Sera moves upright and holds the boy's arm to look into his eyes. "It's all right, Kristo. We're not upset. Why don't you get another one and have Venitria clean you off if she has the time."

Kristo lets out a breath, nods, and carries the empty bucket back in his tired arms.

Sera moves the full bucket inside and grabs a loose cloth to drench it in the water. "Tunic off and tell me about your night."

Garrick obeys and talks of the charge and how he went into the woods. "Do you remember the name of the bearded man whose house we used to throw eggs at?"

"Phern, I think."

"That sounds right. . . . He would get so mad and chase us about the town. I remember your mother sent us right back after she found out and had us clean his house and weed his garden."

Sera splashes her rag in the bucket of water and smiles. "We did other things to him too, like smudging his windows with grease after he cleaned them." Sera gives a little laugh at the memory. "There was that time we—"

"I killed him last night."

Sera abruptly stops, her smile shattered.

"I killed him, Sera. I saw his eyes turn back to see his fortune right before I struck him. One final prank, right?"

Sera cleans the rag in the bucket to rub Garrick's back and soothe him. "I'm sorry, Garrick. I can't begin to imagine how that felt."

Garrick looks up at the ceiling of the tent to focus his eyes on something that isn't there. "I've killed . . . twenty men now. Thirteen tonight alone. I've so much sin on my hands I can't even begin to think of how to wash it off or that those stains can ever leave my being. How can I ever claim before heaven that I lived a moral life after I've robbed the earth of such goodness?"

Sera shakes her head and pulls her husband back into her so he can rest his head upon her lap. Running her hands through his hair, she says, "You can put it back together. One sin at a time, we will find a way for you to be forgiven for each life. Your soul is in my keeping, and if you claim to be sullied, I will help you wash the grime tainting you." She grabs the rag once more, moving it to clean Garrick's chest. "Both literally and otherwise."

Garrick's tone becomes a little less dour. "I would like that. Once this is over, my life will be a quiet one where I help instead of harm. I would use my days to ensure the next generation will live what our childhoods were like their entire lives—so filled with joy that a bed felt like torment and the morning was like unwrapping a present."

Sera nods down at him, scanning his eyes that now gaze back into her own. "Kristo is a good start to your dream."

A long breath comes into Garrick's chest, releasing a touch of his worries. "Kristo is a wonderful child. I would wish to see him become a jewel of Halmin."

Sera hums her approval.

Soon Kristo returns with a cleaned body and another bucket of water, which Sera uses to wash herself while Kristo waits outside. Once she finishes, they all find sleep in the tent till afternoon.

At this time, rebel soldiers are moving through the camp, collecting bodies, and salvaging what they can of wagons. Nature weavers are singing wood from nearby trees to act as fixes for redeemable crates and carts, with the remains of nails being hammered to hold them in place.

Garrick gets up for the day, putting on the clothes Sera cleaned for him, and then exits the tent to get food. Then he reports to Lenfro at his own tent, a large creation of hide supported by stone poles struck up from the ground. The inside, free of ash, has tables and chairs also sung from stone. Many of the knights are inside, convening at a long grey table with a map of Halmin and its surrounding farms. When Garrick walks in, a squire pulls him to the side and offers the knight his armor, the mail having been tended to.

While Garrick is putting on his gear, Kendir, standing next to Lenfro, reads a report. "We suffered relatively few casualties last night. Of our eight thousand men, sergeants report we lost only three hundred due to the great work of the women supplying the eastern wall with medical aid. General Nirkin's army is estimated to have lost close to three thousand men all told. I imagine he and his staff are in disarray at our victory, just as General Bushan's army was when we defeated them here. Though, with the tactics we employed then, the killing was far greater."

"Yes," Lenfro says, "if there weren't an angry tender at our tail, I would have burned another section of this forest. That whole blasted army of his would be nothing but food for the next growth by now."

Garrick joins the table now, fully dressed and adjusting the scabbard at his side.

Kendir continues his report. "Now for the bad news. We have lost more than half of the squires as they were directing the flow of medicine and supplies last night. May their souls find peace. The cavalry charge that hit the western wall also burnt most of our food and medicine. This leaves the assault on Halmin to be our only viable option, lest we incur the wrath of the forest and turn back. The tender here clearly despises us already."

Lenfro pats Kendir and then motions to a man wearing a purple armband.

The man picks up a piece of charcoal and goes to the map of Halmin. He draws a wavy circle, cutting through farms and over the river that curves about the east portion of town. He puts a second one inside the first circle that encompasses the town proper. "Our scouts have reported that mages have built defenses through farmlands to keep us from taking the town easily. Nirkin's army clearly means to hold Halmin with what remains of their manpower. Their attack last night was merely by chance, most likely from the tender's foul appraisal of us. Our expectation is they are trying to hold out for reinforcements from the west. If the loyalists manage to gain uncontestable control of Halmin, the east will starve before the autumnal equinox." The man taps the map on the table. "The dwarfs to the far north and the elves to the east have declared themselves neutral in the matter of our kingdom's fate and will not offer either side trade while a winner is not readily apparent."

The man with the purple band points at a little dot on the eastern side of Asmeria. "We have a new batch of recruits coming in under the command of Lord Duban. They are scheduled to arrive in two weeks as they are marching from Plick. The last report from the north is still that Lord Joc Strixwi is trying to keep the badland's dragonbornes at bay, making his aid impossible."

Lenfro pats the illusionist's shoulder, ruffling his purple band, and takes control of the meeting. "Meaning we are in it alone and time is our enemy. We must strike while the loyalists under Nirkin are weak. We are two days' march from Halmin and expect our attack to be on the fourth. A few of you will be set into the ranks of our men to help relay orders. This battle is to be precise." Lenfro points to the south portion of the outer wall of Halmin on the map. "Our forces will be divided into two. Our main army will be attacking from here. When we breach the walls, the loyalists will be forced to retreat to the town where we will give chase. I would have liked some support from my father, but it seems his hands are tied."

Lenfro moves his finger along the map's wall to where the river flows next to the town. "On our right will be many of you on horseback. You are to breach the wall and run down the soldiers falling back to their second position. Keep the damage in these fields to a minimum. Lighting crops on fire and upending farmland are the opposite of what we intend to do here. That being said, we must do all we can to take the town. Ensure you do what is needed to win the day." Lenfro then picks up a heavy bag from next to the table, placing it on top of it and spilling out a dozen books, each bound tightly with leather straps. "Most of the mages will be with the main force. The cavalry will be using these to breach the town's wall. In these pages are explosive runes. Cut the straps around the book and throw it at a target, or set them all at once to explode."

Lenfro gives a moment for the men to process everything before speaking again. "With so many of the squires killed, we require people of the wagon train to step forward to join us in supporting our forces. Due to the nature of the upcoming battle and the weight it will carry on the war, I have no choice but to ask the women and children of the convoy to help run arrows, administer medicine, and care for the wounded, much like they did last night."

Garrick and the other knights, stunned at the request, shift about uncomfortably.

Lord Lenfro places a hand on the map of Halmin, right over the town. "For our will to be known to the world, we must succeed here. If we don't, we will be remembered as fools for all eternity, glossed over in some archaic tome. That is not what we are destined to become. We are a rising glory, meant to guide Asmeria to better days. It may seem cruel what I'm asking, but it is the way things are."

He goes quiet to let the knights mull over his words. When a decent amount of time has passed and no one has offered a counterargument, Lenfro motions to the exit of the tent. "You're all free to go. I will send soldiers about to inform everyone."

The knights all give light bows to leave, going off to pack up whatever they have.

When Garrick is about to leave, Lenfro motions towards him. "Sir Garrick, I have an assignment for you."

"Yes, My Lord?"

Lenfro motions out towards the camp. "The dead need to be buried. We don't have the luxury of time. Find a few stone singers and soldiers and put the bodies in the ground." Lenfro pats Garrick's shoulder then makes it clear he is dismissed with a flick of his head.

"It will be done, My Lord."

While Garrick is going about his work, the encampment is broken down at a rapid pace. With the destruction of the hauling carts, many people must discard cherished and other possessions. Soldiers also inform women and children of their new roles, causing more than a few to look about in a fearful realization of their futures.

When Sera and Kristo are approached, they agree to join the medical logistics. Once their items are packed on one of the remaining chef's carts, they join in helping others sort through their belongings. By mid-afternoon, all have finished, and the convoy is ready to march on. People move out towards the trees and back on the road leading towards Halmin. The whole convoy passes by Garrick, directing the burials. Brown mages have made an incredibly deep hole, into which the bodies are placed. As the people go by, many say silent prayers for their departed friends and neighbors.

When the last body is brought and the soil covers the dead, an acorn is placed into the loose soil. Three nature speakers gather around it. With their hands glowing a wispy green, they call to the acorn, forcing it to take root and grow. A trunk and body grand enough to make the oldest oak pale in comparison is sung into existence, springing high above the other trees that line the ash field. Great branches are brought forth to reach for the sky, giving way to leaves that will soak in as much sunlight as possible. On every open branch, the over-tunics of the fallen are placed, causing the fabric to drape and catch the breeze. Red and specks of yellow flow in the wind for all to observe, a testament to the thousands of lives lost in this place twice over. As a final gesture, the extra swords and spears of the dead are stabbed into the ground, to remain around the tree forever.

Garrick looks at the tunics flowing in the breeze for a moment. Then he and those who helped him mount their horses and gallop to catch up with the convoy. Garrick reaches Lenfro at the head and slows Pilosus to match his lord's pace. "Done, My Lord."

Lenfro acknowledges the knight. "May Sutri reclaim the souls of those that would die such wasteful deaths."

The pace is slower than when they set out from Effilnem as more goods are carried in arms. Despite this, the journey through the rest of the forest proves an easy endeavor for the army. The signs of the loyalists' retreat are clear, causing many to feel less fearful of an ambush. Green and white mages make treks into the forest, bringing back baskets full of herbs to stuff into carts and wagons where they can fit. After two long days of travel with an uneventful night of rest between, the army makes its way downhill through a thinning of trees. Before them lie the open farms of Halmin. But instead of the vast fields extending to the town proper, a wall of stone and wood cuts through Tennly farm near the tree-grown barn. A second wall of similar construction surrounds the town, blocking its view.

As the rebel army makes camp in the thinning of trees, movement happens on the outer wall and bells ring to alert the town. Lenfro, Garrick, and the attending knights look at both walls as black dots take to the sky. The winged-horse riders, now on patrol, fly over to the south wall. Lenfro reaches down into one of his saddlebags, produces a hand telescope, and stretches it to look at the enemy. "Garrick, I'm going to need your aid to piece out how to best assault the town."

"Yes, My Lord. We will have to regroup to break the second wall, My Lord."

Lenfro eyes Garrick and then relaxes in the saddle. Turning to two of the knights behind him, Lenfro speaks, "Tell the mages to erect the tent here and raise two watchtowers."

The knights ride off, and soon the mages are raising towers for men to occupy and watch the loyalists' maneuverings. Once Lenfro's tent is raised, the knights, mages, and Lenfro discuss potential routes and tactics for the upcoming battle until the selections for the cavalry charge are made.

A mage with a white band on her arm and a mask depicting a flower steps forth to discuss the details. "The menders should be made to stay with the main force to ensure our troops have the strength and numbers to reach the inner wall. Those on horseback should be accompanied by members of the medical team, whose sole purpose is to heal men that can continue to fight."

Kendir snorts at this, dismissively waving his hand. "That is ridiculous. We can send the cavalry in with potions on them so they can cure themselves of their wounds."

The white mage nods at the proposal but offers an open hand with her words. "You're right, we could. But if your horse is killed and you are trapped under it, there is no guarantee you would be able to access the potion to save yourself. Designating members to ride with the cavalry ensures the fallen will be tended to without ruining the formation. The men will also ride harder, knowing they are accompanied by those whose sole purpose is to keep them alive." The mage then looks from Kendir to Lord Lenfro. "Lord Lenfro, this tactic is already in place with your main force. It will not be hard to integrate it with your horsemen. Perhaps they could take up the rear."

Lenfro runs his hand through his hair, humming to himself. "Yes, it will be done. We can't afford potions to be lost or scattered on the field. Even if one of the medical personnel dies, the body with its red band will be easily identified for intended recovery. Ensure the smallest of our medical personnel ride with our cavalry. Our horses are already in use, so they will have to ride with the cavalry. But they should be towards the back. Halflings will have priority, followed by young men."

Garrick steps forward. "My Lord, are you asking children to ride with the cavalry?"

"I am."

As if struck, Garrick's body moves back. "They are children, My Lord! They are the whole reason we are fighting! They suffer enough just by traveling with us. I would have thought they'd tend to the wounded brought back, not this!"

Lenfro puts his hand out to stop Garrick. "Yes, and we must ask for more from them. We have no alternative. Everyone in the camp will be doing their part. They are to hold the potions and administer aid as they see fit. They will be given full rein to heal themselves as many times as they need."

"But, My Lor—"

"Garrick! You try my patience! This will be the last time I allow such an outburst. If this were in front of the men, you'd be struck of rank and title! This battle has consequences far too consequential for your moralities!"

With eyebrows twitching, Garrick silently stews.

Calm has returned to the meeting. Lenfro motions at Kendir. "You will oversee the cavalry. You'll be required to designate bannermen and who in the regiment will ride with the medics."

Suddenly, the call of a horn rings through the entire camp. Knights and mages leave to see what is happening. On a hill, the knights watch a group of loyalist horsemen waving a red-and-green striped flag ride into the open field of Tennly farm.

Seeing the action, Lenfro calls for horses, pointing at various mages and knights, including Garrick, to come with him. Kendir takes up the rebels' own green-and-yellow banner, and the summoned knights ride with Lenfro. On arrival to the loyalists, the mounted rebel knights make a half-circle with Lenfro in the center. The loyalists do the same, the dwarf

General Nirkin in a gilded tunic and plate mail at the center of their formation. A loyalist horseman with a pulled-down helmet forces his way to the forward position of the *U* shape near Garrick. Both the dwarf and Lenfro stare at each other while the knights move forward, forming a circle of knights around both generals.

When the formation is finished, the loyalist who moved to be next to Garrick pulls his visor up to reveal his deep-brown eyes and long black hair. "Garrick, good to see you again, friend."

"I didn't know you were this high up in the winged scouts, Demio. Congratulations."

Demio gives a light bow of his head in thanks. "Thank you. I owe a lot of my skill to how we used to practice together."

"Yes," Garrick says with a smile of remembrance, "I owe my station to that as well. We shouldn't interrupt any further. Let's talk after."

Lord Lenfro and General Nirkin, having graciously waited for the private conversation to end, now inspect the knights lining the other's half-circle.

Lenfro extends his hand to indicate Nirkin should open parley. "Let us hear what you rode out here to say, Nirkin."

The dwarf strokes his beard, flicking his eyes from the white mage in Lenfro's service to Lenfro, looking the rebel general over with a callous eye. "Leave Halmin. Your soldiers coming through the town are the reason for our enforcement here. We loyal to the crown would like to see no harm done to its inhabitants and the crops they grow to feed every Asmerian, traitor or otherwise."

"Our soldiers never moved through Halmin. The only person other than supply officials to venture into this town was Sir Garrick Marmuin, this man here." Lenfro gestures to Garrick.

"It's true," Garrick says. "This is my hometown. I had stumbled across a child slave named Kristo during the siege of Effilnem. I brought him home to my wife to adopt him only a few days ago."

Nirkin waves his hand at the statement. "Nonsense. I have seen a letter detailing multiple rebel soldiers into Halmin. Any talk of child slavery is also a farce. The young man must have done something grievous to warrant his arrest."

A flush of anger rushes to Garrick's face before he calms himself. "General, any document of that nature is a falsehood."

"Hmph! A rebel such as yourself would tell me of treachery?"

"My Lord," Demio volunteers to the surprise of all, "Garrick may be a rebel, but he is no liar."

Nirkin eyes Demio and motions for him to stay quiet. "I have proof of what your friend is." General Nirkin reaches down into a saddlebag, pulls out a letter, and extends it to be taken.

Lenfro points at one of his knights that rides to take the letter and delivers it to their lord. Lenfro takes a minute to read it and then crumples it, shaking it in the air. "Are you serious? You're wagering war in Halmin over a letter from a daughter to her father? You've lost your mind!"

Nirkin points his finger at Lenfro. "That document clearly paints the picture of a planned scouting for the taking of Halmin. Your knight Garrick managed to evade capture. How many more of your scouts have slipped our nets?"

Lenfro's hand glows red to incinerate the letter, letting the ashes drift onto the ground. "That letter was written by a frightened girl calling for her loyalist father to be a hero and come back to town! It's a piece of fiction and cannot be trusted!"

Nirkin points his finger at Lenfro as if cursing him. "Don't talk to me about trust! You who swore fealty to the king and then stabbed him in the back. You were being groomed to be the next minister of war!"

Lenfro slashes his hand in the air. "Enough! I won't hear anything more from a deranged mind such as yours! You would walk with eyes open into a pit of spikes if the so-called king told you to! His reign was a farce to begin with. The figureheads of each church were bribed by his father's coin! You clearly wish for war. Why hold such a ridiculous parley when you won't see reason?"

The dwarf's face is red with anger, the fists clenched on his horse's reins flowing with red energy similar to Lenfro's. "*I* wish for war? *You* caused this entire rebellion! *You* let murderers and rapists spring free from capture! You do not fight for freedom; you fight to put every person living in this kingdom under the boot of savages once more! A pox upon you, Lenfro Strixwi! If your name happens to be remembered through history, may it be used to define lesser men!" General Nirkin spits on the ground. "There's one more proposal since you refuse to let those who know the meaning of loyalty safeguard Halmin. It's from the church of Sutri here. The women of the church wish to be among the soldiers as an independent party. They will be on the battlefield to offer confessions and to hear the last words of the dying, regardless of side. They ask that anyone flying a pink flag on top of a thick wooden parasol not be harmed."

Lenfro pauses for a moment and then nods, wiping his hand down his face as if to wash himself from his rage. "Yes, we agree. Word will be spread through our camp. We wouldn't want your men to pass without a proper goodbye."

Nirkin whistles, causing his men to start breaking the formation. "Your head will make a fine ornament on a pike. I will carry it back to the capital city myself when I get hold of it." With the final insult, Nirkin rides off back to the wall.

Lenfro turns with his knights to return to camp.

Garrick and Demio remain. They turn their horses to look at one another properly.

"Seems ego and past deeds force this fight, Garrick."

Garrick gives a few pats to Pilosus's neck, acknowledging Demio's point. "Liana and your unborn child . . . should you die, I will make sure they will not go hungry. You have my word."

Demio chuckles, despite Garrick's dark demeanor. "I remember you being a lot more fun, Garrick. But, yes . . ." He goes closer to Garrick, riding shoulder to shoulder. Demio takes out a dagger, strips his left hand of his mail glove, and cuts his palm. He holds the dagger for Garrick to take.

Searching Demio's eyes and finding nothing but trust in them, Garrick takes the dagger and similarly cuts himself.

Demio then holds his hand out for Garrick. "I also swear that if you should die, your family will not starve or be left out in the cold. They will live long happy lives for as long as I draw breath."

Garrick grabs Demio's hand, and they shake them. "I will see you on the battlefield then."

Demio gives a wide grin. "Oh, yes. I'll be trying to find you. Make sure you watch the skies for me."

Garrick cracks a smile at Demio's grave joke.

Once their blood is properly mixed, the two let go, nod at each other, and turn away, riding to their respective armies.

Back at the camp, Kendir is waiting for Garrick, holding a long pole with various flags. Garrick rides up to the standing man, hails him, and dismounts Pilosus to talk to him.

Kendir notes the blood on Garrick's hand. "Making oaths with loyalists will not look favorable to the men."

"It is an oath to protect and guide each other's families should one of us die. He is my oldest friend."

Kendir grunts and then gives the pole and flags to Garrick. "These are signaling flags. I'm appointing you to oversee their use." Handing Garrick a piece of parchment, Kendir adds, "Here's what they mean. I heard you can read. They might not be necessary as we'll be communicating by flare, but if our accompanying mage dies, relaying information is on you." Kendir pats Garrick on the side, holding his arm. "Your boy will be riding with us. He's under your care."

Garrick stares into Kendir's eyes from this news, who looks back with remorse.

Kendir lets go of Garrick's arm and walks off into camp.

Garrick leads Pilosus to be taken care of by one of the few remaining squires. With his horse stabled, he moves through the camp, going towards where the chefs have set up. Spotting the tallest woman, he walks towards her and touches his wife's side to have her turn and look at him. "Where is he?"

Sera looks down at her husband, putting a hand on his cheek, and then flicks her head towards their tent.

He gives his wife a hug, goes to the tent, and moves the flap.

Inside the tent, Kristo is standing, wearing an open-faced helmet and a chain shirt, kept tight with a belt. Over his chainmail is a red-and-white striped tunic to indicate his role, and draped around him is a satchel, stuffed with hay and potions. The child beams up at Garrick. "I'm going to save people, just like Iva."

Running his eyes over Kristo, Garrick drops the banners, kneels to Kristo, and grabs him in a tight hug.

The short half-elf grunts from such a tight grip but returns the hug. "Uh . . . Garrick? Are you all right?"

Garrick nods, pulling himself back and patting Kristo's cheek. Without a word, he departs, leaving Kristo standing in the tent confused. Sera looks at Garrick. The two to stare at one another until Garrick turns away, walking off to a thicker part of the forest. When at last there is no one near him, he touches a tree, kneeling before it, his head bent and eyes closed. "Mother Sutri, hear my prayer . . ."

19

MOTHERS OF MERCY

As the sun comes up, it cracks through the flap of the Marmuin tent. Yelling rings through the encampment as sergeants call for all medical personnel to gather outside of Lord Lenfro's tent. Sera, rubbing her eyes open, pushes on Kristo until he rises. The two leave Garrick in the tent to be fully rested for the coming day. Walking through the rows of white tents, they see other women and similarly aged children moving towards Lenfro's campsite. When they make it up to the cresting of the hill, everyone can see Lenfro is waiting for them next to a series of crates that a few knights are sitting on. The female white mage with a flower mask is also here, eyeing the growing crowd.

When the crowd reaches an ample size, Lenfro raises an arm to ensure everyone is paying proper attention. "Ladies and youths, it is good to see you here. I understand what you are about to do might shake you to your core, but it is a necessity." Lenfro points off to the walls surrounding Halmin. "These monsters would let every man, woman, and child east of this point go through a winter without food. They're willing to starve innocent Asmerians to death just to kill us. What future does this kingdom hold for its people where, by order of our lords, we would at a whim live our lives below even the dirtiest beggar? What future is there in a kingdom that would enslave half its population just to hold power for its greed-driven lords? This battle will decide the fate of this love-filled land. You all do so much for us by being here. I, for one, am immensely proud for Asmeria to have grown such women and children that stand for themselves. Your jobs are simple—keep the men alive to fight for this free land, and ensure you do not die yourselves." Lenfro motions to the white mage sitting on one of the crates. "This is Lady Kela Holstim. Her parents are the lords of the capital coast, but she is loyal to this cause. She will be informing you on your assignments."

Lenfro extends his arm to her and then moves out of the way to attend to other matters. The porcelain-masked mage moves forward talking loud enough to ensure her voice can be heard, though the mask doesn't seem to dampen her words. "Your assignments for the battle are simple. You report to the menders' unit that will be dispersed through the army's ranks. You'll be expected to give basic medical attention to get people back on their feet and drag out people if needed. The loyalist medical corps is not integrated into their ranks; it moves behind their army. Having all of you present to rescue soldiers and push them back into the fray gives us a huge advantage, not just in numbers. The men will fight harder knowing there is someone like all of you around to save them if things go wrong."

Lady Kela pauses briefly. "The members of the menders' unit picked the forest clean of healing plants on our march here from Kurin's Retreat, but now they need more hands to brew potions. It is also your duty to help make these before battle begins. They should be cooking potions as we speak. Go and report to them. Also, before any of you step onto the battlefield, make sure you are wearing your healer's band. Healers are meant to be spared. It won't save you from a barrage of arrows, but men will know not to slash someone wearing it. I won't obscure facts from you, though. In the last battle when we were hit in the baggage train, two mender bodies were recovered without arrows in them. Make sure you all stay safe." Lady Kela motions to the mender's part of the encampment and waves the crowd towards it. "You have your tasks. May Sutri guide you."

Sera pushes on Kristo's shoulders to have him move with the rest of the crowd down the hill. At the menders' camp, numerous fires are going with men and women dropping herbs and berries into pots hanging over the flames. The fresh recruits from the convoy mingle with the menders at each of their tents, offering aid as instructed. Kristo's eyes scan through the area until he spots Iva carrying a basket of herds to her fire. He points her out for Sera who goes with Kristo to Iva. "Hello, Iva."

Faking a smile at him, she drops to her knees and hugs Kristo. "Hello, you lovely boy." Iva tilts her head at Sera, who in turn shakes her head. Iva pulls back from Kristo, holding him about the shoulders. "My, you save one person, and they dress you like a hero!" She pats his cheek and stands back up. "What are you doing here, Kristo?"

Puffing his chest out, he says, "We're supposed to help the menders make healing potions."

"Did you come over to offer me help?"

"Yup!"

Iva offers her hand to Kristo, who takes it, letting himself be led to Iva's tent with Sera walking behind. There, a cauldron half-filled with water rests on stones around her fire to let it stand directly over the flames. Iva lets go of Kristo's hand to take a seat on the ground by the fire, setting her basket of herbs down. She motions for the other two to do the same. "Healing potions can be made of a variety of ingredients. Different regions produce potions with what they have on hand. Who knows how many trials and errors have happened over the years." Iva gives a hum, showing her affection for the topic. "Lady Kela has instructed us to use these plants from the region." Iva takes some herbs from her basket and shows each to the pair.

First in her hands is a branch of a bush with dark green serrated leaves and blue oval berries.

"Are we boiling the leaves?"

"Yes, how did you know?"

Kristo gives a shrug, plucking at the grass next to him. "Lady Amelia taught me that. She said the berries were poisonous too."

"This Lady Amelia knew her plants. Sometimes warriors coat their weapons in a poison made from these berries, plus a few other plants. The men of both these armies don't do such a thing. At least I haven't had a poison victim come through my care."

Sera relaxes, enjoying being the one taught for a change.

Iva puts the cutting down. "That bush is called the bellfire bush. Next, we have white wart, a moss that blooms little white flowers with a yellow center on birch trees." Iva shows it to the pair. "Everything green from this plant goes in the brew; anything white or yellow ruins it." Iva then takes out her final plant, the one that takes up the most space in her basket—an oddly small tree that has been plucked from the ground with its root system intact. "Margrove tree. It grows like weeds deeper in the forest where humans aren't allowed. You put both cut roots and the leaves in the pot."

Iva pulls a knife from the basket and hands it to Sera. "Why don't you cut the roots, and Kristo can pull the leaves off. These are the proper portions: five parts margrove tree, two parts white wart, and one part bellfire leaves. Boil and reduce until it's syrupy. Men will be coming around with bottles soon for us to fill. Then Lady Kela and the other white mages will collect the containers after they do mana activations on them." Iva takes the moss, cutting off the flowers, while Kristo and Sera work with the margrove trees. When the ingredients are being added to the pot, Iva says, "Kristo, we might need some more water. Why don't you go find Venitria?" Iva taps a bucket near her.

Kristo takes it. "I guess I'll always have to run water." Then he goes off.

While the women work, Iva says, "He shouldn't be here, going to war like this."

"Yes . . . he deserves more than this. He's suffered enough."

Iva gets up to stand over the cauldron and stir its ingredients. "His fate isn't decided. You could take him away from this cruelty."

Sera stops her cutting completely. "You want us to flee?"

Iva shakes her head. "Is it fleeing? The life of your son could end tomorrow. He looks as if he's barely seen thirteen winters. He deserves more than being thrown to war. He is strong and courageous. I doubt many boys his age would have ventured out from under the cart."

"There are other children in the camp too. What about them?"

Iva nods, doubling the sternness of her tone. "There is only one mother in front of me to talk to now."

"I'm not his real mother; not even the person we're taking care of him for was."

Iva's expression softens. "That isn't what makes you his mother. I've seen you do more for him at Kurin's Retreat than my mother ever did for me. It's in the heart. That boy loves you, clear as day, and you love him."

Sera looks off to where Kristo went, trying to see him.

Iva continues to speak, looking for him as well. "We're sacrificing the generation that we are supposed to be protecting. Lord Lenfro had time to grow and develop, to become great. We are robbing these children of that chance."

"You may be right, but if we're branded traitors, where would we go?"

Iva sees the approaching child and understands their conversation has ended.

Kristo places the bucket by Iva.

She knocks on his helmet and says, "Help Sera put the ingredients she prepares into the cauldron."

Kristo does as asked. Then his attention turns to all the women and children making their own potions. "There's a lot of brewing happening." Kristo looks to Iva and then Sera but gets no response from either. "Is it really going to be that bad?"

Sera moves to the boy, kneeling in front of him. "Kristo, tomorrow is going to be very difficult for everyone here. We are all going to be fighting so that there won't be places like the pit in Effilnem. Remember in the ash field, where lots of people were killed? It will be just like that."

Kristo gives a few blinks, looking at Sera with a frown on his face. "Are we going to be safe?"

Sera shakes her head, looking down at the ground. "I can't promise that, Kristo. Garrick will do all in his power to keep you safe."

Kristo's eyes are red, turning redder as he rubs them. "I don't want to be killed! I don't want you or Garrick to die!"

Sera pulls Kristo into her, pulling off his helmet so he can rest on her shoulder. She looks up at the sky, watching the clouds move and holding Kristo until she feels he has calmed down a bit. "I'm sorry, Kristo . . . but . . . do you want other people to have to grow up the way you did?"

"No . . . what would . . . who would . . . why would anyone want to live like that?"

Sera lets Kristo go, rubbing him on the side. "That is why we're fighting, for everyone like you, since we could easily have been you if we had crossed the wrong person."

Kristo shakes his head. "But it's different. You all . . . you don't deserve to die. Garrick doesn't deserve that. Nobody here deserves that."

"I say you're absolutely right, no-one deserves to die on a field when they could be at home. Everyone makes sacrifices; the people here would rather be dead than be enslaved." Sera pulls back slightly to look at Kristo's face. "Aren't you the same?"

Kristo nods. "But still this shouldn't of happened, this army shouldn't exist. The loyalists shouldn't exist."

Sera pats Kristo side. "A lot of things shouldn't of happened, but now we're here. It's unfair, I know." Sera pokes Kristo's chest. "But now that you're here, you can make a difference. You can help decide what is fair. Standing to the side means your fate will be written by someone elses hand. You have the chance to grab the quill and add your own line to the way the world is unfolding. You're a strong boy, I'm sure that people will read the great exploits of 'Kristo the Hero'. Sera's hands move to exaggerate the pretend title."

Kristo can't help but smile, looking over at Iva. "I already got to save one person."

Iva has an unsure expression on her face, but she soon catches a look from Sera, causing her to act confident. "I'd write your tales myself, but I'm afraid I can't read."

Sera raises her eyebrows at Kristo. "I can teach her, but I'd need my school back. How about it Mr. Hero? Want to take your home back?"

Kristo gives an affirmative hum. "Absolutely. Iva can be my classmate when we get it back."

Iva cracks a smile, then touches the top of her head out of worry, but doesn't say whats on her mind. "Lets get these potions done."

Kristo nods, rubbing his eyes a final time and steadying his breath. "I will fight too for people out there like Mabel."

Given that Kristo has found his spirit again, the two get back to helping Iva until midday comes around when men can be seen riding through the menders' camp on a horse-drawn cart. In the back are various bottles, ones for potions, some for ale, and even bottles fit for wine. Once they get to Iva's tent, a man climbs down from the wagon to inspect Iva's cauldron.

"Can I help you?" she asks him.

The man shakes his head, going back to the cart and pulling bottles from it, a few of which still seem to have alcohol inside. "Nope, but I can help you.

When your brew is finished, put what you've made in here. The white mages will be by later to activate your potions." He places bottles by Sera.

She inspects them. Confused, she says, "Some of these are still filled with beer and wine."

"Yes, they are. Drink 'em or spill 'em, makes no difference. Just make sure they're cleaned out before you fill 'em. Have fun, ladies." Back on the cart, he has his partner take him to the next stop.

Iva and Sera raise a brow at one another, noticing how those working at other tents have already popped open beer and wine bottles to enjoy. Mimicking their fellow menders', the two pop open bottles to drink. By the time the brews have been reduced properly, the menders' tents are buzzing with conversation. Iva and Sera are ladling their potions into bottles Kristo helped clean with water, each of them drinking from their own bottle of wine every now and again.

When their cauldron is empty, Kristo looks at a few of the proper potion bottles that are filled, seeing the fluid is a yellow-brown color. "Um, Iva? Are healing potions supposed to be this color? Mine are red."

Iva gives the boy a pat on the back, picking the bottle out of his hand and placing it back with the others. "Yes, yes, potions are normally colored with dye rocks during their brewing to designate them. We just don't have any." Iva brings up her wine bottle to drink from, finishing the contents and getting another bottle. A few of the other menders are wandering about to get extra bottles for their brew, leading to Sera passing out wine and beer to them. When the other menders finish their filling, they return to Iva's tent. All the women make merry by playing guessing games or gossiping about others in the army while sitting in the grass and drinking what is left in their bottles.

Kristo, with little to do, starts drawing in the dirt with a stick while the women go about their conversations.

When night draws near, the women say their goodbyes.

Three white mages, each with her own mask, come by with a cart to each pile of potions, illuminating them in a glorious white glow of their hands and loading the bottles into their cart. Lady Kela is among the mages and addresses Sera and Iva. "Hello, ladies. I hope you are feeling jolly."

The two women nod at her.

"I'm happy to hear it. I assume you all know what you're doing with a regular healing potion, but some of you might receive a larger bottle tomorrow that isn't portioned properly. In that case, you are to instruct the wounded to bite their cheeks or tongues to have their blood in their mouths. After that, pour about three spoonsful of the potion into their mouths—the blood in their mouths will activate the potion—and then have them swallow."

The two women say they understand, and Lady Kela goes off with her fellow mages to the other tents.

"Something the matter?" Iva asks in seeing Sera's dour expression. "Live while you can; you might not get the chance to tomorrow."

Eyeing the dying moon coming into the sky, Sera leans up from her spot on the ground. "We should stay by each other tomorrow . . ."

Iva straightens now too. "I had already planned on it; I owe you and your son an immense debt. I'd be proud to stand by you."

Both women turn to look at each other, clinking their bottles together. When the world turns dark and the moon takes its firm hold, Sera stands and eyes Iva, who is looking off at the walls surrounding Halmin. Soon Iva feels Sera's eyes, and the mender flicks her head towards the main camp.

Sera puts down her bottle and motions for Kristo to come to her. "Kristo, let's get something to eat."

A few of the other menders have the same idea too, their drinks having kept their minds occupied until night settled. Every now and then, a stream of light comes across the sky of Halmin's walls and illuminates the farm fields for the loyalists to search for unwanted guests.

When Sera and Kristo have their food, they walk to a place near the crest of the hill, resting beneath a tree that looks out on the walls and farmland of Halmin, plus the forest beyond. To the northwest, the forest around the walls has a pale green glow to it, mixed with dots of reds and blue. Kristo points to it, waiting to finish a bit of bread before speaking. "Why is the forest glowing?"

Sera pats Kristo's head and drinks some water. "That is the Forest of Slumber where Halmin buries its dead. Other towns, cities, and even kingdoms bury their dead in its borders if the person had a deep love of the goddess Sutri."

"But why is it glowing?"

"Hush. I'm getting to that; you have to understand one thing to know another sometimes." Sera taps Kristo's wooden plate to tell him to eat. "The lights you are seeing are hundreds of little balls called sap songs. Where the dead rest, the trees can cast spells. A sap song is used to help keep a tree's neighbors healthy by giving them energy. Other times, it's used to spread seeds. That's what my mother tells me. You should see the town in late spring—dancing lights, people out in their best clothes moving along with the tree's magic to music played in the town center."

Sera has a smile on her face, but it soon disappears as her eyes wander over the erected walls and flying knights, her eyebrows twitching. "Spring was Mabel's favorite time of year for that reason." Sera goes silent for a long time, looking down at the rebel camp to watch people moving around. "I was the reason for her imprisonment, you know."

Kristo looks up at her but says nothing.

"She was stealing books from the library. I loved books, and when I caught her doing it, I told the librarian. I didn't think . . ." Sera lets her eyes go to the ground. "I didn't want what happened to Mabel to come to pass. It wasn't even her fault really; it was her parents'. Still, I didn't want them to go like that either. I thought they might get their library card suspended or have to do community service. She was my best friend, and I made her go to that hell hole. I didn't want that. The gods above every day since her leaving knew I didn't want that."

The two sit, looking out on the divided fields of Halmin till Kristo puts a hand on Sera's arm. "She told me she was mad at you."

Sera's eyes snap to Kristo's.

"She told me she hated you with everything in her heart when she was younger. She also told me that it wasn't how she felt anymore and how she would have wanted to talk to you, to ask why you did it. She told me that based on your answer she would make up her mind then." Kristo takes his hand back, fidgeting with his food. "I think she would have forgiven you, and I know best. I was her best friend after you."

Sera leans over into Kristo, giving him a hug, which sends the trays of food spilling onto the ground. Kristo's arms go about her until she pulls away, wiping her eyes. "Looks like I ruined dinner, huh?"

Kristo looks down in sorrow at the meal in the dirt and then back at Sera. "Food isn't everything."

Sera shakes her head. "No, let's go back, and I'll tell them I dropped it. I don't want you going hungry." Sera pats Kristo's back, and they both get up. Sera waits for a moment, looking back down at the armored child. "Garrick and I love you very much. I know you might not want to join our family just yet, but our door and hearts will always be open for you."

"I know." Kristo says with a smile on his face.

At the chef's station, Sera and Kristo apologize and get more food. But instead of going back to the hill, Sera guides Kristo to their tent. On arrival, Garrick is taking his armor off to comfortably sit by a fire with a few other people whose tents are nearby. Sera sits against him, leaning her weight onto his shoulder as he's placed in a hug from the side.

Garrick returns the hug, having to brace an arm against the ground to hold her. "I heard they gave the menders the alcohol stores we had and the ladies were having parties around the cauldrons like witches in that evil story."

"Yes, I cast some very vile curses and even danced with a demon."

"Yeah, that sounds like you."

Sera gives a playful slap to Garrick's chest. The two ignore the others about the fire who are similarly engaged with their loved ones or friends.

Kristo finds a seat to Garrick's left,.

"That armor looks like it was well cared for, Kristo. It should keep you safe tomorrow."

Kristo looks himself over, taking off his helmet to examine it. "It's pretty heavy."

Garrick gives a short nod to the comment, moving his supportive arm to rustle the links of Kristo's mail. "Good, that means it's made right."

Soldiers are moving through the tents, relaying messages to those they pass by. A blond soldier approaches the threesome's fire, rests on his spear, and speaks. "The horsemen are being summoned. Report to Kendir on the hill with your charge if you have one." The soldier then gives a small bow of his head to Garrick, leaving to address other men of camp.

Sera looks up to Garrick's eyes, staring with such a longing.

Garrick can't help but look down at her and tightens both arms about her body as she is against his chest now. "Kristo and I will be as safe as we can be. I'm to ride near the rear of the formation with him."

Sera nods against Garrick's chest and, after a bit, moves to let her husband up.

Garrick reaches around him, grabbing the armor he took off only a short time ago and puts it on again. Sera calls up at him, and he offers her a hand. When she takes it, Garrick pulls her up into his arms and forces her to lean into a kiss. Sera's arms cling to her husband as she pushes back, the two of them sharing their feelings without a care of the audience.

When at last Garrick moves to part, Sera holds him. He touches her waist with a gentle push, to which she nods down at the ground and lets her husband go. Garrick watches Sera's eyes for a time and then looks down to Kristo. "Come, Kristo. We are needed."

Kristo gets up, puts his helmet back on, and adjusts his satchel. He then looks up at Garrick, showing that he's ready. "More walking . . ."

Garrick gives the half-elf a smile, knocking on Kristo's helmet. "I'd throw you if I could, but I'm not as big as the giants Theotis stays around." Garrick looks back to Sera. "I was thinking. A knight could use a favor from the lady he loves, you know, something to remind him of her when things seem dark."

Sera gives a look at the ground and then smiles at Garrick.

"What? I'm serious, you know. I'd take the amphitheater, but it's kind of big."

The request has Sera thinking for a bit, having nothing to give him. She then approaches Garrick, putting her hand out. "I'll need your dagger."

Garrick lifts his right leg, pulls a dagger from his boot, and places it in Sera's hand.

Gripping the blade, she cuts a bit of hair from her head, ties a simple knot in it, and offers it to Garrick, handing the dagger back as well. "This should give my knight a constant reminder of my love." Garrick takes off his mail glove, and Sera pushes her gift into the palm of his hand. "Stay safe."

Garrick holds onto the lock of hair, looking into Sera's eyes. He puts his arms around his wife, stealing another embrace. A good number of men pass by the two until Garrick lets her go. "You stay safe too." Putting his hand on Kristo's shoulder, the knight guides the boy up the hill towards Lenfro's tent.

Sera watches them leave, and once they're out of sight on the crest of the hill, she sighs and rubs her head, looking at her family's empty tent. Going inside she finds no comfort on the hides that were laid down. When sleep finally comes, the moon moves too quickly, and soon the muster horn sounds from the hill.

20

The Tree of Liberty

Sera rushes to get up, seeing the light of the world pouring through the flap of her tent. She also sees soldiers and women alike rushing about to get ready. Watching for only a moment, she crawls out of her tent, joining the frantic scene.

Sergeants move through the camp, shouting orders for all to hear. One goes through Sera's section, swatting at tents. "Move people! Move! Down the hill and form ranks! Women and menders report to the carts! Get up!"

Turning her head in all directions, Sera spots the carts down the hill near where the men are forming a conglomeration of shimmering metal armor. People are pouring down the hill to make their lines. Sera goes to the carts, joining other women and children as they move in a line of sorts to the carts. Going forward, she sees bottles of the potions she made yesterday are being dispensed to the women and children who are then directed where to go. Sera calls, trying to be heard above the loud conversations around her. "Iva! Iva!" Despite repeated calls, Sera is unable to find the woman. Now at the front of the line, Sera receives a wine bottle of the potion and asks the man distributing the bottles, "Have you seen a short, black-haired woman in a green dress? Her name is Iva."

The man shakes his head, passing out bottles beside her. "I've seen dozens of black-haired women. Move on. I need to get these potions out." The man shoos Sera away with a flick of his wrist.

She holds the bottle by the neck and walks slowly by the cart down towards the massing army and is bumped in the side.

"Hello, Sera," Iva says.

Sera smiles down at her and puts her in a hug. "Thank the goddess you're here. I thought I was going to have to do this without you."

Iva pats her back, then gets let go. "Not a chance, I made a promise."

The two turn to the army, trying to pick out where to go.

"How did you find me?" Sera asks. "I could have walked by a different cart."

"It was pretty easy. All I had to do was wait for the tallest woman in camp to come by."

She points out a position within the army near the center, and the women move to join the refined formation, moving between soldiers who are eyeing them. Sera shrugs, and both try to find a good spot in the array of men. Other women and menders have taken the better positions, so Sera and Iva must take a spot near the front of the formation. Ahead, they stare out onto a wall of rock and wood with men atop the formation wielding bows. The loyalists' winged riders are absent from the skies, leaving all the soldiers here on alert, each one occasionally scanning the surroundings for treachery. To the side of the formation, brown-cloaked mages are shaking the ground, summoning up great balls of rock through combined efforts to rest on the surface of the earth.

Lenfro flies over his mass of soldiers, having traded his stallion for a flying mount whose white wings beat in the air, soaring above his troops. Two other mages—Lady Kela and the purple-cloaked rider from the ash field—accompany him on their own flying steeds. After circling, the three land at the front of the formations of soldiers.

The lord's fiery red hand touches his neck as he speaks, causing Lenfro's voice to carry to the back ranks of soldiers. "My father, Lord Joc Strixwi, is dead."

Whispers of worry run through the ranks of the rebels. Sera and Iva glance at one another, shifting in their places.

"His fate was at the hands of dragonborne tribesmen. He died facing down enemy shamans, trying to give cover for his retreating soldiers. My father will go to heaven a proud and uncompromised man. I have only one regret upon hearing of his passing, and that is that I was not in his place. Asmeria's freedom rests upon the shoulders of such sacrifice. If today is my day of sacrifice, then so be it! I would gladly give my life to live in a free and just world, just as my father did!"

Lenfro lets his words sink in, watching his soldiers shake their weapons and bash their shields. "Before you all lies the heart of Asmeria, where all hope to the future of this great kingdom lies. The loyalists would see you barred from its glory. These very walls they've made are a testament to their fearful and crazed minds. The men behind these walls are dogs of the king, choosing to dine on the scraps thrown from an abusive master's table. They would see you starving for not accepting the shackles of slavery! They would watch as your children's faces grow gaunt and bodies turn to nothing but bones! There can be only victory today! Any other outcome means the damnation of a once-free kingdom!"

The group of soldiers around Iva and Sera cry out in rage. "I'll kill every man on the other side of that wall if it means never returning to the mine!" says one.

A dwarf with a waist-length beard shakes his war pick in the air in agreement. "I'd die a thousand deaths to see these bastards have their heads cut off!"

Iva leans into Sera to whisper. "Are these the slaves from Effilnem?"

"They aren't slaves anymore."

"True, they aren't," Iva says with a proud smile on her face. She nudges the dwarf next to her, who turns to look at her with a grunt and blood-thirsty glare. "You're not going to be able to die a single death with us here."

The dwarf gives a wicked grin. Tightly gripping his pick, he yells to the men around him. "Today we fight like the damned! The menders refuse to let us die!"

All the men around the dwarf roar in anger, years of planned revenge written in the snarls of their faces.

The dwarf gives a respectful nod to Iva. "You and your compatriot best be swift. The slaves of Effilnem are free once more, and they're out for the key-keepers' blood." He laughs in anticipation, causing both women to look with concern to each other.

Lenfro turns his winged horse around, drawing his blade and pointing it at the walls of Halmin. "Let the heavens know your anger by the countless dead in your wake! To war!" Lenfro and his accompanying mages charge forward on their winged horses and then take to the sky, flying to the enemy fortifications.

With every man, woman, and child seeing their leaders move in such a brazen fashion, the entire army surges forward to close the distance between them and the wall. Calls for blood and glory reach high over the outer walls to into Halmin proper, causing more than a few men on the ramparts to look for assurance at their fellow soldier.

Above the ramparts, Lenfro and both his mages fly to look over the wall at the enemy positions and hastily dive back in front of the wall as the men at the tops of the walls fire arrows at them. Lenfro's hand goes to his neck to again project his voice. "Raise shields! Launch the boulders!"

The rebel men raise their shields over their heads while charging. When those around Sera and Iva see the women ducking, unprotected, the men attempt to cover them. Loyalist arrows soon fly over Halmin's walls, and the rebels let fly giant stones in return. The large mass of rocks slung by the rebel earth mages knocks great swaths of arrows from the sky and collides with the top section of the wall that the rebel army is charging. The wood-and-stone wall cracks from the weight of the mighty boulders. As massive chunks of the top wall break, the loyalists on the section are blown backwards and off it. In retaliation, loyalist pyromancers on the wall cast fireballs to the rebel brown mages, who summon cover for themselves from the earth.

The onslaught continues as loyalist arrows find their place in either flesh or the wood of shields. Those that catch an arrow in their body are immediately tended to by the menders. They rip out the arrows and administer potion to the wounded, ordering them to get back into the fray. Sera and Iva have been keeping up with the crazed men of Effilnem, their pace far outstripping the rest of the army and having avoided the archers' fire.

The loyalists who fell from the boulders collapsing the wall are soon pounced upon as a flurry of steel-clad men break their bodies.

Lenfro shouts at his men. "Deploy the books! Break the walls!"

The dwarf shouts his affirmation, ripping his pick from a dead loyalist's neck. "Aye! Who brought the party favors? Bring them to the front!"

Two strong-backed men run forward with numerous satchels dangling on them.

Fearful shouting from the walls draws the dwarf's attention. Looking to the source, he sees blue mages along the wall are suspending black oil in the air above the rebel forces with pyromancers stopping their barrage to cast flames and boil the oil. The dwarf throws the nearest man next to him backwards and moves away from their attack. "Get back! Oil!"

The ex-slaves push their way against one another to put distance between them and the outer wall but are hit with the rest of the rebel line that are trying to advance. Too many are too late to escape. The oil is dropped, drenching unlucky rebels in the molten liquid. Screams of terror rip through the front lines from those hit with the oil, and they collapse in extreme pain. One such man staggers with a hand out to Iva and then falls in front of her. She looks at the man, drops to her knees, being careful not to touch him, and says, "You're going to be fine. Bite your tongue." After doing so, Iva pours a bit of her bottle in his mouth. But he cries out in renewed pain from the burning liquid scorching his skin once more. Iva looks at the act taking place in horror and calls towards the men. "Get him back! He needs treatment!" Two men come forward, grabbing the soldier by the legs where the oil isn't covering him, and drag him into the rebel lines. "Healer!" Iva cries. "Where are the goddamn white mages?"

Similar shouts are called by other men, who are dragging the still burning men away from the front.

The dwarf returns his attention to the men with satchels of the books. "Birkin! Are we to throw the books?" The dwarf points his pick at the wall.

"Aye. Bring them to their knees! We're going to water these fields with their blood!"

Rebels ready the explosives.

On the wall, archers are peppering the rebel soldiers below, but only a few shots manage a kill since any blow is soon corrected by menders pulling the arrows from wounded men and dispensing the healing potion. The loyalist pyromancers are now throwing balls of fire at the men on the ground.

Lenfro calls to his mages. "Loose boulders on the wall once more! Target the red mages!"

The book-carrying rebels grab their weapons by the spines, readying to toss them. At the same time brown mages throw their boulders at the walls to cover the rebels' advance. The wall breaks at the top while great explosions rock the base of the wall.

Birkin yells at his men, seeing the damage. "Keep throwing. It's breaking!"

The book carriers toss as fast as they can. Birkin joins them and rips books from their packs to aid in the destruction. The ground around the walls has numerous holes blown into it, and when another boulder from the brown mages collides with the wall, the area undercut by the explosions collapses. Debris and men rain on the ground, leaving a pile of bodies and stone for the rebels to climb on.

Before the dust of the broken stone has a chance to settle, Birkin rushes across the broken ground. "It's time for the men of Effilnem to show their teeth! Off with the slavers' heads!"

All the men under Birkin's command cry in agreement and charge with their sergeant. Sera and Iva are forced to keep up, moving with them through the breach where a mass of rebel soldiers with spears at the ready braces for their charge.

"Throw the books! Break their line!" Birken yells.

The satchel men take ground on the debris of the wall and hurl their explosives at the spearmen, blowing massive holes in their lines. Through those gaps, Birkin leads his men to take the loyalists' heads. Sera and Iva are in the third line, pushing men from their side to attend to the fallen. Archer fire comes from the back ranks of the loyalists, spilling the blood of rebels climbing over the breach. To ensure the safety of the men, Lenfro rides over the wall, sending flames down onto those that still line the ramparts. The enemy pyromancers attempt to shield themselves and their troops. When boulders target their position, the walls break underneath, sending them on a one-way trip downward.

Sera and Iva are still pulling people from the fray, establishing a healing line, and are now pulling rebel soldiers across the bodies of loyalists.

Birkin shouts from the front to whoever can hear him. "Foul white magic! Spike the heads of the dead!"

A chilling black fog swirls by the feet of those standing and seeps into the slain bodies around them, causing the arms of the dead to twitch back to life. At Birkin's command, the rebels stab the heads of corpses to stop their dark return.

Sera and Iva hear the loyalist bodies they are moving across groan to life. The women scramble, trying to get back from the line, but the arm of an undead catches Sera's leg. She trips and is dragged back over other slain loyalists who are similarly starting to stir. "No! No! Help! Iva!"

Iva looks back at Sera screaming and turns to go to her aid. Iva kicks the helm off the dead man and stomps on its arm with her heel. "A weapon, Sera! Grab a weapon!"

Sera looks about the stirring remains of the dead, spots an axe, and rips it from the fallen. She lurches round to swing the weapon and embeds it into the head of her attacker. Taking a moment to breathe, she suddenly screams from the top of her lungs, fresh blood staining every part of her. She gets up, drawing the axe out of her enemy's skull, and swings it down on the heads of bodies that are twitching in the black fog.

Iva stands for a moment, dumbfounded at the sight of Sera, until her senses return from the cry of a fallen rebel. The rebel line continues to surge forward, creating a pocket where the loyalists surround them. Coming about the side, a loyalist soldier sees Sera chopping at fallen loyalists. Immediately, he charges at her.

In wide-eyed terror, Sera sees the man coming at her. He slashes his sword from the left. In defense, Sera puts out her axe, and his blade notches the wood near the head and is turned away. Then she brings her axe back up, swipes down the side and strikes where the mans shoulder meets his neck. The man attempts to raise his shield in defense, but Sera is too quick, sinking the axe head into the mans flesh. The man falls forward to the ground, Sera having felled him in one hit. She screams once more and brings her axe up to strike again, splitting his skull on the ground so he can't come back to haunt her.

Watching the large woman kill one of their own, loyalist soldiers look to close the noose on the rebel line.

Seeing the men eyeing the situation, Sera looks down at them, readying the axe in front of her to defend Iva, who is tending to the fallen behind her. "I'm going home," Sera yells, "and none of you are stopping me!"

The man Iva has just aided gets up and thrusts his sword in the air. "Aid the red lady!"

Men form around her, pushing forward into the line of loyalists ahead of her. The giantess continues to eye everything for a for a moment and then rushes forward, delivering an overhead chop across the line of rebels in front of her to crush the arm of a loyalist. Sera looks at her feet, still seeing the black swirling mist across them. "We need a mage!"

Across the line, men relay back. "Mage to the front!"

The rebel line keeps at a standstill as the order is relayed back. Coming forth through the ranks of rebels, an elven figure in all blue strides over the rubble, a wall of transparent ice floating in front of her to guard against incoming arrows. Men move around her, letting Venitria make her way to the front where Birkin and his most bloodthirsty men are bogged down by the undead. Venitria looks about the dead in front. She turns her ice to water, has it rush about the undead's feet, and snap freezes the bodies, holding them in place for the rebels to kill them for good.

"Where is the caster?" Birkin looks back and up at the elf while his men move forward.

The dwarf motions to the northwest of their formation. "Bloody menace is hiding among the sea of soon-to-be corpses. You'll have to look for their black mist. It's been a blessing getting to kill these people twice, but I'm getting sick of it!"

Venitria calls to melt the bloody water that she froze and has it rush back to her to summon a tower of liquid about herself. Her hands roil blue, and she fires herself out of the top of the tower and into the sky. Her outer clothes having been soaked turn into a hard ice from her magic. The elf in freefall uses her magic to pull on the ice formed about her body, diving in the direction of her prey. Venitria's other hand calls to the water she had blasted herself out of, washing it around the loyalists' forces to knock them aside for Birkin and his men to slaughter the fallen.

With Birkin's men moving in, the rebel soldiers advance to the front to aid in the fighting. A few look in disbelief at the sheer carnage the ex-slaves caused—many red-tunicked men lie slain with holes through their eyes or their heads clean off. A scant number of yellow-clad men, most still moving, are peppered among the swath of bodies and groan as their bodies go through the healing process.

Lenfro swoops in front of his troops at seeing their progress. "Forward! Kill as many as possible before they regroup!"

The regular soldiers soon find their stomach again, pressing on to join the melee. Sera pulls the wounded out of the way to be treated by Iva. Mages from the ramparts are fleeing now, blasting off by fiery infernos to get away from the crumbling defenses. Other blue mages are flying out, trying to get back to town as they've seen the defenses overrun and surprise tactics in shambles.

Venitria runs upon her prey and lands in front of the mask-wearing necromancer. A gauntlet of ice forms about her hand with a spike at the end. Attempting to skewer the white mage, Venitria thrusts forward, but the masked mage moves back and avoids the blow. His black shrouded hand grabs the gauntlet of ice. His hand glows a brilliant white as he grips it and shatters the ice. Before he can grab her arm, Venitria wills the ice of her clothes to shove herself back, standing away from the masked mage.

The man's mask depicts a blue flower in bloom, surrounded by ice. Behind this mask a deep voice emerges. "Those of the immortal woods have no business in the realm of mortals. Return to the wilds, elf."

Venitria takes a split second to see the retreating men, turns back to the mage, and pulls inward the water she used to knock over the loyalists, surrounding herself in a large wave. "Half-elves were found to be in the labor camps of your kingdom. Those blessed by the eternal light are to suffer no bondage save by a court of their own kin."

"Your land's laws are not ours. The jurisdiction you take over another kingdom's populace is an overreach."

Venitria shakes her head. "It won't trouble you then that a half-elven child was liberated from Effilnem?"

"This news does trouble me, but what of the other thousands of criminals? I also can't let you dethrone our king."

Venitria shakes her head, putting her hands up. "You would defend a tyrant?"

The man nods, one hand beaming a brilliant white while the other is shrouded in darkness, still calling those that have fallen to fight and slow the rebels. "I sacrifice for those who know honor and the code of law. Tyrants must be uprooted, but this rebellion has a hold of the reins of tyranny far greater than King Brenan. Lenfro would seize the throne for himself by right of conquest. You must see this outcome. You must have seen this outcome many times, elf."

"Better to be free under a ruthlessly ambitious man than to be shackled by a grand jailor. Surrender. House Winterbloom shouldn't have to lose its lord. You are soon to be overrun."

The white mage shakes his head. "I am the line between you and my men. I would see them live to bury you all. Noble birth should not dictate the mercy you refuse to show them. I will not accept it."

Venitria sees that her conversation is causing the loyalists to escape and flicks her hand forward, the water about her rushing towards the man. "A glorious death to you then!"

Accepting his role, the white mage's feet glow white, and he jumps twenty feet to the side of the rushing water. "We shall see." The white mage draws a bastard sword from his side and bounds forward with strides that would put a charging stallion to shame.

Venitria's eyes widen from the speed of the mage, and she barely has time to form ice in front of her to deflect the blow. The white mage is upon her now, and he slashes at her with trained strikes. The elf pulls herself back by focusing her magic on her frozen clothes, causing the blows to miss. To escape her foe, she pulls herself into the air, her eyebrows straining from concentration to do such a feat. While up, she witnesses Lenfro fire from his hand a green flare into the sky.

Venitria moves a hand above her head, readying to throw a support flare into the sky. But the white mage grabs weapons from the fallen and, with glowing hands, launches them at the elf, a flurry of steel shooting through the sky at her. Venitria moves out of the way, having to sacrifice the flare she readied to control her flying. The mage flings more weapons with the might of a catapult and the accuracy of a marksman, keeping the elf from signaling for reinforcement.

In a desperate, determined, and draining effort, Venitria calls to the water on the ground to chase the man out of the combat zone. A trail of water forms a circle, which she attempts to close on him. As white light pools at his feet, he redraws his bastard sword, and with a loud snap from the man's legs, he bounds into the air, leaping to Venitria in the sky. She dodges his strike, and as the mage falls, she attempts to call water into the sky. Still tumbling through the air, he rears back his arms, gripping his sword by the guard and blade, and throws it at Venitria's back, causing his body to somersault on his fall back to earth.

The elf turns around in the sky, the bloody water of the ground having reached her, and looks at the man to encapsulate him on his fall. For a second, she glimpses the bastard sword hurtling to her. With no time to react, she feels it break her clothes, pierce her torso right below her ribcage, and cut through to the other side. Her body hangs in the air for a moment and then plummets to the ground.

Sera and Iva catch the sight above them, tracking Venitria's fall. Without hesitation, they are shoving at the men around them to urge them forward. Sera points her axe at where Venitria is going to land. "Cut a path to Venitria! She needs our help!"

The white mage is behind the elf in the fall, and when he collides with the earth, his body breaks but refuses to die. His hands are akin to beacons, engulfing his being in healing magic and blinding those who look at him. His body mends, bones set, and legs straighten, and he is soon back on his feet after the perilous fall. His eyes shift to the combat next to him and then towards the elf who is staring at the sky, her body sitting up somewhat as she landed on a corpse. Rebel soldiers rush towards her, not caring about the man's power as they call Venitria's name. The white mage walks to her, and their eyes meet. Lord Winterbloom grabs the hilt of the blade stuck through her chest.

Venitria stares into the holes in the man's mask, seeing his green eyes through the shadow. "I offered you mercy, Dendric. Now I am at yours."

The man's hand hesitates on the hilt of the blade, watching a small group of rebels come in and the women running at their fore. Dendric moves in close, peering into Venitria as if to examine her soul. "Why? Why should I grant you your life?"

Venitria continues to stare into Dendric's eyes.

Dendric sees the search and puts a hand near where his blade is piercing her. "You will remember this. The heavens did not put you on this earth with the years and the powers you have to collect the souls of others. The freedom you claim to fight for is but another shackle. Those who were criminals had their chance. Perhaps a few souls did not deserve it, but no system will ever be perfect. Asmeria prospered as those who wronged her toiled for her glory."

With indignation, Venitria says, "Freedom is worth any price for those robbed of it. When the time comes to figure out its cost, it is too late. Life is the only currency that will buy it back. If it is my place to die for others to live full, unfettered lives outside the shadow of fear or tyrants, so be it." Her eyes move from the man's, spying the forest that is just within the walls sung up by the loyalists. "The lady's garden doesn't seem so bad."

Dendric looks up once more, seeing the thirty or so soldiers nearly upon them. Yet his calm demeanor gives no hint of being in danger. "In twenty years, regardless of this war's outcome, you will come to the Rose Court to be tried. If you have not atoned, judgment shall reign." Dendric lets a white light come to his hand by Venitria's stomach, and his other pulls the bastard sword from her belly.

The elf gasps for air as she is being healed and the blade removed. Then she lies there, her eyes unfocused and looking at the sky.

Dendric stands and points the tip of his blade at Venitria's left eye. "Your soul is now in my keeping, elf." He turns, running off at the speed of a race horse, and catches up with his men.

Sera and Iva reach Venitria and take her under their care. But Iva finds no evidence of a wound from the sword.

21

THE CHARGE

To the east, near the river that gives Halmin all its life, the rebel knights lie in waiting. The walls here are unmanned, all personnel having been moved to deal with the mustering rebel force. The men here are in neatly aligned ranks. Horsemen idly wait in their saddle. At the front, Kendir is directing the planting of the books as men set them along the wall, a pyromancer ready to detonate them all at once with the single cast of a spell. Then a great cry for battle arises from the south wall. The men's heads turn to listen to it.

Kristo and Garrick are in the back of the formation, the two of them sitting atop Pilosus. Kristo is trying to find a comfortable way to hold a rebel banner that has a secondary green fabric. "Garrick?"

The knight turns his torso to look at Kristo. "What's wrong? Is the banner heavy?"

"No. I was wondering. Are you and Sera still okay with adopting me?"

Garrick stabs his lance into the ground, dismounts his horse, and stands beside Kristo. "Sera and I would love to adopt you."

"Is it still because of Mabel?"

Before he can answer, Kendir, spying Garrick dismounted and riding up to him, says, "Something the matter, Sir Garrick?"

"No, sir. Tending to family matters."

Kendir points at Pilosus. "Then mount your horse, Garrick. We could be summoned at any moment." And Kendir trots back to the front of the line.

Garrick sighs but remains standing. "Yes and no, Kristo. We may have originally wanted to take you in because of our want to honor Mabel, but there is more to it now. You are a wonderful child, full of thought and consideration. We want you with us because, quite simply, we love you."

"I want to be a Marmuin."

Garrick grabs Kristo's shoulder, jostling him slightly and smiling widely. "Then from now on you are. You are Kristo Marmuin, the son of a baker and a teacher." He pulls Kristo toward him and knocks his helmet against his son's. "Your mother is going to be ecstatic at the news." Then Garrick climbs back onto Pilosus's saddle, straightening himself upright and grabbing his lance.

Kristo's eyes look at Garrick with reverence and then drift over to the sight of flying debris. "Mom is in that?"

"Yes."

"She will be safe."

With a smile on his face, Garrick turns slightly to look at Kristo. "You're right. You're absolutely right." Garrick knocks on Kristo's helm. "Do you remember all the flag colors?"

Kristo gives an affirming hum.

As the long minutes pass, the men become increasingly anxious, as do their horses, flapping their lips and pawing at the dirt. Finally the signal comes, a glowing ball of green light shooting high in the air above the obscuring height of the walls. Kendir at the front slaps the side of the pyromancer next to him, spurring him into action. The pyromancer raises a hand, forming a mass of flame in it, and lobs it at the books. The next moment, an ear-ringing blast causes a few horses to buck and try to throw their riders. A rain of wood and stone comes down on the earth, and when it stops, Kendir moves forward, riding over the debris with his horsemen following.

Going into the open farmland, the horsemen witness the retreating loyalists, and Kendir calls to his men, putting his horse into full gallop. "Do not let them reinforce the town! Slay them, and the day is ours!" One of the men behind Kendir sounds a horn, and the other men all set their horses into a run, beating their steeds through the farmland, crushing cabbages, and breaking vines. Kristo has his hands wrapped tight about the banner, leaning forward against Garrick so as to not lose balance. Garrick himself is tight at the reins, forcing Pilosus forward as they rush over the land.

When they are halfway across the field, a horn sounds from the town, and great wings take to the sky, loyalists forming ranks as their winged horses in the sky cast broad shadows on the ground. With zeal in their voices, the regiment of flying cavalry comes over the walls to fly at the charging rebel horsemen.

Kendir continues to press on, regardless of the threat. "Our lives are for this great kingdom's renewal! Stay your course!"

As the rebels continue to ride, the fliers from their right are moving in, each holding a package.

Kendir spots the packages and calls to his riders. "Loosen formation!"

The men scream the orders for everyone to hear and break apart to the best of their ability. Now the fliers are upon them, throwing their packages upon the rebel riders and blowing craters into the earth. Booms echo through the farmland, causing horse and man to be spread across the fields. A well-aimed throw hits Kendir, blowing his horse's legs from one side and blasting the knight's body to bits. His corpse scatters over the battlefield, leaving the men without their captain.

The horses buck, a few breaking from their riders and running away from combat. Other knights are screaming for retreat at the devastating effects of the counter charge. With a bomb hitting only a few feet away, Garrick and Kristo narrowly miss a cruel fate. After calming Pilosus, Garrick looks at the loyalist soldiers who are nearing the walls. Loyalist mages are opening the stone and wood walls for their soldiers arrival. Garrick looks back at Kristo with wild fervor, and after a second, Kristo nods, holding the banner in his arms proudly.

Garrick turns Pilosus around and urges the mare into a gallop as she curves around the fleeing horsemen. In the run, he points his lance at the formation, yelling to the men, while Kristo flies the rebel banner high overhead, "Are you cowards? Death awaits every man at the end! Should I die, I will die giving all to the cause of free men!" Garrick turns his horse back towards the loyalist soldiers. Fleeing knights turn their beasts to follow Garrick. "Ride with me!" He cries. "Ride to your dooms and a better tomorrow for it!" Pilosus's hooves churn the tilled dirt, with the other horsemen breaking their route to follow behind. The shouting coming from every horseman causes the retreating loyalists to look back with utter terror from their ramshackle spear lines.

With the loyalists having to form ranks or be decimated, the chasing rebel soldiers have time to catch up. Birkin's voice calls for the loyalists' deaths as he and his men draw close.

Garrick's lance falls into position, picking out a man to deliver the point to. "Drop lances!" he calls. The nearby horsemen repeat his words through the ranks, and they set their lances on their targets or ready their swords. The final distance is broken, and Garrick watches the man he's picked attempt to get his spear into proper placement, fumbling with its direction. The man holds his spear tight and turns his head away, closing his eyes in fear. A cry of anger comes from Garrick as he nears the line of loyalists. The men behind him yell for blood, their voices ringing over the sounds of the battlefield. The rebels bear down, and the loyalists' line cracks. Those in the back break and scramble to the walls, wild fear in their eyes as they look at the rebel horsemen advancing upon them.

Pilosus charges into the loyalist line, and Garrick's lance holds true. The loyalist spearman's weapon scrapes across Pilosus's barding as Garrick's lance skewers the man below the collar bone. Garrick lets go of his lance from the dead weight and moves deeper into the ranks of men, emerging out on the other side of them. Indiscriminate slaughter is upon the loyalists. The horsemen draw blades after the initial charge and begin rending the loyalists' souls from the earth.

When the horsemen reach the other side of the men, they turn and see the winged knights giving chase, readying parcels once more to avenge their brothers in arms. When Garrick sees this, he turns Pilosus about and runs through his ranks of horsemen. "Run! Run! Scatter yourselves!"

Every man is of the same mind. The cavalry ranks split and tear across the farmland to escape the bombs. A white rider soars above the field, cursing and calling for the damnation of all rebels, his black hair flowing from under his helm. When he spots Garrick out of the pack, he gives chase. "Garrick! The reaper comes for you! The leader of these men is to die today!"

Garrick looks back over his shoulder at the flier who has raised his mask to show his face. Demio. Garrick tells Kristo, "Raise the red flag!"

In shock, Kristo looks at Garrick for a moment.

"Do it, Kristo!"

The child frantically pulls his banner down, leaning to take a red cloth from Pilosus's saddlebag in exchange.

In that moment, Demio throws his package at Garrick, a fiery boom on his right that forces Pilosus to turn towards the outer wall where the rebels came in from.

"Garrick! You will answer to me!" Demio's voice thunders over the both of them.

Kristo puts up the red banner.

Garrick sees this and grabs it from Kristo. "Get off!" he yells.

Kristo is terrified, looking at the ground rushing past.

"Now," Garrick screams. "Get off the horse, Kristo!" He pushes Kristo back, causing the half-elf to fall back, tumbling into the dirt with his helmet rolling off. Another ear-rendering boom shakes the ground behind Garrick from Demio's second assault on him.

"Noble of you to get rid of your charge, Garrick!"

While bounding forward, Garrick raises his banner as high into the air as he can manage. "Demio! Stop this!"

A third boom shakes the earth. "Never! I saw you rally a whole broken regiment! You are these men's spirit! They must lose their soul!"

Overseeing the scene, Lenfro watches his horsemen scatter and Garrick riding with a red banner. The lord then calls to his men. "Ready archers. Fire upon the fliers!"

Lady Kela, next to him, shouts. "We'll be firing on our own men!"

"They'll die anyway, Kela!" Lenfro raises his hand to give the order to the rebel archers scattered through the battlefield.

Garrick witnesses the men ready to fire and looks back at Demio. "Turn back! The archers will slaughter you!"

Demio shakes his head, nearly over Garrick, carefully aiming his toss. "Then we shall both die together!"

The order to fire rings across the farmland, and hundreds of bowstrings send thorns into the sky. Demio hurls his fourth load at Garrick, but as it leaves the flier's hands, Garrick yanks the reins, and Pilosus immediately digs her hooves into the soil, causing the boom book to sail in front of Garrick and destroy only crops.

With the arrows coming in, Demio attempts to turn, but the thorns find their mark, plunging into his steed's side and eye. The man plummets. Garrick watches the fall and then kicks Pilosus to move to where Demio fell. Garrick gets off Pilosus to kneel near Demio, pinned under his dead winged horse. Demio still draws breath, and Garrick holds his friend's head.

At this time the pink-flagged wooden parasols are moving out from the town, signaling the women of the church coming to attend to the dead.

"Why, Garrick? Why betray me? Why . . . betray the laws . . . of a land . . . that let us live such great lives?"

"Those laws imprisoned our friend Mabel. There was no need for such strict laws, Demio. The rulings were unjust."

Demio coughs blood and a haze sets into his eyes. "She . . . was stealing. She . . . chose . . . her fate."

"No one deserves the life of a slave for such a crime. Not her or her parents."

Demio weakly grabs Garrick's tunic. "You . . . could have been . . . a great man. But . . . you fight . . . to let . . . criminals run free. I fight . . . I fought for . . . a world free . . . of such people. You . . . you have become an instrument of pain . . . against all that is good and just. You . . . this rebellion sends . . . good honorable people to their deaths . . . over the lives of a scarce few."

"Kristo!" Garrick shouts. "Kristo come quickly!"

Demio's eyes roll down from Garrick's face, looking at the carnage of the battle, at the broken wall, at all the dead loyalists on the ground. "Look . . . Garrick . . . at your better world."

Garrick turns his eyes to witness the dead and all the destruction about him.

Kristo runs, his satchel flopping on his waist, and tears through stakes of vines.

Demio notices Garrick's understanding and relaxes. "I fear for the future . . . for what world . . . a good, misguided man . . . like you . . . might help create."

Reaching the two men, Kristo drops to his knees, looking at the dying man.

"Potion, now!"

In confusion, Kristo looks at the loyalist in Garrick's arms, but Garrick pushes his hand into the boy's chest, getting the child to hand one over. Garrick uncorks it, gets blood in it from Demio's lips, and pours the liquid in Demio's mouth, who swallows it. "Come on. You're going to be all right, Demio. You can make sure Lania and your kid are protected yourself."

From Halmin, a bestial roar explodes. New bodies line the inner walls near where the rebel army has started to reform. The noise is not of man nor creature, and it reverberates through the entire area. Demio looks at the walls and the bodies moving to man it. "So . . . the dragonbornes did not forsake us. Good. Perhaps the day is not lost."

"You mean the barbarians from the north?"

"You won't get to win the day . . . this easily, my friend." Despite the potion, Demio coughs blood down his chin. "The fiery pits of hell . . . await me, same as you. . . . Let's hope we aren't dooming . . . those we intend to save."

Garrick grabs at Demio's hand, holding it as his friend's grip weakens. "No! Demio! You can stay! Just hold on a little longer, and you'll live!"

With a final effort, Demio flexes his arm, bringing Garrick into the same grip they had when they swore their oaths, and looks Garrick in the eyes.

Garrick nods and lets his eyes fall to Demio's chest as his lifelong friend draws his last breath, sighs, and stares off at the sky for his final sight.

Garrick stays with his friend for a moment and then gets up. As he looks at the body of his friend, his brows twitch with anger. He screams at the world, draws his blade, and walks along the length of the winged horse. In a swift and violent motion, Garrick brings his blade down on the animal, slicing its stomach open, and continues to slash at the beast, screaming until his breath gives out. Blood from the beast splatters along his blade, on his tunic, and across his face, which he wipes away with the back of his glove.

Having watched all, Kristo gets up and hugs Garrick around the waist.

Garrick's arms are open for a moment, and then one of his hands comes to hold Kristo's back, patting him. "I don't know what's right anymore,

Kristo. I have no regrets freeing you . . . but . . . the cost. Demio is right. Is this worth it?" He turns to look at the destruction of the fields and the women of the church tending to the fallen. "This is the result of freedom? Good men caught in the middle? Death brought home? There are only a handful of men who deserve death for this cruelty, yet we must pile the bodies of others in the way to reach the truly guilty." Garrick looks up at the sky to see vultures already circling the battlefield. The knight's legs give out from under him. As he sinks to the ground, he stabs his blade into the earth, tapping his helm against the pommel repeatedly. "My purpose is to nourish those who want to live. Not this. Not this."

Kristo puts his hand on Garrick's shoulder, just being there with him.

A minute passes, and Garrick gets up, turning to Kristo. "Let's just get through the day. We free Halmin and go from there."

Kristo nods up at Garrick, and the man moves to Pilosus, helping Kristo back on before getting up on the mare himself looking one last time at his deceased friend.

22

THE COST OF A DREAM

GARRICK TURNS PILOSUS AROUND, RIDING BACK to the reforming ranks of rebel horsemen. Lenfro is calling for Kendir to report to him. After his third call with no response, he flies over the horsemen. "Where is Kendir?"

One of the men speaks up. "Kendir is dead, My Lord, killed by the loyalist fliers."

Lenfro immediately looks down at the ground, closing his eyes to center himself. Then he looks at the man. "Who led the charge?"

"It was Sir Garrick, My Lord. We followed his banner into battle."

Having reached the group, Garrick moves his way to the back to his original position in the formation, trying to ignore the conversation.

The dragonbornes on the wall wait for the second assault to begin, while the rebels regroup out of range of the wall.

"Garrick, report!"

The knight reluctantly rides to the front. Lenfro lands his steed on the ground, goes to Garrick, and in a hushed voice, says, "These men followed you?"

Garrick raises his voice to let the men hear him. "They rode with valor when duty called, yes."

Lenfro looks at the men, who are waiting on orders, and then back at Garrick. "You are their captain; they follow you willingly. You will lead them for the remainder of this battle. The forces inside the wall aren't many, but they have plenty of ways to hide. About two thousand of these beasts plus the remaining loyalists lurk behind the walls. They are all but routed. Take your men round, blow the walls from behind, and line the streets with cavalry. We march on the front. Look for my signal."

Garrick and Lenfro move to go to their positions, but Lenfro stops for a moment, calling back to Garrick. "The beast-men are known for their cunning. They won't fight the same way men do, and if you make them, watch out for fire or acid from their mouths."

"I've heard of their abilities."

Lenfro turns to leave but sees no salute from Garrick. "You need to acknowledge my departure."

Garrick turns his head back to Lenfro and puts a hand over his chest to salute him. "Fight well, My Lord."

Lenfro's eyes survey Garrick for a moment. Then he turns his winged horse to take off, flying to look over the main force.

Walking to a position in front of the cavalry, Garrick turns to his son. "Kristo, put the green flag up." Garrick looks at all the men under his command, who rode with him through broken spirit. Taking a moment, he stares at their faces, observing their expressions if they aren't hidden behind visors. When Kristo raises the banner of the rebellion, Garrick points off to the north above the walls. "We ride to the north side. Be on the lookout for the enemy, and trust your senses. The beast-men of the north are said to be great hunters. They will not engage us in honorable combat unless forced. We will force them to, and we are superior at it. But be warned, these warriors from the north have the ability to spew fire or acid from their mouths at will, so take care to avoid it." Garrick nods to the men in assurance, with each of them seeming a bit sterner in their saddle.

Garrick turns Pilosus and points his sword in the direction he intends for them all to go. They move through the wheatfields of the west and around to the north to avoid archers and mages. Loud booms come from the south wall, followed by the cries of angry men as the horsemen reach their intended target. Instead of opposition there, the back walls have large portions missing. Entrances have been made by brown and green mages, yet no one is manning the ramparts. Staying away from the wall, Garrick surveys it, trying to inspect every detail. Garrick then looks back at Kristo, holding the banner pole. "Either they just arrived and had to make entrances, or this is a trap."

Kristo looks up at Garrick. "We could blow up the top of the wall to make sure."

Garrick knocks on Kristo's helm. "That's a good suggestion. I'm not sure if I should be proud of your idea or concerned at how you came up with it at your age." Garrick turns round in the saddle, calling to the men. "Where is our pyromancer?"

At his call, a man dressed in red robes rides to Garrick's side. "Sir?"

Garrick points at the top of the wall. "Blow a hole in the top. I want to see if we're being tricked."

The pyromancer walks his horse forward with spell blazing in hand. With a thrust forward, he launches a ball of fire to blow crenelation from the wall, revealing nothing beyond it but the roof of a house inside the walls.

Garrick spies this and motions forward with his arm. "Fill the streets, and face southward! Look for the green signal flair from Lenfro. Then charge!" He rides to the pyromancer and says, "Stay near the center. Back up whoever gets hit."

The pyromancer salutes and rides through an entrance in the wall.

Garrick swings his arm forward to usher his men onwards, riding through with them and taking to the front of the leftmost formation. As they march through, the men, women, and children of Halmin peer out of windows at the rebels. Parents quickly shoo the children away to safer parts of their house.

One window opens with a bang. A curly red-haired old man hurls obscenities at the riders in the street. "You traitors couldn't leave well enough alone! Now war is here! You all ought to be ashamed of you—"

A woman grabs him around the mouth and pulls him back inside, and a younger man slams the window shut.

Garrick and Kristo turn from the scene and look ahead down the grassy street where the path turns due to the layout of buildings. Men are shouting down the street, and as the shouting gets louder, a green flair flies up over the buildings. Garrick holds his gifted blade high in the air to point forward. "Sound the horn! We send these barbarians to see their gods!"

A horn rings throughout the town, and hooves trample the syrup-filled grass as the horsemen charge southward through the streets. Turning along with the street, Garrick can see loyalist men fleeing into the cavalry charge and readies to hit their line. Kristo on the back of the saddle steadies himself so as to not fall off.

The line of men running in retreat look at Garrick's men and rush to set up spears at the fore with a sense of duty, not fear, in their eyes. The line has barely any dragonbornes in its ranks, and the ones that are there are standing proud, taunting the horsemen that are positioned near the butchery. Garrick continues the charge but stays watchful. When his horsemen near the loyalists, the roofs of buildings distort, thatch and wood moving in impossible turns. In the next moment, dragonborne illusionists end their deceptions to expose numerous lizard-like warriors lining the tops of buildings to surround the cavalry charge. Wide-eyed, Garrick at the front tries to pull Pilosus around. "Turn back!" he yells. "Flee to the north wall!"

Men at the back of the rushing formation pull their reins, their horses churning the ground to turn around and gallop past the church of Sutri.

Garrick and the other men deeper in are exposed. Arrows fire on them from the rooftops causing riders to fall from their mounts as they are hit from the surprise barrage. Men yell up at the sky from the pain of arrows stuck into their bodies. The dragonbornes near the edge of the roofs start heaving their chests, stirring a fire behind their sharpened teeth, and spew flames from their mouths to immolate rebels in the street. Garrick forces Pilosus to move near one of the buildings. He and Kristo helplessly watch as the front formation of men and horses under Garrick's command are burned alive. As the heat rises around him, Garrick looks back to see the Kristo has dropped the rebel standard to hold him. With his men running off, Garrick kicks Pilosus forward and down a side street by the butchery to avoid the ceaseless flames behind him. The dragonbornes track them, jumping from rooftop to rooftop, and attempt to shoot Garrick and Kristo. One arrow collides with the chainmail on Garrick's shoulder and slides off. He grunts, rolls his shoulder to check for damage, and feels none. "Sutri can't have us yet." Garrick darts across streets, makes turns down familiar alleys, to throw off his pursuers, riding his way back out of town to his retreating men. "Hold and turn!"

As the orders are relayed through the men, one man's mount falls over, the creature having been hit, burned skin showing to the world. Its rider shouts through the ranks. "We must find another way! Man and horse alike will die to that cursed fire!"

Garrick rubs his chin, his eyes flicking to random men under his command. "We must aid the foot soldiers, or they will walk into the same trap." He points at a rider in front. "Lenfro must have already seen what happened. Regardless, relay him our problem so his men won't rush such a formation. Tell him I am coming up with a new strategy."

The horseman nods, ready to ride off, but looks behind Garrick at the sky, pointing at it. "Lord Lenfro has already seen our plight, sir."

Garrick turns to look at Halmin. A great ball of fire is being summoned near a flying white steed. The ball is then sent downward onto the roofs near Halmin's south wall, debris and bodies flying into view of the cavalry. After Lenfro's attack, other balls of fire and giant stones break the southern homes of Halmin from the rebels' indiscriminate attacks. Houses are brought to rubble. The bodies of soldiers and sheltering villagers are caught in the destruction. Garrick's eyes trace the arc of each attack, watching the destruction of a familiar home or shop. "No . . . no . . ."

But behind him, the horsemen are cheering, seeing their enemy blown to pieces. A flare shot by Lenfro signals his call to advance.

Garrick doesn't move. He just watches the mage's artillery roll through the town to chase after the retreating loyalists under Lenfro's direction.

The pyromancer trots up to Garrick's side. "Sir Garrick? Your orders?"

Garrick's eyes snap to the man, examining the lack of concern in them. "We . . . stay here."

The pyromancer turns his head in confusion. "Sir?"

Garrick disregards the man for a moment. "Kristo, hand me your potion pouch and get off the horse."

Kristo hesitates.

Garrick snaps, "Give me the pouch and get off, Kristo!"

The sharp tone tenses Kristo, but he hands over the pouch and gets off the horse. "Dad, I—"

"You all," Garrick says to the cavalry behind him and pointing to several horses carrying medical supplies, "medical personnel, dismount and give your potions to your riders."

The boys look confused but comply, giving their supplies over.

Garrick then motions the riders to come to him. "You all come with me. The rest of you stay behind; go to the tree line. If the loyalists retreat, they'll do so through there. Charge them when they're in the open. These men and I are going to treat any civilians we can find." Garrick points at the pyromancer. "You're in charge." Garrick then looks down at Kristo and the other children. "Go hide in the trees to the west. No army should be going that way. When you all think it's safe, enter the town. Kristo . . ." Father and son hold their gaze for a moment. "Keep the other children and yourself safe."

Kristo gives Garrick a nod.

The knight motions his selected men forward, and they ride through the arches, taking a sharp right after entering the town. "We'll avoid the loyalists by staying near the east side. Then we'll sweep from east to west through the rubble for survivors." Garrick's men ride in, shouts of retreat filling the air with loyalist horns sounding their need to flee. Man and dragonborne alike are running from combat through Halmin's fruited streets. A white-clad figure dashes through the town, attempting to cover the retreat. Garrick and his horsemen stick to side paths, staying out of the way and traveling through vine-covered alleys. Once the troops pass, Garrick's riders move freely as he and his men approach the destroyed southern portion of the town. A few menders already are tending to the rebel wounded.

Houses here are toppled, their wood and stone strewn into the grassy streets, breaking the spines of the Almenian grass to fill the air with the scent of sugar and blood. Strong support beams stand splintered near the tops where boulders smashed through them, while roofs hit by fire still smolder or have open flames consuming them. Parts of unfortunate soldiers and dragonbornes are cast about the debris, painting the area in more blood and sinew than anyone should ever have to witness. Garrick looks at the sight in disbelief, rubbing the side of his head. He quickly dismounts Pilosus, motioning towards the rubble. "Search the area! Save anyone left drawing breath!"

The men with him obey the order, moving into the ruins of buildings, trying and failing to avoid the blood. Garrick calls to the ruins of the house he's in, moving over portions of wood to see if anyone is under them. No one responds. In the ruins of the house across from him, he hears retching from the soldier who went to examine it. Exiting the building, the man throws up in the rubble-covered street. He locks eyes with Garrick and shakes his head. After steadying himself for a moment, he goes to search another home.

As Garrick and his men search, a figure in a green dress flowing in vines and grey-blond hair braided behind her sifts through the houses. Her hands glow green to call to the wood of the houses and have it move the stone rubble. Other regular green-dressed women come through with pink flags atop wooden parasols, approach the dead, and offer prayers for the departed. The searching turns somber, as only a handful of people are found living, all of them near the body of a loved one they are clinging to. People are slowly coming out from homes as the violence has passed. When they see what has happened to Halmin's southern portion, people rush to the broken houses of close family and friends, and mourning cries fill the town.

Garrick and his men are still searching the houses as the townsfolk come. They watch as he and his men comb through the rubble to save whoever is trapped. The woman in flowing green vines comes to Garrick with the people she finds, floating them on a thin piece of wood. Looking at her, Garrick smiles weakly to her. "Good to see you're safe, Yuna."

Yuna nods and motions to the woman she's brought. "It's good to see you safe as well."

Garrick takes a bit of the injured woman's blood into a potion vial and administers it to her.

Yuna looks back over everything, her face touched somewhere deep inside at the sight of the ruins. "Where is Lord Lenfro? He caused this, did he not?"

Garrick looks out on the sight of the townspeople. "Yuna, this isn't the time."

Yuna's sight turns to him, as she appraises his being. "You would stay loyal to a man that would do this for victory? I saw children riding with the cavalry. I see families slain from wanton destruction. I foresee that Lenfro will be king, and I cannot tell you if that king will be better than the one who's done such horrible things to cause this violence. The gods will question, the same as I do, if such a man truly deserves divine rule." Yuna's chin then dips slightly. "They will also have questions for the people who follow him."

Garrick's arms hang by his sides, his head turned upward to look at the sky. "How beautiful it must be to live up there, and how miserable are we to be born here. A world where others would rather live on the labors of those they deem lesser. Where the only counterargument is violence, where innocents must die for such a disagreement." Garrick turns his eyes to the bodies of those around him, noting more than a few recovered dead. "And a world where leaders will trample those that deserve protection underfoot. In trying to free the people of the kingdom, we've put them on the field of battle and killed them. I cannot tell if this is a victory or if we've lost our cause seeking it."

Garrick looks at Yuna, who is still staring at him. "I do not know where Lenfro is. I'm here searching for survivors on my own orders. He will go back to the baggage train eventually to get everything moving into town. He is a fan of speeches and will likely show himself to address the town and his men."

Yuna nods to this, looking back over the rubble to the north, near where the center of town is. "If I were a minister of war, I would give my speech there."

Garrick looks to where Yuna indicates. "Yes, he'll be on his flying horse too. Are you sure you want to question him in front of everyone?"

Yuna casts her arms out at the ground around her. The grass grows around her waist and carries her towards Garrick, who is caught up in a mess of plants, flowing like a wave from the new growth. "Seldom is it that good things grow in the dark." Yuna transports them both through the town, placing herself and Garrick on top of a house to wait. Below them, people run buckets of water through the town to douse the smoldering ruins of houses.

Lenfro's arrival is timely as victory is clear to everyone left on the field. The lord then takes to the sky near the center of town to address his men, his fiery red hand causing his voice to boom for all to hear while positioning the great white wings of his steed clear for all to witness. "To all true sons and daughters of Asmeria! The loyalists are beaten yet again! These weak-willed and weak-armed men would have starved all of you and had you on your knees!"

Garrick is about to speak, but Yuna puts a hand on his chest, still listening. She looks back up to Lenfro, her eyes narrowed and her demeanor wrought with anger.

Lenfro continues. "These cowards will learn from their ways by having it thrust upon them. All food shall be transported east, to feed those loyal to freedom and her designs. All your families shall be eating feasts for your work here today!"

Cheering comes from most of the soldiers left in town while others murmur about relations to the west.

Before Lenfro can continue, Yuna's hand glows wispy green. Vines coil around her waist and raise her into the sky across from Lenfro. Using her own magic to project her voice, filled with the tone of a teacher tempered by hundreds of lessons, she says, "What you plan to do is treasonous, not against the crown but against the very people of Asmeria herself. Do not condemn the west to starvation, Lenfro. You have caused enough devastation here today."

"What the west has earned," Lenfro says, "they shall receive. Their cruelty towards us cannot go unpunished. We deserve justice!" He points down at Garrick. "Your very adoptive son was a slave of this system. Does he not deserve peace of mind that those that would abuse him and use him got their reward?"

Garrick shakes his head, and while his voice is not loud enough for all to hear, it does reach Lenfro. "My son did not deserve the life he had, and I would see justice delivered."

Lenfro nods at this, content with the response.

But Garrick continues to speak. "But this is not justice. This will breed a new form of hate and cruelty. A kingdom divided cannot come back together through mistreatment. They will be our brothers and sisters again once the war is over. We've already ruined numerous families. By enslaving the old guards of Effilnem and by the houses destroyed in the south of this town, we would ruin all families of the west with this unfeeling decision."

During the debate, a crowd filled with soldiers and citizens has formed. Sera has pushed through it and is near the house Garrick sits upon. She looks upward now, listening to Lenfro.

"The cruelties of war are a fact of life. They cannot be avoided. What happened to the south of Halmin was necessary to ensure a victory that would cause an untainted peace to reign through Asmeria! Soldiers understand this; the citizenry are blind to it. Even my own life is forfeit for the future. So long as the future will be brighter than before, their deaths were not in vain."

Yuna points her finger out to Lenfro. "Soldiers give of themselves willingly. Those that died from your destruction are those you should have been striving to protect. How are you better than a tyrant that would cast those under him into chains if you would cast these people so quickly into a fire or under a falling rock for a so-called better future? Surely King Vanari thought the same about slavery!"

Lenfro jabs his hand down at the ground to point at it, a furious temper showing on his brow. "The fires of war care not for whom they scorch! Why would General Nirkin let his allies position themselves on the roofs of innocents? War is cruelty! What matters is that the days after the war will be better ones, where leaders do not cast innocents into harm's way!"

Garrick shouts up now, raising his gifted blade to point at his lord. "What about the innocents we sent into combat today? What about the women sent to be in the lines? What about the children we sent to be with the cavalry? What future are we gaining when we sacrifice it?"

Lenfro points down to Garrick, as if to curse him. "Know your loyalties and lower your blade! The women and children were put at risk to save the future! Are men not equal parts responsible for the state of the world? The women and children helped save lives!"

"They were sent defenseless!" Garrick says, keeping his blade steady and pointing it directly at Lenfro's head in an accusatory manner. "My son was given armor, but how many others went in bladeless and without even a shield? Men are part of the future, it's true, but you sent untrained women and children in to save military power by sacrificing the safety of innocents! I saw the bodies of horse, child, woman, and man alike litter the farmlands today! You similarly gave the enemy no choice but to kill them or risk defeat!"

"I won't stand for treasonous accusations," Lenfro says, drawing his sword and pointing it at Garrick. "I did what I did for the best future possible! Leaders face impossible decisions. I've studied war for years. There is no way a bread maker such as yourself could ever understand such complex concepts. Lower you blade, Garrick Marmuin, or stand a traitor to the free people of Asmeria!"

Garrick looks to his sword, takes a deep breath, and stretches his arm holding his sword further out towards Lenfro. "I am no traitor to the people of Asmeria! I am true to the values of freedom and peace. I am a traitor to a worthless man who would sacrifice children to attain victory. I am a traitor to one who would burn the bounty of his kingdom for so-called justice! I am a traitor to a person who would see half his kingdom starve for the sake of a warped sense of fairness. If anyone has betrayed the people of Asmeria, it is you, Lenfro! You have become a tyrant in your own right, and it is the duty of all free men to take the head of such a man!"

23

WHERE WORDS FAIL

"ENOUGH, GARRICK!" LENFRO'S SWORD ARM comes back while his hand glows red. A ball of raging red flame grows near the tip, and he swings it downward at Garrick. "Your services to this house are over, Sir Marmuin!" The ball of flame flies to Garrick, who raises an arm to block the intense light of the orb. "May you rest firmly in hell, where traitors and oath breakers belong!"

As the ball of fire comes in, an arm of vines shoots from the stalk that is holding Yuna in the sky, coming right into the path of the fireball. It bursts with unbridled fury, blowing plant flesh across the town and down onto the crowd of bystanders.

Lenfro switches his gaze to Yuna, readying his sword. He makes a flame consume the blade, and it drips and oozes downward into a long whip. "Never would I have thought Yuna of the Grand Garden would stand to be my enemy. It is your grave then!" Lenfro urges his winged horse forward, gripping the flame-whip of his sword to lash at Yuna.

Yuna twitches her fingers, and the mass of vines holding her droop to move her out of the way of the strike. She animates the vine once more, and a leaf on it grows to the size of a house. With a powerful wave of her hands, her stalk of vines waves the leaf at Lenfro, causing a gust of wind to hit his mount, and the flying horse loses its balance. Understanding what is happening, Lenfro frees himself from the animal and jumps to the tailor's house directly below. Continuing to tumble in the blast of wind, the horse screeches as it collides with the roof of the home behind Lenfro and one of its wing snaps and folds over.

Garrick witnesses this and looks for sure footing to jump across the buildings. With a reckless leap, he lands with a thud, falling forward into the thatch of the next building and stabs his sword into the hay to help himself get upright.

"Garrick! Garrick!?" From the crowd below, Sera calls up to her husband.

"Sera?" Garrick looks questioningly down at his blood-stained wife and then shakes his head. "Sera! We need to help your mother. I need a bow. I'm heading north on the roofs."

She looks at the people around her.

One of the soldiers grabs her arm. "You're not helping an enemy of this cause!"

The soldier next to him then grabs the shoulder of his brother-in-arms, turning him round. "That man is no enemy! You heard his argument at the trial. He is of noble mind"

"He is a traitor to turn sword on Lenfro!"

"Lenfro has abandoned the true purpose of this rebellion. He will ruin Asmeria!"

The argument grows, and soon the entire street erupts into anger. Fingers jab into the chest of comrades; voices reach high in the sky.

Sera eyes the men arguing with each other and then slips away, moving through the mob to a side alley. Her eyes scan the bodies of the fallen, looking for a bow. As she moves through the town, voices behind her rise out of control. She uncorks the wine bottle dangling at her hip, hoping to find someone living among the dead. Turning into one of the southern streets, she looks over the bodies of fallen loyalists and sees snapped bow-strings and rent shields.

Down one of the alleys, a small girl is looking over the body of a loyalist, who is rubbing her back with his bloody hand. "Go. Go back inside. Get off the streets, Thea."

The girl shakes her head, clutching the man's chest. "No! No! I'm so sorry. I shouldn't have been out, Dad. I'm sorry."

Sera hurries to the pair and drops to her knees.

Thea looks up and then hugs her dad's chest, causing him to groan. "No! Get away! No rebel will hurt my dad!"

Sera gives the girl a pat on the back and a forced smile, showing her wine bottle. "Hello, Thea. I've missed you in classes. I have a potion here to help your dad. I just need him to bite his tongue for me."

The girl looks at the bottle and then wipes her eyes, moving back on her knees. "You promise?"

Sera nods and looks at the man on the ground.

"I don't know by what grace you come here," he says, "but I'm grateful."

The man bites his tongue, and Sera pours the potion into his mouth, letting the man's wounds heal. "You and your daughter need to get off the street. Take off your colors. The loyalists have retreated."

The man relaxes back on the ground, nodding while his strength returns.

Thea moves next to her dad's head, putting a hand on his chest. "Thank you, Mrs. Marmuin. I'm sorry for skipping classes."

Sera puts a hand on her head and looks at the father again. "I need a bow. Did any of your allies carry one?"

The man points to a ruin of bodies. Sera gets up and goes to it.

Overhead, mages have taken to the tops of houses to have a better vantage. Yuna's stalk is being assaulted by a healer, who bounds from rooftop to rooftop and then leaps onto the mass of plants holding Yuna aloft. A black mist flows from the white mage's hand as she thrusts her arm into the plant, making it turn a dead brown, and the withering travels through the stalk. Moments later, the upper part of Yuna's stalk turns downward to swat the mage off. But, anticipating the strike, the white mage pulls her arm back and jumps back to a rooftop. Yuna moves her arms to turn her leaf around to where the white mage leapt. The head priestess's right hand comes up, and hundreds of spikes grow on the underside of the giant leaf. With a clutch of her fist, the foot-long spikes shoot from the leaf down upon where the white mage stands. The white mage bounds left but is struck through the leg and pinned to the roof while she forces herself to heal, trying to pull the spike from her body. Yuna clasps her hands together in a prayer, and from the spike in the white mage's leg, branches bloom, decorated in cherry tree leaves. The white mage shrieks in terror as roots dig through her body until they reach through her neck, causing her pain to end. "May you be one with her glory, my wayward child."

Mages are firing at one another on the rooftops, some casting off their colors while others rain death upon perceived betrayers. The scene in the streets is no different. Citizens have fled to their houses once again as a sea of fighting fills the streets, friends becoming foe for a second time in Asmeria.

Lenfro, still on the roof of the tailor's shop, raises one hand to the sky and fires a blue flare into it. Soon two mages come, Lady Kela, who bounds up onto the roof, and a purple-robed mage that rides in on his winged horse. Lady Kela goes over to Lenfro. Her hands glow a brilliant white over him, causing a cracking sound from his ribs as they snap back into place. Lenfro grunts from the pain and then turns over to get up. Witnessing Yuna in combat with other mages, ruthlessly killing those that oppose her will while saying prayers for their souls, he says, "So it is true. She was once one of the great tenders."

Kela looks at the spire of vines. "It matters not, My Lord; she stands opposed to us now. Servant of the goddess or not, she must not be allowed to stand in the way of a truly free Asmeria. The cause will undoubtably fail if these traitors win."

"Agreed. These traitors know nothing of sacrifice. The throne must be mine. No other knows the pain behind each choice made."

Lady Kela puts her hands out, eyeing the light they cast. "The magic in the air thins. Mages here have consumed too much mana. The area will become a dead zone soon enough."

Lenfro looks away now towards his winged horse that has fallen from the roof into a side street. "Ensure she is healed." Then he motions to the man robed in purple. "Tengin, I need you to distract Yuna while Estu is being mended."

The man nods and sends a purple mist from his hands to shroud his body. As the mist dissipates, he is a perfect copy of Lenfro. Out from it walk numerous copies of Lenfro. As one, they look at Lenfro and speak. "Your will be done, My Lord." The Tengin-Lenfro copy moves over the crest of the rooftop, and the other Lenfro copies join him in jumping about the houses around Yuna's vines where she is taking care of a pyromancer. The Lenfro copies on various nearby roofs have a faux flame in hand and cast the illusory fire about Yuna's vines and past her vision to get her attention. Every copy of Lenfro opens its mouth to speak, pointing up to her. "The goddess deals in death's renewal, but she does not cause it, rogue priestess! Your teachings only mean to convert people to your mindset!"

Yuna's head moves to inspect the Lenfro copies on houses, and her vines stop their assault. "I've seen illusion magic before, mage."

Again all the copies speak at once. "Then you know what happens if you guess wrong."

Yuna's fingers flick out, and the vines of her stalk grow pink flowers with long yellow stamens. The effort sends beads of sweat rolling down her forehead. Yuna's eyes move about the copies, trying to note the movements of each as they raise a fiery fist, casting fake flame that hits the stamens and vines directly but has no effect on the stalk holding Yuna up. "Is the real one even among you?" Yuna's hand rises, and the green wind flows down over her stalks as the stamens of the flowers shed yellow fog into the surrounding area.

Those fighting in the town below in the fog-enshrouded area cough in fits, trying to battle through the thick cloud of pollen enveloping them. The Lenfro copies move away from the cloud, haphazardly jumping from one building to another, most of them fading a foot or arm through a roof as the illusionist escapes the area.

Yuna ignores these fakes and readies her leaf. Spikes grow on its surface once more. She aims them at the group of copies near the edge of her pollen cloud. "Skilled, but unimaginative. It takes creativity to win fights as a mage. You'll learn that in the afterlife."

From between the houses of Halmin, Lenfro's wide-winged horse takes flight.

Yuna sees them and turns the leaf of her vine to rain a torrent of spikes on him and his mount. In preparation, both of Lenfro's hands are out, casting roaring flames ahead of himself. Yuna's needles rain onto nearby buildings and into the inferno cast by Lenfro, which catch fire and incinerate down to harmless ash. Lenfro soars through the ash, leaving a trail of dust behind him and his mount.

He draws his sword with red hands, and once again, a flame drips from its length to form a long lash. Coming close to Yuna's vine, he cracks his whip in the air, coiling it about Yuna's flowers and stalk. The flames ignite the plant on contact and spread down the vines as if consuming the driest of tinder. Lenfro has his flames tighten about the stalk. The whip becomes solid white and slices through the vines, causing the portion holding Yuna to begin to topple. In mid-fall, her hand crosses over her chest. "So you've come to burn my grove as well then?" Yuna's eyes track Lenfro's flight as a green glow envelopes her. The last of the vines about her turn a dark brown. From the death around her, a budding flower with pink petals grows to the size of a small carriage, envelopes Yuna in its petals, and then breaks off. On its independent tumble, the bud hits a roof and then bounces off to plop into the street. The severed vine stalk lolls over and then falls from its own terrible weight, laying waste to houses in its path. Roofs splinter and foundations crack under its fall, trapping some men underneath its shadow.

Garrick, who is still going from roof to roof, steadies his balance as the ground shakes from the vine's fall. He shouts into the din of combat. "Give me a bow! One of you, a bow!"

In the crowd of men fighting, a rebel with a bow strung across his back, calls back, "I'll give you a bow!"

Garrick holds his hand out to catch it from a toss.

Instead, the rebel soldier nocks an arrow, aiming it at Garrick. "Arrows first, traitor!"

Garrick moves back over the crest of the house he's on, ducking behind the arch as the rebel's arrow strikes the thatch.

"Stand and take what you deserve, coward!"

Garrick peeks over the crest of the house.

The man fires again when he spots Garrick's head. The arrow whizzes by his left ear before he ducks again.

Sera's voice reaches him over the sound of combat. "Garrick! Garrick, where are you?"

"I'm over here, atop the Gullan house!"

Sera hears his words and moves through the streets, avoiding the men clashing with one another. When she reaches the side of the house, she raises her arms up to the edge with a bow and arrows.

Garrick crawls down, remaining out of sight of his attacker, and takes them. Looking at his wife in the eyes, he says, "Now get off the streets. It's too dangerous."

"I—"

"Sera, I need you to take care of Kristo."

She puts her arm up again. "I love you."

Garrick puts the arrows down on the roof to hold her arm as her lips are out of reach. "I love you." The pair stare at each other for just a moment, and then Garrick pulls his arm back, grabbing the arrows once more. "Go. Kristo should be on the western outskirts."

Getting up to a crouch, Garrick nocks an arrow. He shows himself for a moment to the bowmen and then gets back down as an arrow whizzes where his head was. He then stands proper, watching his mark as the rebel is getting another arrow ready. With a twang, Garrick lets loose, his arrow cracking the chainmail of the man and bouncing off.

But the man topples over, despite the bounce, and grabs at his ribs. "Gah!"

Garrick eyes his foe who is similarly looking at him and trying to get back on his feet. Turning his head to look over the houses, Garrick sees Lenfro in the distance diving with Estu to where Yuna landed and the houses in the area blanketed in yellow fluff. With no choice, Garrick moves back to run, jumps to the next house, and continues over the rooftops, escaping from the man below who fails to draw his bow in time.

Lenfro directs Estu to land on a house close to where Yuna fell and looks down on her. His hands stretch out and immediately let loose a blaze of fire meant to melt the flesh of plant and woman alike. The fire hits the budding flower and sets it ablaze with Lenfro continuing to pour on the heat.

Inside the pod, Yuna closes her eyes, and the grass underneath the pod grows to cup the flaming bloom and launch it in the air away to the south part of Halmin. In its flight, the flower bud opens fully, revealing a beautiful pink blossom lit with a hateful fire. As it soars above the heads of men, Yuna emerges and then drops from it, falling to the earth with her arms outstretched. The grass below her grows tall and lush and gently catches her. Meanwhile, the flaming pink flower smashes into the ruins of south Halmin, lighting leftover wood on fire once more.

Lenfro mounts Estu, and they fly about as he searches for Yuna. Below, Garrick notices Lenfro in flight, raises his nocked bow, and fires an arrow, which sinks deep into the unarmored horse's chest. The steed cries from the blow, huffing as air becomes impossible to take in. As rider and steed fall from the sky, Lenfro abandons Estu once more, and the horse crashes against the corner of a house, its whining coming to an end as it lifelessly drops to the ground. While falling, Lenfro sends the roiling fire in his hands to his feet that shoot flames and let him land softly on a roof. He takes a moment to check himself and then looks at Garrick to the north. The two men lock eyes. Lenfro's deep scowl condemns even the sight of Garrick.

Choosing action over grimaces, Garrick has nocked another arrow and readies it. He maintains an expression of duty, his lips showing no curl and his eyes like steel, never moving from Lenfro. Garrick lets loose his arrow, and Lenfro effortlessly raises his hands to spout fire that turns the arrow to ash.

Staring at Garrick again, Lenfro raises a red fist in the air, and the fire pluming from inside escapes through the cracks of his grip. He gets ready to throw the ball of flame, but the fire sputters and dies. All about the battlefield, mages experience the same loss of power. Most retreat.

Garrick, still holding his bow, draws back another arrow and aims it at Lenfro.

The lord draws his sword, pointing it towards Garrick to challenge him.

24

WELCOME HOME

To the west, children are scurrying through brush and needle to find a suitable hiding place. Kristo, at the front of them, urges everyone forward. After he and the children find proper hiding spots, they look back on the town and see Yuna's stalk grown tall enough to appear over the wall. Then they stare wide-eyed as it, having been cut by Lenfro, falls and smashes through the west wall, providing an open view into Halmin. In front of him, Kristo sees the ruins of Sera and Garrick's house, the vine having smashed through the building, destroying the side where his room was, as well as a good portion of the main house. Smoke rises from the rubble, turning into a dense cloud on the ground that then runs away to go deeper into the forest. The children cry out in fright as they see fighting happening in the town once more. Confused, Kristo looks up at Lenfro, watches him fly forward, and then sees the lord's winged horse shot down by Garrick on a rooftop.

Kristo takes a few steps towards the ruined wall.

One of the children grabs his arm. "We're supposed to stay here."

Kristo looks at the boy and yanks his arm away, pushing the kid back and causing him to fall over. Kristo looks at the boy apologetically, but the half-elf's expression turns to determination. "If people always did what they are supposed to do, I wouldn't be here." He turns now and runs into the backyard of the bakery, looking about. To his right, he spots his fighting stick and grabs it. He goes further into town, hearing Garrick get challenged by Lenfro.

At that moment, Garrick tosses his bow to the side and grabs his sword from its sheath. Both men move across rooftops to meet.

Kristo shakes his head in disbelief. "Dad, no."

Lord and knight reach the flat stone top of the town's blacksmith. The end of its roof and wall have been blown in.

Kristo pushes forward through the town towards the two, keeping away from the fighting wherever possible.

Eyes not leaving Lenfro, Garrick steadies himself from his last jump, pulls his shield from his back, and undoes the twine to ready it in his off-hand. "There was a time when I would have liked nothing more than to have your house crest painted on this shield. You were a hero in my eyes. You were a hero in thousands of eyes."

Lenfro readies his sword by holding it by its handle in his right hand and the middle of its blade in the left. "You can still have it. You are an influential person, Garrick, able to capture the hearts of those you've spoken to. Asmeria could become great under our combined leadership. The loyalist armies have failed; their ally is on the run. They could make a last effort, but we have the manpower. Let this pointless insubordination end."

"No, I can't let you become king. I followed you to free Asmeria from its jail master, but I see now that we would earn a lord of smoke and rubble, willing to justify the great pain he commits."

"Smoke and rubble are what I'll make of you and your resting place, baker. Who are you to deny me my right, my reward for the sacrifices I've made? You are no one, a pissant who gave into his ego when challenged by someone who studied war and combat all his life. You've lost by meeting me here, and history will forget you."

Lenfro surges forward, bringing his blade up horizontally to smack into Garrick's. The knight goes around with his shield and hits Lenfro, pushing him back a step. The lord touches his chest plate where he was struck and punches it. Then he takes up his sword, swings it overhead with two hands, and cuts into Garrick's wooden shield to imbed his blade near the center.

Garrick twists his shield arm, tears away Lenfro's sword from his hands, and tosses the sword-laden shield off the blacksmith's roof to the ground near Kristo. "Don't claim the bodies of those you tricked into following your banner as your sacrifices!"

After the shield smashes into the ground, Kristo runs to the ruined side of the building, tosses his stick onto the roof, and starts to climb its rubble to the top. Near the roof, his foot slips on a loose stone, causing the boy to scramble up.

Lenfro draws a dagger from his belt, and beckons Garrick to come at him. Garrick grips his sword with both hands and slashes sideways. Lenfro jumps back. Unrelenting, Garrick attempts to stab as a recovery, which lets Lenfro move to the side. From this position, Lenfro stabs his dagger into Garrick's left wrist where his chain shirt doesn't quite meet his glove. Garrick screams, pulling his wounded arm back while keeping his good arm forward, his weapon pointed at Lenfro.

Lenfro flicks his dagger down, splattering the stones with drops of Garrick's blood. "Did you think your morals would give you an advantage in a duel? You should have fired on me."

Garrick's eyes flick for a moment from Lenfro to Kristo, who has now reached the rooftop. "I should have, a mistake I won't make again."

Lenfro wags a finger at Garrick. "A mistake you won't get a chance to repeat."

Kristo stands, grabs his carved stick, and moves to Lenfro.

Garrick motions back at the soldiers fighting in the streets. "After I kill you, how do you think I should rally the troops?"

"After *your* death, I will simply tell them you were an agent of the crown and the men should be brought together in vigilance."

Kristo is right behind Lenfro now and winds his stick back. "Raghh!"

Startled, Lenfro looks back as Kristo swings with all his might at Lenfro's knee but only breaks the wood in two around Lenfro's plate armor. Lenfro, ripe with wrath, balls a fist and strikes Kristo across the jaw, sending him to the ground.

Garrick advances, grabs Lenfro around his upper chest, and brings his blade to the lord's neck. Before Garrick can slice him, Lenfro's gauntleted hands grip the blade, and he throws his weight forward, flipping Garrick onto the stones and relinquishing him of his sword. Lenfro doesn't waste a moment and stabs down at Garrick with the sword. Garrick's arms swing, swatting the strike away with his chainmail. Lenfro eyes Garrick on the ground, who is trying to see where Lenfro may strike with the blade.

Instead, Lenfro kicks Garrick in the side whenever there is an opening. "Is being a knight all you hoped for, Garrick? Is being a moral man everything it's cracked up to be?" Lenfro delivers a hard kick to Garrick's face and then drops on top of him, trying to angle the blade of the sword into the knight's neck. Garrick struggles to keep it away.

On the ground, Kristo shakes his head and pushes himself up. He grabs a rock from the rubble. As Garrick is struggling, Lenfro puts his weight into the sword, managing to cut into Garrick's neck as Kristo comes over. With another yell, Kristo brings the stone up with both hands and strikes Lenfro on the back of the head, causing him to slump over, face up, on the roof. He groans, trying to get up. When Kristo gets on top of him, the noble's eyes flutter as he watches the stone crack into his face. Again and again, Kristo strikes, grunting each time, smashing Lenfro's face and soaking the stone in noble blood.

Garrick's eyes widen at the sight. His fingers flick about next to him, trying to open the satchel at his side. A gurgle of blood comes from his lips, causing Kristo to look over. The boy tosses the rock away as he goes to Garrick. The man's eyes lock with his son's for a moment.

The child reaches into the satchel to bring out a vial. "You're okay, Dad. I'm here. We're going to have lots of roasts, and you can dance with Mom as long as you want. You can teach me how to bake bread too. How does that sound?" Kristo uncorks the vial, lifting Garrick's head to pour it in his mouth.

But with his neck sliced by Lenfro, the potion fails to help. Garrick can only sputter after receiving the liquid. In a final effort, he reaches at Kristo's chest. "No . . . Kristo, you . . . you didn't . . . kill?"

Kristo reaches into the satchel again and uncorks and pours another one down Garrick's mouth.

Unable to speak now, Garrick squirms in a death throe, one of his legs kicking absently.

For a third time, Kristo goes into the satchel for a vial, looking at the cut in Garrick's neck to see if he can pour the potion in there. "Dad? Dad! Please! Please! Don't go yet!"

JAMES MANGANAIS HAS WRITTEN AND TOLD STORIES since he was little. Over the years, he developed a creative passion for high fantasy after reading books, watching movies and television series, and playing games related to the genre. He is a new father and lives in New Hampshire where he works as a card dealer in a charity casino. In his free time, Manganais enjoys board games, the occasional television binge, video games, Texas Hold 'Em poker, trying new foods, and daydreaming of stories. The last of which has resulted in these pages. He hopes to one day be able to afford his own place to raise his new family and give back to the world as he feels grateful for what he's been given.